# TOMORROW
### or
# TOMORROW
### or
# TOMORROW

## JAMES BLISH
imagines a tomorrow when there are too many
of us, according to the statisticians. But what
can a statistician do? One finds out.

## JOHN BRUNNER
imagines a tomorrow when the psychologists
must learn to deal with a new kind of patient—
more (or less) than human.

## HARRY HARRISON
imagines a tomorrow when teachers can teach
history by taking their students into yesterday. But students are as students ever have
been.

# SCIENCE AGAINST MAN

### Edited by
## Anthony Cheetham

AVON
PUBLISHERS OF
DISCUS • CAMELOT • BARD

This is the first American publication of
*SCIENCE AGAINST MAN* in any form.

AVON BOOKS
A division of
The Hearst Corporation
959 Eighth Avenue
New York, New York 10019

First Avon Printing, December, 1970

AVON TRADEMARK REG. U.S. PAT. OFF. AND
FOREIGN COUNTRIES, REGISTERED TRADEMARK—
MARCA REGISTRADA, HECHO EN CHICAGO, U.S.A.

Printed in the U.S.A.

# CONTENTS

# INTRODUCTION

TEN YEARS ago a collection such as this would have been a series of technological nightmares—crazy robots, poisoned wastelands, megalomaniac computers, fiendish subliminal advertising techniques, mega-death dealing microbes and warheads. These would have been the true heroes, or antiheroes while the human puppets danced to their tune. Today these nightmares are no longer the preserve of the science fiction writer. They are part of our daily lives. The contributors to SCIENCE AGAINST MAN have therefore chosen to concentrate on the human aspect. Man has altered beyond recognition the environment in which he evolved. How will he now meet the challenge of his new environment?

*NORMAN SPINRAD*, author of BUG JACK BARRON, THE MEN IN THE JUNGLE and the award winning short story THE BIG FLASH, is perhaps more than any other major science fiction writer concerned in his work with politics. THE LOST CONTINENT tilts ambitiously at the two most potent issues of the 70's: environmental pollution and racial conflict. The United States survives only as a gigantic outdoor monument to the Space Agers whose technological miracles poisoned the earth and the sky. The rich African tourists who gawp nervously at the remains can never quite reconcile their feelings of superiority as the survivors with the knowledge that the Space Agers represented the summit of human achievement—a form of schizophrenia already familiar to big city dwellers who curse the noise, the fumes and the dirt but wouldn't dream of moving out into the sticks.

## THE LOST CONTINENT

### By Norman Spinrad

I FELT a peculiar mixture of excitement and depression as my Pan African jet from Accra came down through the interlocking fringes of the East Coastal and Central American smog banks above Milford International Airport, made a slightly bumpy landing on the east-west runway, and taxied through the thin blue haze toward a low, tarnished-looking aluminum dome that appeared to be the main international arrivals terminal.

Although American history *is* my field, there was something about actually being in the United States for the first time that filled me with sadness, awe, and perhaps a little dread. Ironically, I believe that what saddened me about being in America was the same thing that makes that country so popular with tourists, like the people who filled most of the seats around me. There is nothing that tourists like better than truly servile natives, and there are no natives quite so servile as those living off the ruins of a civilization built by ancestors they can never hope to surpass.

For my part—perhaps because I am a professor of history and can appreciate the parallels and ironies—I not only feel personally diminished at the thought of lording it over the remnants of a once-great people, it reminds me of our own civilization's inevitable mortality. Was not Africa a continent of so-called Underdeveloped Nations not two centuries ago when Americans were striding to the Moon like gods?

Have we in Africa *really* preserved the technical and scientific heritage of Space Age America intact, as we like to pretend? We may claim that we have not repeated the American feat of going to the Moon because it was part of the overdevelopment that destroyed Space Age civilization, but few reputable scientists would seriously contend that we could go to the Moon if we so chose. Even the jet in which I had crossed the Atlantic was not quite up to the airliners the Americans had flown two centuries ago.

Of course, the modern Americans are still less capable than we of re-creating twentieth century American technology. As our plane reached the terminal, an atmosphere-sealed extensible ramp reached out creakily from the building for its airlock. Milford International was the port of entry for the entire northeastern United States; yet the best it had was recently obsolescent African equipment. Milford itself, one of the largest modern American towns, would be lost next to even a city like Brazzaville. Yes, African science and technology are certainly now the most advanced on the planet, and some day perhaps we will build a civilization that can truly claim to be the highest the world has yet seen, but we only delude ourselves when we imagine that we have such a civilization now. As of the middle of the twenty-second century, Space Age America still stands as the pinnacle of man's fight to master his environment. Twentieth century American man had a level of scientific knowledge and technological sophistication that we may not fully attain for another century. What a pity he had so little deep understanding of his relationship to his environment, or of himself.

The ramp linked up with the plane's airlock, and after

a minimal amount of confusion we debarked directly into a customs control office, which consisted of a drab, dun-colored, medium-sized room divided by a line of twelve booths across its width. The customs officers in the booths were very polite, hardly glanced at our passports, and managed to process nearly a hundred passengers in less than ten minutes. The American government was apparently justly famous for doing all it could to smooth the way for African tourists.

Beyond the customs control office was a small auditorium in which we were speedily seated by courteous uniformed customs agents. A pale, sallow, well-built young lady in a trim blue customs uniform entered the room after us and walked rapidly through the center aisle and up onto the little low stage. She was wearing face-fitting atmosphere goggles, even though the terminal had a full seal.

She began to recite a little speech; I believe its actual wording is written into the American tourist-control laws.

"Good afternoon, ladies and gentlemen, and welcome to the United States of America. We hope you'll enjoy your stay in our country, and we'd like to take just a few moments of your time to give you some reminders that will help make your visit a safe and pleasurable one."

She put her hand to her nose and extracted two small transparent cylinders filled with gray gossamer. "These are government-approved atmosphere-filters," she said, displaying them for us. "You will be given complimentary sets as you leave this room. You are advised to buy only filters with the official United States Government Seal of Approval. Change your filters regularly each morning, and your stay here should in no way impair your health. However, it is understood that all visitors to the United States travel at their own risk. You are advised not to remove your filters except inside buildings or conveyances displaying a green circle containing the words 'Full Atmosphere Seal'."

She took off her goggles, revealing a light red mask of welted skin that their seal had made around her eyes. "These are self-sealing atmospheric goggles," she said. "If you have not yet purchased a pair, you may do so in the main lobby. You are advised to secure goggles before leaving this terminal and to wear them whenever you venture out into the open atmosphere. Purchase only goggles bearing the Government Seal of Approval, and always take care that the seal is airtight.

"If you use your filters and goggles properly, your stay in the United States should be a safe and pleasant one. The government and people of the United States wish you good day, and welcome you to our country."

We were then handed our filters and guided to the baggage area, where our luggage was already unloaded and waiting for us. A sealed bus from the Milford International Inn was already waiting for those of us who had booked rooms there, and porters loaded the luggage on the bus while a representative from the hotel handed out complimentary atmosphere goggles. The Americans were most efficient and most courteous; there was something almost unpleasant about the way we moved so smoothly from the plane to seats on a bus headed through the almost empty streets of Milford toward the faded white plastic block that was the Milford International Inn, by far the largest building in a town that seemed to be mostly small houses, much like an African residential village. Perhaps what disturbed me was the knowledge that Americans were so good at this sort of thing strictly out of necessity. Thirty percent of the total American Gross National Product comes from the tourist industry.

I keep telling my wife I gotta get out of this tourist business. In the Good Old Days, our ancestors would've given these African brothers nothing but about eight feet of rope. They'd've shot off a nuclear missile and blasted all those black brothers to atoms! If the damn brothers didn't have so much loose money, I'd be for riding every one of them back to Africa on a rail, just like the Space Agers did with their black brothers before the Panic.

And I bet we could do it, too. I hear there's all kind of Space Age weapons sitting around in the ruins out west. If we could only get ourselves together and dig them out, we'd show those Africans whose ancestors went to the Moon while they were still eating each other.

But, instead, I found myself waiting with my copter bright and early at the International Inn for the next load of customers of Little Old New York Tours, as usual. And I've got to admit that I'm doing pretty well off of it. Ten years ago, I just barely had the dollars to make a down-payment on a used ten-place helicopter, and now the thing is all paid off, and I'm shoveling dollars into my stash on every day tour. If the copter holds up another ten years—and this is a genuine Space Age American Air Force helicopter restored and converted to energy cells in Aspen, not a cheap piece of African junk—I'll be able to take my bundle and split to South America, just like a tycoon out of the Good Old Days. They say they've got places in South America where there's nothing but wild country as far as you can see. Imagine that! And you can buy this land. You can buy jungle filled with animals and birds. You can buy rivers full of fish. You can buy air that doesn't choke your lungs and give you cancer and taste like fried turds even through a brand-new set of filters.

Yeah, that's why I suck up to Africans! That's worth spending four or five hours a day in that New York hole, even worth looking at Subway Dwellers. Every full day tour I take in there is maybe $20,000 net toward South America. You can buy ten acres of prime Amazon swampland for only $56 million. I'll still be young ten years from now. I'll only be forty. I take good care of myself, I change my filters every day just like they tell you to, and I don't use nothing but Key West Supremes, no matter how much the damn things cost. I'll have at least ten good years left, why I could even live to be fifty-five! And I'm gonna spend at least ten of those fifty-five years someplace where I can walk around without filters shoved up my nose, where I don't need goggles to keep my eyes from rotting, where I can finally die from something better than lung cancer.

I picture South America every time I feel the urge to tell off those brothers and get out of this business. For ten years with Karen in that Amazon swampland, I can take their superior civilization crap and eat it and smile back at 'em afterward.

With filters wadded up my nose and goggle seals bruising the tender skin under my eyes, I found myself walking through the blue haze of the open American atmosphere, away from the second-class twenty-second century comforts of the International Inn, and toward the large and apparently ancient tour helicopter. As I walked along with the other tourists, I wondered just what it was that had drawn me here.

Of course Space Age America is my specialty, and I had reached the point where my academic career virtually required a visit to America, but aside from that, I felt a personal motivation that I could not quite grasp. No doubt I know more about Space Age America than all but a handful of modern Americans, but the reality of Space Age civilization seems illusive to me. I am an enlightened modern African, five generations removed from the bush; yet I have seen films—the obscure ghost-town of Las Vegas sitting in the middle of a terrible desert clogged with vast mechanized temples to the God of Chance, Mount Rushmore where the Americans carved an entire landscape into the likenesses of their national heroes, the Cape Kennedy National Shrine where rockets of incredible size are preserved almost intact—which have made me feel like an ignorant primitive trying to understand the minds of gods. One cannot contemplate the Space Age without concluding that the Space Agers possessed a kind of sophistication which we modern men have lost. Yet they destroyed themselves.

Yes, perhaps the resolution of this paradox was what I hoped to find here, aside from academic merit. Certainly, true understanding of the Space Age mind cannot be gained from study of artifacts and records—if it could, I would have it. A true scholar, it has always seemed to me, must seek to understand, not merely to accumulate knowledge. No doubt it was understanding that I sought here. . . .

Up close, the Little Old New York Tours helicopter was truly impressive—an antique ten-seater built during the Space Age for the military by the look of it, and lovingly restored. But the American atmosphere had still been breathable even in the cities when it was built, so I was certain that this copter's filter system would be of questionable quality, no doubt installed by the contemporary natives, in modern times. I did not want anything as flimsy as that between my eyes and lungs and the American atmosphere, so I ignored the "Full Atmosphere Seal" sign and kept my filters in and my goggles on as I boarded. I noticed that the other tourists were doing the same.

Mike Ryan, the native guide and pilot, had been recommended to me by a colleague from the University of Nairobi. A professor's funds are quite limited of course—

especially one who has not attained significant academic stature as yet—and the air fares ate into my already meager budget to the point where all I could afford was three days in Milford, four in Aspen, three in Needles, five in Eureka, and a final three at Cape Kennedy on the way home. Aside from the Cape Kennedy National Shrine, none of these modern American towns actually contained Space Age ruins of significance. Since it is virtually impossible and at any rate prohibitively dangerous to visit major Space Age ruins without a helicopter and a native guide, and since a private copter and guide would be far beyond my means, my only alternative was to take a day tour like everyone else.

My Kenyan friend had told me that Ryan was the best guide to Old New York that he had had in his three visits. Unlike most of the other guides, he actually took his tours into a Subway station to see live Subway Dwellers; there are reportedly only a thousand or two Subway Dwellers left, they are nearing extinction. It seemed like an opportunity I should not miss. At any rate, Ryan's charge was only about $500 above the average guide's.

Ryan stood outside the helicopter in goggles helping us aboard. His appearance gave me something of a surprise. My Kenyan informant had told me that Ryan had been in the tour business for ten years; most guides who had been around that long were in terrible shape. No filters could entirely protect a man from that kind of prolonged exposure to saturation smog; by the time they're thirty, most guides already have chronic emphysema, and their lung-cancer rate at age thirty-five is over fifty percent. But Ryan, who could not be under thirty, had the general appearance of a forty-year old Boer; physiologically, he should have looked a good deal older. Instead he was short, squat, had only slightly-graying black hair, and looked quite alert, even powerful. But of course he had the typical American grayish-white pimply pallor.

There were eight other people taking the tour, a full copter. A prosperous-looking Kenyan who quickly introduced himself as Roger Koyinka, traveling with his wife; a rather strange-looking Ghanaian in very rich-looking old-fashioned robes and his similarly clad wife and young son; two rather willowly and modishly dressed young men who appeared to be Luthuliville dandies; and the only other person in the tour who was traveling alone, an intense young man whose great bush of hair, stylized dashiki, and gold earring proclaimed that he was an Amero-African.

I drew a seat next to the Amero-African, who identified himself as Michael Lumumba rather diffidently when I introduced myself. Ryan gave us a few moments to get acquainted—I learned that the Ghanaian was named Kulongo, that Koyinka was a department store executive from Nairobi—that the two young men were named Ojubu and Ruala—while he checked out the helicopter, and then seated himself in the pilot's seat, back toward us, goggles still in place, and addressed us without looking back through an internal public address system.

"Hello ladies and gentlemen, and welcome to your Little Old New York Tour. I'm Mike Ryan, your guide to the wonders of Old New York, Space Age America's greatest city. Today you're going to see such sights as the Fuller Dome, the Empire State Building, Rockefeller Plaza, and even, as a grand finale, a Subway station still inhabited by the direct descendants of the Space Age inhabitants of the city. So don't just think of this as a guided tour, ladies and gentlemen, you are about to take part in the experience of a lifetime—an exploration of the ruins of the greatest city built by the greatest civilization ever to stand on the face of the earth."

"Stupid arrogant honkie!" the young man beside me snarled aloud. There was a terrible moment of shocked, shamed embarrassment in the cabin, as all of us squirmed in our seats. Of course the Amero-Africans are famous for this sort of tastelessness, but to be actually confronted with this sort of blatant racism made one for a moment ashamed to be black.

Ryan swiveled very slowly in his seat. His face displayed the characteristic red flush of the angered Caucasian, but his voice was strangely cold, almost polite: "You're in the *United States* now, *Mr*. Lumumba, not in Africa. I'd watch what I said if I were you. If you don't like me or my country, you can have your lousy money back. There's a plane leaving for Conakry in the morning."

"You're not getting off that easy, honkie," Lumumba said. "I paid my money, and you're not getting me off this helicopter. You try, and I go straight to the tourist board, and there goes your license."

Ryan stared at Lumumba for a long moment. Then the flush began to fade from his face, and he turned his back on us again, muttering "Suit yourself, pal. I promise you an interesting ride."

A muscle twitched in Lumumba's temple; he seemed about to speak again. "Look here, Mr. Lumumba," I whispered at him sharply, "we're guests in this country and you're making us look like boorish louts in front of the natives. If you have no respect for your own dignity, have some respect for ours."

"You stick to your pleasures, and I'll stick to mine," he told me, speaking more calmly, but obviously savoring his own bitterness. "I'm here for the pleasure of seeing the descendants of the stinking honkies who kicked my ancestors out to grovel in the putrid mess they made for themselves. And I intend to get my money's worth."

I started to reply, but then restrained myself. I would have to remain on civil terms with this horrid young man for hours. I don't think I'll ever understand these Amero-Africans and their pointless blood-feud. I doubt if I want to.

I started the engines, lifted her off the pad, and headed east into the smog bank trying hard not to think of that black brother Lumumba. No wonder so many of his ancestors were lynched by the Space Agers! Sometime during the next few hours, that crut was going to get his. . . .

Through my cabin monitor (this Air Force Iron was just loaded with real Space Age stuff), I watched the stupid looks on their flat faces as we headed for what looked like a solid wall of smoke at about 100 miles per hour. From the fringes, a major smog bank looks like that— solid as a steel slab—but once you're inside there's nothing but a blue haze that anyone with a halfway-decent set of goggles can see right through.

"We are now entering the East Coastal smog bank, ladies and gentlemen," I told them. "This smog bank extends roughly from Bangor, Maine in the north to Jacksonville, Florida in the south, and from the Atlantic coastline in the east to the slopes of the Alleghenies in the

west. It is the third largest smog bank in the United
States."

Getting used to the way things look inside the smog
always holds 'em for a while. Inside a smog bank, the
color of everything is kind of washed-out, grayed and
blued. The air is something you can see, a mist that
doesn't move; it almost sparkles at you. For some reason,
these Africans always seem to be knocked out by it.
Imagine thinking stuff like that is beautiful, crap that
would kill you horribly and slowly in a couple of days if
you were stupid or unlucky enough to breathe it without
filters.

Yeah, they sure were a bunch of brothers! Some executive from Nairobi who acted like just being in the same
copter with an American might give him lung cancer and
his wife. Two rich young fruits from Luthuliville who
seemed to be traveling together so they could congratu-
late themselves on how smart they both were for picking
such rich parents. Some professor named Balewa who had
never been to the States before but probably was sure he
knew what it was all about. A backwoods jungle-bunny
named Kulongo who had struck it rich off uranium or
something taking his wife and kid on the grand tour. And
of course, that creep Lumumba. The usual load of African tourists. Man, in the Good Old Days, these niggers
wouldn't have been good enough to shine our shoes!

Now we were flying over the old State of New Jersey.
The Space Agers did things in New Jersey that not even
the African professors have figured out. It was weird
country we were crossing: endless patterns of box-houses,
all of them the same, all bleached blue-gray by two
centuries of smog; big old freeways jammed with the
wreckage of cars from the Panic of the Century; a few
twisted gray trees and a patch of dry grass here and there
that somehow managed to survive in the smog.

And this was western Jersey; this was nothing. Further
east, it was like an alien planet or something. The view
from the Jersey Turnpike was a sure tourist-pleaser. It
really told them just where they were. It let them know
that the Space Agers could do things they couldn't hope
to do. Or want to.

Yeah, the Jersey Lowlands are spectacular all right, but
why in hell did our ancestors want to do a thing like that?
It really makes you think. You look at the Jersey Low-

lands and you know that the Space Agers could do about anything they wanted to. . . .

But why in hell did they want to do some of the things they did?

There was something about actually standing in the open American atmosphere that seemed to act directly on the consciousness, like kif. Perhaps it was the visual effect. Ryan had landed the helicopter on a shattered arch of six-lane freeway that soared like the frozen contrail of an ascending jet over a surreal metallic jungle of amorphous Space Age rubble on a giant's scale—all crumbling rusted storage tanks, ruined factories, fantastic mazes of decayed valving and piping—filling the world from horizon to horizon. As we stepped out onto the cracked and pitted concrete, the spectrum of reality changed, as if we were suddenly on the surface of a planet circling a bluer and grayer sun. The entire grotesque panorama appeared as if through a blue-gray filter. But we were inside the filter; the filter was the open American smog and it shone in drab sparkles all around us. Strangest of all, the air seemed to remain completely transparent while possessing tangible visible substance. Yes, the visual effect of the American atmosphere alone are enough to affect you like some hallucinogenic drug: distorting your consciousness by warping your visual perception of your environment.

Of course the exact biochemical effects of breathing saturation smog through filters are still unknown. We know that the American atmosphere is loaded with hydrocarbons and nitrous oxides that would kill a man if he breathed them directly in a matter of days. We know that the atmosphere filters developed toward the end by the Space Agers enable a man to breathe the American atmosphere for up to three months without permanent damage to his health and enable the modern Americans—who have to breathe variations of this filtered poison every moment of their lives—to often live to be fifty. We know how to duplicate the Space Age atmosphere filters, and we more or less know how their complex catalytic fibers work, but the reactions that the filters must put the American atmosphere through to make it breathable are so complex that the only thing we can say for sure of what comes out the other side is that it usually takes about four decades to kill you.

Perhaps that strange feeling that came over me was a combination of both effects. But for whatever reasons, I saw that weird landscape as if in a dream or a state of intoxication: everything faded and misty and somehow unreal, vaguely supernatural.

Beside me, staring silently and with a strange dignity at the totally artificial vista of monstrous rusted ruins, stood the Ghanaian, Kulongo. When he finally spoke, his wife and son seemed to hang on his words, as if he were one of the old chiefs dispensing tribal wisdom.

"I have never seen such a place as this," Kulongo said. "In this place, there once lived a race of demons or witch-doctors or gods. There are those who would call me an ignorant savage for saying this thing, but only a fool doubts what he sees with his eyes or his heart. The men who made these things were not human beings like us. Their souls were not as our souls."

Although he was putting it in naive and primitive terms, there was the weight of essential truth in Kulongo's words. The broken arch of freeway on which we stood reared like the head of a snake whose body was a six-lane road clogged with the rusted corpses of what had been a region-wide traffic-jam during the Panic of the Century. The freeway led south, off into the fuzzy horizon of the smog bank, through a ruined landscape in which nothing could be seen that was not the decayed work of man; that was not metal or concrete or asphalt or plastic or Space Age synthetic. It was like being perched above some vast ruined machine the size of a city, a city never meant for man. The scale of the machinery and the way it encompassed the visual universe made it very clear to me that the reality of America was something that no one could put into a book or a film.

I was in America with a vengeance. I was overwhelmed by the totality with which the Space Agers had transformed their environment, and by the essential incomprehensibility—despite our sophisticated sociological and psycho-historical explanations—of why they had done such a thing and of how they themselves had seen it. "Their souls were not as our souls" was as good a way to put it as any.

"Well, it's certainly spectacular enough," Ruala said to his friend, the rapt look on his face making a mockery of his sarcastic tone.

"So it is," Ojubu said softly. Then, more harshly: "It's probably the largest junk-heap in the world."

The two of them made a half-hearted attempt at laughter, which withered almost immediately under the contemptuous look that the Kulongos gave them; the timeless look that the people of the bush have given the people of the towns for centuries, the look that said only cowardly fools attempt to hide their fears behind a false curtain of contempt, that only those who fear magic need openly to mock it.

And again, in their naive way, the Kulongos were right. Ojubu and Ruala were just a shade too shrill, and even while they played at diffidence their eyes remained fixed on that totally surreal metal landscape. One would have to be a lot worse than a mere fool not to feel the essential strangeness of that place.

Even Lumumba, standing a few yards from the rest of us, could not tear his eyes away.

Just behind us, Ryan stood leaning against the helicopter. There was a strange power, perhaps a sarcasm as well, in his words as he delivered what surely must have been his routine guide's speech about this place.

"Ladies and gentlemen, we are now standing on the New Jersey Turnpike, one of the great freeways that linked the mighty cities of Space Age America. Below you are the Jersey Lowlands, which served as a great manufacturing, storage, power-producing and petroleum refining and distribution center for the greatest and largest of the Space Age cities, Old New York. As you look across these incredible ruins larger than most modern African cities—think of this: all of this was nothing to the Space Age Americans but a minor industrial area to be driven through at a hundred miles an hour without even noticing. You're not looking at one of the famous wonders of Old New York, but merely at an unimportant fringe of the greatest city ever built by man. Ladies and gentlemen, you're looking at a very minor work of Space Age man!"

"Crazy damn honkies ..." Lumumba muttered. But there was little vehemence or real meaning in his voice, and like the rest of us, he could not tear his eyes away. It was not hard to understand what was going through his mind. Here was a man raised in the Amero-African enclaves on an irrational mixture of hate for the fallen

Space Agers, contempt for their vanished culture, fear of their former power, and perhaps a kind of twisted blend of envy and identification that only an Amero-African could fully understand. He had come to revel in the sight of the ruins of the civilization that had banished his ancestors, and now he was confronted with the inescapable reality that the "honkies" whose memory he both hated and feared had indeed possessed power and knowledge not only beyond his comprehension, but applied to ends which his mind was not equipped to understand.

It must have been a humbling moment for Michael Lumumba. He had come to sneer and had been forced to gape.

I tore my gaze away from that awesome vista to look at Ryan; there was a grim smile on his pale unhealthy face as he drank in our reactions. Clearly, he had meant this sight to humble us, and just as clearly, it had.

Ryan stared back at me through his goggles as he noticed me watching him. I couldn't read the expression in his watery eyes through the distortion of the goggle lenses. All I understood was that somehow some subtle change had occurred in the pattern of the group's inter-relationships. No longer was Ryan merely a native guide, a functionary, a man without dignity. He had proven that he could show us sights beyond the limits of the modern world. He had reminded us of just where we were, and who and what his ancestors had been. He had suddenly gained second-hand stature from the incredible ruins around him, because, in a very real way, they were *his* ruins. Certainly they were not ours.

"I've got to admit they were great engineers," Koyinka, the Kenyan executive, said.

"So were the ancient Egyptians," Lumumba said, recovering some of his bitterness. "And what did it get *them?* A fancy collection of old junk over their graves—exactly what it got these honkies."

"If you keep it up, pal," Ryan said coldly, "you may get a chance to see something that'll impress you a bit more than these ruins."

"Is that a threat or a promise, Ryan?"

"Depends on whether you're a man ... or a *boy,* Mr. Lumumba."

Lumumba had nothing to say to that, whatever it all

had meant. Ryan appeared to have won a round in some contest between them.

And when we followed Ryan back into the helicopter, I think we were all aware that for the next few hours, this pale, unhealthy American would be something more than a mere convenient functionary. We were the tourists; he was the guide.

But as we looked over our shoulders at the vast and overwhelming heritage that had been created and then squandered by his ancestors, the relationship that those words described took on a new meaning. The ancestral ruins off which he lived were a greater thing in some absolute sense than the totality of our entire living civilization. He had convinced us of that, and he knew it.

That view across the Jersey Lowlands always seems to shut them up for a while. Even that crut Lumumba. God knows why. Sure it's spectacular, bigger than anything these Africans could ever have seen where they come from, but when you come right down to it, you gotta admit that Ojubu was right—the Jersey Lowlands are nothing but a giant pile of junk. Crap. Space Age garbage. Sometimes looking at a place like that can piss me off. I mean, we had *some* ancestors, they built the greatest civilization the world ever saw, but what did they leave for us? The most spectacular junk-piles in the world, air that does you in sooner or later even through filters, and a continent where seeing something alive that people didn't put there is a big deal. Our ancestors went to the Moon, they were a great people, the greatest in history, but sometimes I get the feeling they were maybe just a little out of their minds. Like that crazy "Merge With the Cosmic All" thing I found that time in Grand Central—still working after two centuries or so; it must do *something* besides kill people, but *what?* I dunno, maybe our ancestors went a little over the edge, sometimes. . . .

Not that I'd ever admit a thing like that to any black brothers! The Space Agers may have been a little bit nuts, but who are these Africans to say so, who are they to decide whether a civilization that had them beat up and down the line was sane or not? Sane according to who? Them, or the Space Agers? For that matter, who am I to think a thing like that? An ant or a rat living off their garbage. Who are nobodies like us and the Africans to judge people who could go to the Moon?

Like I keep telling Karen, this damn tourist business is getting to me. I'm around these Africans too much. Sometimes, if I don't watch myself, I catch myself thinking like them. Maybe it's the lousy smog this far into the smog bank—but hell, that's another crazy African idea!

That's what being around these Africans does to me, and looking at Subway Dwellers five times a week sure doesn't help either. Let's face it, stuff like the Subways and the Lowlands is really depressing. It tells a man he's a nothing. Worse, it tells him that people who were better than he is still managed to screw things up. It's just not good for your mind.

But as the copter crested the lip of the Palisades ridge and we looked out across that wide Hudson River at Manhattan, I was reminded again that this crummy job had its compensations. If you haven't seen Manhattan from a copter crossing the Hudson from the Jersey side, you haven't seen nothing, pal. That Fuller Dome socks you right in the eye. It's ten miles in diameter. It has facets that make it glitter like a giant blue diamond floating over the middle of the island. Yeah, that's right, it floats. It's made of some Space Age plastic that's been turned blue and hazy by a couple centuries of smog, it's ten miles wide at the base, and the goddamn thing floats over the middle of Manhattan a few hundred feet off the ground at its rim like a cloud or a hover or something. No motors, no nothing. It's just a hemisphere made of plastic panels and alloy tubing and it floats over the middle of Manhattan like half a giant diamond all by itself. Now *that's* what I call a *real* piece of Space Age hardware!

I could hear them suck in their breaths behind me. Yeah, it really does it to you. I almost forgot to give them the spiel, I mean who wants to, what can you really say to someone while he's looking at the Fuller Dome for the first time?

"Ladies and gentlemen, you are now looking at the world-famous Fuller Dome, the largest architectural structure ever built by the human race. It is ten miles in diameter. It encloses the center of Manhattan Island, the heart of Old New York. It has no motors, no power source, and no moving parts. But it floats in the air like a cloud. It is considered the First Wonder of the World."

What else is there to say?

We came in low across the river toward that incredible floating blue diamond, the Fuller Dome, parallel to the ruins of a great suspension bridge which had collapsed, and now hung in fantastic rusted tatters half in and half out of the water. Aside from Ryan's short guidebook speech, no one said a word as we crossed the waters to Manhattan.

Like the Moon Landing, the Fuller Dome was one of the peak achievements of the Space Age, a feat beyond the power of modern African civilization. As I understand it, the Dome held itself aloft by convection currents created by its own greenhouse effect, though this has always seemed to me the logical equivalent of a man lifting himself by his own shoulders. No one quite knows exactly how a dome this size was built, but the records show that it required a fleet of two hundred helicopters. It took six weeks to complete. It was named after Buckminster Fuller, one of the architectural geniuses of the early Space Age, but it was not built till after his death, though it is considered his monument. But it was more than that; it was staggeringly, overwhelmingly beautiful.

We crossed the river and headed toward the rim of the Fuller Dome at about two hundred feet, over a shoreline of crumbling docks and the half-sunken hulks of rusted-out ships; then over a wide strip of elevated highway filled with the usual wrecked cars; and finally we slipped under the rim of the Dome itself, an incredibly thin metal hoop floating in the air, from which the Dome seemed to blossom like a soap-bubble from a child's bubble-pipe.

And we were flying inside the Fuller Dome. It was an incredible sensation—the world inside the Dome existed in blue crystal. Our helicopter seemed like a buzzing fly that had intruded into an enormous room. The room was a mile high and ten miles wide. The facets of the Fuller Dome had been designed to admit natural sunlight and thus preserve the sense of being outdoors, but they had been weathered to a blueish hue by the saturation smog. As a result, the interior of the Dome was a room on a superhuman scale, a room filled with a pale blue light—and a room containing a major portion of a giant city.

Towering before us were the famous skyscrapers of Old New York, a forest of rectangular monoliths hundreds of feet high; in some cases well over a thousand feet tall. Some of them stood almost intact, empty concrete boxes transformed into giant somber tombstones by the eerie blue light that permeated everything. Others had been ripped apart by explosions and were jagged piles of girders and concrete. Some had had walls almost entirely of glass; most of these were now airy mazes of framework and concrete platforms, where the blue light here and there flashed off intact patches of glass. And far above the tops of the tallest buildings was the blue stained-glass faceted sky of the Fuller Dome.

Ryan took the helicopter up to the five hundred foot level and headed for the giant necropolis, a city of monuments built on a scale that would have caused the Pharaohs to whimper, packed casually together like family houses in an African residential village. And all of it bathed in a sparkly blue-gray light which seemed to enclose a universe—here in the very core of the East Coastal smog bank, everything seemed to twinkle and shimmer.

We all gasped as Ryan headed at 100 mph for a thin canyon that was the gap between two rows of buildings which faced each other across a not-very-wide street hundreds of feet below.

For a moment, we seemed to be a stone dropping toward a narrow shaft between two immense cliffs—then suddenly, the copter's engines screamed, and the copter seemed to somehow skid and slide through the air to a dead hover no more than a hundred feet from the sheer face of a huge gray skyscraper.

Ryan's laugh sounded unreal, partially drowned out by the descending whine of the copter's relaxing engines. "Don't worry folks," he said over the public address system, "I'm in control of this aircraft at all times. I just thought I'd give you a little thrill. Kind of wake up those of you who might be sleeping. Because you wouldn't want to miss what comes next: a helicopter tour of what the Space Agers called 'The Sidewalks of New York'."

And we inched forward at the pace of a running man;

we seemed to drift into a canyon between two parallel lines of huge buildings that went on for miles.

Man, no matter how many times I come here, I still feel weird inside the Fuller Dome. It's another world in there. New York seems like it's built for people fifty feet tall, it makes you feel so small, like you're inside a giant's room, but when you look up at the inside of the Dome, the buildings that seemed so big seem so small; you can't get a grasp on the scale of anything. And everything is all blue. And the smog is so heavy you think you could eat it with a fork.

And you know that the whole thing is completely dead. Nothing lives in New York between the Fuller Dome and the Subways where a couple thousand Subway Dwellers stew in their own muck. Nothing can. The air inside the Fuller Dome is some of the worst in the country, almost as bad as that stuff they say you can barely see through that fills the Los Angeles basin. The Space Agers didn't put up the Dome to atmosphere-seal a piece of the city; they did it to make the city warmer and keep the snow off the ground. The smog was still breathable then. So the inside of the Dome is open to the naked atmosphere, and it actually seems to suck in the worst of the smog, maybe because it's about twenty degrees hotter inside the Dome than it is outside, something about convection currents the Africans say. I dunno.

It's creepy, that's what it is. Flying slowly between two lines of skyscrapers, I had the feeling I was tip-toeing very carefully around some giant graveyard in the middle of the night. Not any of that crap about ghosts that I'll bet some of these Africans still believe deep down; this whole city really *was* a graveyard. During the Space Age, millions of people lived in New York; now there was nothing alive here but a couple thousand stinking subhuman Subway Dwellers slowly strangling themselves in their stinking sealed Subways.

So I kind of drifted the copter in among the skyscrapers for a while, at about a hundred feet, real slow, almost on hover, and just let the customers suck in the feel of the place, keeping my mouth shut.

After a while, we came to a really wide street, jammed to overflowing with wrecked and rusted cars that even filled the sidewalks, as if the Space Agers had built one of their crazy car-pyramids right here in the middle of Manhattan, and it had just sort of run like hot wax. I hovered the copter over it for a while.

"Folks," I told the customers, "below you you see some of the wreckage from the Panic of the Century which fills the Sidewalks of New York. The Panic of the Century started right here in New York. Imagine, ladies and gentlemen, at the height of the Space Age, there were more than one hundred million cars, trucks, buses, and other motor vehicles operating on the freeways and streets of the United States. A car for every two adults! Look below you and try to imagine the magnificence of the sight of all of them on the road all at once!"

Yeah, that would've been something to see all right! From a helicopter, that is. Man, those Space Agers sure had guts, driving around down there jammed together on the freeways at copter speeds with only a few feet between them. They must've had fantastic reflexes to be able to handle it. Not for me, pal, I couldn't do it, and I wouldn't want to.

But God, what this place must've been like, all lit up at night in bright colored lights, millions of people tearing around in their cars all at once! Hell, what's the population of the United States today, thirty, forty million, not a city with 500,000 people, and nothing in all the world on the scale of this. Damn it, those were the days for a man to have lived!

Now look at it! The power all gone except for whatever keeps the Subway electricity going, so the only light above ground is that blue stuff that makes everything seem so still and quiet and weird, like the city's embalmed or something. The buildings are all empty crumbling wrecks, burnt out, smashed up by explosions, and the cars are all rusted garbage, and the people are dead, dead, dead.

It's enough to make you cry, if you let it get to you.

We drifted among the ruins of Old New York like some secretive night insect. By now it was afternoon, and the canyons formed by the skyscrapers were filled with deep purple shadows and intermittent avenues of pale blue light. The world under the Fuller Dome was composed of relative darknesses of blue, much as the world under the canopy of a heavy rain forest is a world of varying greens.

We dipped low and drifted for a few moments over a large square where the top of a low building had been removed by an explosion to reveal a series of huge cuts and caverns extending deep into the bowels of the earth, perhaps some kind of underground railway terminal, perhaps even a ruined part of the famous New York Subways.

"This is a burial ground of magics," Kulongo said. "The air is very heavy here."

"They sure knew how to build," Koyinka said.

Beside me, Michael Lumumba seemed subdued, perhaps even nervous. "You know, I never knew it was all so big," he muttered to me. "So big, and so strange, and so . . . so . . ."

"*Space Age,* Mr. Lumumba?" Ryan suggested over the intercom.

Lumumba's jaw twitched. He was obviously furious at having Ryan supply the precise words he was looking for. "Inhuman, honkie, inhuman, was what I was going to say," he lied transparently. "Wasn't there an ancient saying, 'New York is a nice place to visit, but I wouldn't want to live there'."

"Never heard that one, pal," Ryan said. "But I can see how your ancestors might've felt that way. New York was always too much for anyone but a *real* Space Ager."

There was considerable truth in what they both said, though of course neither was interested in true insight. Here in the blue crystal world under the Fuller Dome, in a helicopter buzzing about noisily in the graveyard silence, reduced by the scale of the buildings to the relative size of an insect, I felt the immensity of what had been Space Age America all around me. I felt as if I were trespassing in the mansions of my betters. I felt like a bug, an insect. I remembered from history, not from instinct, how totally America had dominated the world during the Space Age—not by armed conquest, but by the sheer overwhelming weight of its very existence. I had never before been quite able to grasp that concept.

I understood it perfectly now.

I gave them the standard helicopter tour of the Sidewalks of New York. We floated up Broadway, the street

that had been called The Great White Way, at about fifty
feet, past crazy rotten networks of light steel girders,
crumbled signs and wiring on a monster scale. At a
thousand feet, we circled the Empire State Building, one
of the oldest of the great skyscrapers, and now one of the
best-preserved, a thousand-foot slab of solid concrete,
probably just the kind of tombstone the Space Agers
would've put up for themselves if they had thought about
it.

Yeah, I gave them all the usual stuff. The ruins of
Rockefeller Center. The UN Plaza Crater.

Of course, they were all sucking it up, even Lumumba,
though of course the slime wouldn't admit it. After this,
they'd be ripe for a nasty peek at the Subway Dwellers,
and after they got through gaping at the animals, they'd
be ready for dinner back in Milford, feeling they had got
their money's worth.

Yeah, I can get the same money for a five hour tour
that most guides get for six because I've got the stomach
to take them into a Subway station. As usual, it had just
the right effect when I told them we were going to end
the tour with a visit on foot to an inhabited Subway
station. Instead of bitching and moaning that the tour was
too short, that they weren't getting their money's worth,
they were all eager and maybe a little scared at actually
walking among the *really* primitive natives. Once they'd
had their fill of the Subway Dwellers, a ride home across
the Hudson into the sunset would be enough to convince
them they'd had a great day.

So we *were* going to see the Subway Dwellers! Most of
the native guides avoided the Subways and the American
government for some reason seemed to discourage research
by foreigners. A subtle discouragement, perhaps, but
discouragment nevertheless. In a paper he published a few
years ago, Omgazi had theorized that the modern Americans in the vicinity of New York had a loathing of the
Subway Dwellers that amounted to virtually a superstitious dread. According to him, the Subway Dwellers,
because they were direct descendants of die-hard Space
Agers who had atmosphere-sealed the Subways and set up
a closed ecology inside rather than abandon New York,
were identified with their ancestors in the minds of the
modern Americans. Hence, the modern Americans

shunned the Subway Dwellers because they considered them shamans on a deep subconscious level.

It had always seemed to me that Omgazi was being rather ethnocentric. He was dealing, after all, with modern Americans, not nineteenth century Africans. Now I would have a chance to observe some Subway Dwellers myself. The prospect was most exciting. For although the Subway Dwellers were apparently degenerating towards extinction at a rapid rate, in one respect they were unique in all the world: they still lived in an artificial environment that had been constructed during the Space Age. True, it had been a hurried, makeshift environment in the first place, and it and its inhabitants had deteriorated tremendously in two centuries, but whatever else they were or weren't, the Subway Dwellers were the only enclave of Space Age Americans left on the face of the earth.

If it were possible at all for a modern African truly to come to understand the reality of Space Age America, surely confrontation with the lineal descendants of the Space Age would provide the key.

Ryan set the helicopter down in what seemed to be some kind of large open terrace behind a massive, low, concrete building. The terrace was a patchwork of cracked concrete walkways and expanses of bare gray earth. Once, apparently, it had been a small park, before the smog had become lethal to vegetation. As a denuded ruin in the pale blue light, it seemed like some strange cold corpse as the helicopter kicked up dry clouds of dust from the surface of the dead parkland.

As I stepped out with the others into the blue world of the Fuller Dome, I gasped: I had a momentary impression that I had stepped back to Africa, to Accra or Brazzaville. The air was rich and warm and humid on my skin. An instant later, the visual effect—everything a cool pale blue—jarred me with its arctic-vista contrast. Then I noticed the air itself and I shuddered, and was suddenly hyperconscious of the filters up my nostrils and the goggles over my eyes, for here the air was so heavy with smog that it seemed to sparkle electrically in the crazy blue light. What incredible, beautiful, foul poison!

Except for Ryan, all of us were clearly overcome, each in his own way. Kulongo blinked and stared solemnly for a moment like a great bear; his wife and son seemed to lean into the security of his calm aura. Koyinka seemed

to fear that he might strangle; his wife twittered about
excitedly, tugging at his hand. The two young men from
Luthuliville seemed to be self-consciously making an
effort to avoid clutching at each other. Michael Lumumba
mumbled something unintelligible under his breath.

"What was that you said, *Mr.* Lumumba?" Ryan said a
shade gratingly as he led us out of the park down a
crumbling set of stone-and-concrete stairs. Something
seemed to snap inside Lumumba; he broke stride for a
moment, frozen by some inner event while Ryan led the
rest of us onto a walkway between a line of huge silent
buildings and a street choked with the rusted wreckage of
ancient cars, timelessly locked in their death-agony in the
sparkly blue light.

"What do you want from me, you damned honkie?"
Lumumba shouted shrilly. "Haven't you done enough to
us?"

Ryan broke stride for a moment, smiled back at
Lumumba rather cruelly, and said: "I don't know what
you're talking about, pal. I've got your money already.
What the hell else could I want from *you?*"

He began to move off down the walkway again, thread-
ing his way past and over bits of wrecked cars, fallen
masonry, and amorphous rubble. Over his shoulder, he
noticed that Lumumba was following along haltingly,
staring up at the buildings, nibbling at his lower lip.

"What's the matter, Lumumba," Ryan shouted back at
him, "aren't these ruins good enough for you to gloat
over? You wouldn't be just a little bit afraid, would you?"

*"Afraid?* Why should I be afraid?"

Ryan continued on for a few more meters; then he
stopped and leaned up against the wall of one of the more
badly-damaged skyscrapers, close by a jagged cave-like
opening that led into the dark interior. He looked directly
at Lumumba. "Don't get me wrong, pal," he said, "I
wouldn't blame you if you were a little scared of the
Subway Dwellers. After all, they're the direct descendants
of the people that kicked your ancestors out of this
country. Maybe you got a right to be nervous."

"Don't be an idiot, Ryan, why should a civilized African be afraid of a pack of degenerate savages?" Koyinka
said as we all caught up to Ryan.

Ryan shrugged. "How should I know?" he said. "Maybe you ought to ask Mr. Lumumba."

And with that, he turned his back on us and stepped through the jagged opening into the ruined skyscraper. Somewhat uneasily, we followed him into what proved to be a large ante-chamber that seemed to lead back into some even larger cavernous space that could be sensed rather than seen looming in the darkness. But Ryan did not lead us towards this large open space; instead, he stopped before he had gone more than a dozen steps and waited for us near a crumbling metal-pipe fence that guarded two edges of what looked like a deep pit. One long edge of the pit was flush with the right wall of the ante-chamber; at the far short edge, a flight of stone stairs began which seemed to go all the way to the shadow-obscured bottom.

Ryan led us along the railing to the top of the stairs, and from this angle I could see that the pit had once been the entrance to the mouth of a large tunnel whose floor had been the floor of the pit at the foot of the stairs. Now an immense and ancient solid slab of steel blocked the tunnel-mouth and formed the fourth wall of the pit. But in the center of this rusted steel slab was a relatively new airlock that seemed of modern design.

"Ladies and gentlemen," Ryan said, "we're standing by a sealed entrance to the Subways of Old New York. During the Space Age, the Subways were the major transportation system of the city and there were hundreds of entrances like this one. Below the ground was a giant network of stations and tunnels through which the Space Agers could go from any point in the city to any other point. Many of the stations were huge and contained shops and restaurants. Every station had automatic vending machines which sold food and drinks and a lot of other things too. Even during the Space Age, the Subways were a kind of little world."

He started down the stairs, still talking. "During the Panic of the Century, some of the New Yorkers chose not to leave the city. Instead, they retreated to the Subways, sealed all the entrances, installed Space Station life-support machinery—everything from a fusion reactor to hydroponics—and cut themselves off from the outside world. Today, the Subway Dwellers, direct descendants of those Space Agers, still inhabit several of the Subway stations. And most of the Space Age life-support machinery is still running. There are probably Space Age artifacts down here that no modern man has ever seen."

At the bottom of the pit, Ryan led us to the airlock and opened the outer door. The airlock proved to be surprisingly large. "This airlock was installed by the government about fifty years ago, soon after the Subway Dwellers were discovered," he told us as he jammed us inside and began the cycle. "It was part of the program to recivilize the Subway Dwellers. The idea was to let scientists get inside without contaminating the Subway atmosphere with smog. Of course, the whole program was a flop. Nobody's ever going to get through to the Subway Dwellers, and there are less of 'em every year, they don't breed much, and in a generation or so they'll be extinct. So you're all in for a really unique experience. Not everyone will be able to tell their grandchildren that they actually saw a live Subway Dweller!"

The inner airlock door opened into an ancient square-cross-sectioned tunnel made of rotting gray concrete. The air, even through filters, tasted horrible: very thin, somehow crisp without being at all bracing, with a chemical undertone, yet reeking with organic decay odors. Breathing was very difficult; it felt like we were at the fifteen-thousand-foot level.

"I'm not telling you all this for my health," Ryan said as he moved us out of the airlock. "I'm telling it to you for *your* health: don't mess with these people. Look and don't touch. Listen, but keep your mouths shut. They may seem harmless, they may be harmless, but no one can be sure. That's why not many guides will take people down here. I hope you *all* have that straight."

The last remark had obviously been meant for Lumumba, but he didn't seem to react to it; he seemed subdued, drawn up inside himself. Perhaps Ryan was right—perhaps in some unguessable way, Lumumba *was* afraid. It's impossible to really understand these Amero-Africans.

We moved off down the corridor. The overhead lights—at least in this area—were clearly modern, probably installed when the airlock had been installed, but it was possible that the power was actually provided by the fusion reactor that had been installed centuries ago by the Space Agers themselves. The air we were breathing was produced by a Space Age atmosphere plant that had been designed for actual Space Stations! It was a frightening and at the same time thrilling feeling: our lives were dependent on actual functioning Space Age equipment. It was almost like stepping back in time.

The corridor made a right-angle turn and became a downward-sloping ramp. The ramp leveled off after a few dozen feet, passed some crumbling ruins inset into one of the walls—apparently a ruined shop of some strange sort with massive chairs bolted to the floor and pieces of mirror still clinging to patches of its walls—and suddenly opened out into a wide, low, cavelike space lit dimly and erratically by ancient Space Age permabulbs which still functioned in many places along the grime-encrusted ceiling.

It was the strangest room—if you could call it that—that I had ever been in. The ceiling seemed horribly low, lower even than it actually was, because the room seemed to go on under it indefinitely, in all sorts of seemingly-random directions. Its boundaries faded off into shadows and dim lights and gloom; I couldn't see any of the far walls. It was impossible to feel exactly claustrophobic in a place like that, but it gave me an analogous sensation without a name, as if the ceiling and floor might somehow come together and squash me flat.

Strange figures shuffled around in the gloom, moving about slowly and aimlessly. Other figures sat singly or in small groups on the bare filthy floor. Most of the Subway Dwellers were well under five feet tall. Their shoulders were deeply stooped making them seem even shorter, and their bodies were thin, rickety, and emaciated under the tattered and filthy scraps of multicolored rags which they wore. I was deeply shocked. I don't really know what I had expected, but I certainly had not been prepared for the unmistakable aura of diminished humanity which these pitiful creatures exuded even at a distant first glance.

Immediately before us was a kind of concrete hut. It was pitted with what looked like bullet scars and parts of it were burned black. It had tiny windows, one of which still held some rotten metal grillwork. Apparently it had been a kind of sentry-box, perhaps during the Panic of the Century itself. A complex barrier cut off the section where we stood from the main area of the Subway station. It consisted of a ceiling-to-floor metal grillwork fence on either side of a line of turnstiles. On either side of the line of turnstiles, gates in the fence clearly marked "Exit" in peeling white and black enamel had been crudely welded shut, by the look of the weld perhaps more than a century ago.

On the other side of the barrier stood a male Subway Dweller wearing a kind of long shirt patched together out of every conceivable type and color of cloth and rotting away at the edges and in random patches. He stood staring at us, or at least with his deeply-squinted expressionless eyes turned in our direction, rocking back and forth slightly from the waist, but otherwise not moving. His face was unusually pallid even for an American and every inch of his skin and clothing was caked with an incredible layer of filth.

Ignoring the Subway Dweller as thoroughly as that stooped figure was ignoring us, Ryan led us to the line of turnstiles and extracted a handful of small greenish-yellow coins from a pocket.

"These are Subway Tokens," he told us, dropping ten of the coins into a small slot atop one of the turnstiles. "Space Age money that was only used down here. It's good in all the vending machines, and in these turnstiles. The Subway Dwellers still use the Tokens to get food and water from the machines. When I want more of these things, all I have to do is break open a vending machine, so don't worry, admission isn't costing us anything. Just push your way through the turnstile like this. . . ."

He demonstrated by walking straight through the turnstile. The turnstile barrier rotated a notch to let him through when he applied his body against it.

One by one we passed through the turnstile. Michael Lumumba passed through immediately ahead of me, then paused at the other side to study the Subway Dweller, who had drifted up to the barrier. Lumumba looked down at the Subway Dweller's face for a long moment; then a sardonic smile grew slowly on his face, and he said: "Hello, honkie, how are things in the Subway?"

The Subway Dweller turned his eyes in Lumumba's direction. He did nothing else.

"Hey, just what *are* you, some kind of cretin?" Lumumba said as Ryan, his face flushed red behind his pallor, turned in his tracks and started back towards Lumumba. The Subway Dweller's face did not change expression; in fact it could hardly have been said to have had an expression in the first place. "I think you're a brain-damage case, honkie."

"I told you not to talk to the Subway Dwellers!" Ryan said, shoving his way between Lumumba and the Subway Dweller.

"So you did," Lumumba said coolly. "And I'm beginning to wonder why."

"They can be dangerous."

*"Dangerous?* These little moronic slugs? The only thing these brainless white worms can be dangerous to is your pride. Isn't that it, Ryan? Behold the remnants of the great Space Age honkies! See how they haven't the brains left to wipe the drool off their chins—"

"Be silent!" Kulongo suddenly bellowed with the authority of a chief in his voice. Lumumba was indeed silenced, and even Ryan backed off as Kulongo moved near them. But the self-satisfied look that Lumumba continued to give Ryan was a weapon that he was wielding, a weapon that the American obviously felt keenly.

Through it all, the Subway Dweller continued to rock back and forth, gently and silently, without a sign of human sentience.

Goddamn that black brother Lumumba and goddamn the stinking Subway Dwellers! Oh how I hate taking these Africans down there, sometimes I wonder why the hell I do it. Sometimes I feel there's something unclean about it all, something rotten. Not just the Subway Dwellers, though those horrible animals are rotten enough, but taking a bunch of stinking African tourists in there to look at them, and me making money off of it. It's a great selling-point for the day-tour, those black brothers eat it up, especially the cruts like Lumumba, but if I didn't need the money so bad, I wouldn't do it. Call it patriotism, maybe. I'm not patriotic enough not to take my tours to see the Subway Dwellers, but I'm patriotic enough not to feel too happy with myself about it.

Of course I know what it is that gets to me. The Subway Dwellers are the last direct descendants of the Space Agers, in a way the only piece of the Space Age still alive, and what they are is what Lumumba said they are: slugs, morons, and cretins. And physical wrecks on top of it. Lousy eyesight, rubbery bones, rotten teeth, and if you find one more than five feet tall, it's a giant.

They're lucky to live to thirty. There's no smog in the recirculated chemical crap they breathe, but there's not enough oxygen in the long run either, and after two centuries of sucking in its own gunk, God only knows exactly what's missing and what there's too much of in the air that the Subway life-support system puts out. The Subway Dwellers have just about enough brains left to keep the air plant and the hydroponics and stuff going without really knowing what the hell they're doing. Every one of them is a born brain-damage case, and year by year the air keeps getting crummier and crummier and the crap they eat gets lousier and lousier and there are fewer and fewer Subway Dwellers and they're getting stupider and stupider. They say in another fifty years, they'll be extinct. They're all that's left of the Space Agers, and they're slowly strangling their brains in their own crap.

Like I keep telling Karen, the tourist business is a rotten way to earn a living. Every time I come down into this stinking hole in the ground, I have to keep reminding myself that I'm a day closer to owning a piece of that Amazon swampland. It helps settle my stomach.

I led my collection of Africans further out into the upper level of the station. It's hard to figure out just what this level was during the Space Age—there's nothing up here but a lot of old vending machines and ruined stalls and garbage. This level goes on and on in all directions; there are more old Subway entrances leading into it than I've counted. I've been told that during the Space Age thousands of people crowded in here just on their way to the trains below, but that doesn't make sense. Why would they want to hang around in a hole in the ground any longer than they had to?

The Subway Dwellers, of course, just mostly hung around doing what Subway Dwellers do—stand and stare into space, or sit on their butts and chew their alga-cake, or maybe even stand and stare and chew at the same time, if they're real enterprising. Beats me why the Africans are so fascinated by them. . . .

Then, a few yards ahead of us, I saw a vending machine servicer approaching a water machine. Now there was a piece of luck! I sure didn't get to show every tour what passed for a "Genuine Subway Dweller Ceremony." I decided to really play it up. I held the tourists off about ten feet from the water machine so they wouldn't mess things up, and started to give them a fancy pitch.

"You're about to witness an authentic water machine servicing by a Subway Dweller Vending Machine Servicer," I told them, as a crummy Subway Dweller slowly inched up to a peeling red and white water machine dragging a small cart which held four metal kegs and a bunch of other old crap. "During the Space Age, this machine dispensed the traditional Space Age beverage, Coca Cola—still enjoyed in some parts of the world—as you can see from some of the lettering still on the machine. Of course the Subway Dwellers have no Coca Cola to fill it with now."

The Subway Dweller took a ring of keys out of the cart, fumbled one of them into a keyhole on the face of the machine after a few tries, and opened a plate on the front of the machine. Tokens came tumbling out onto the floor. The Subway Dweller got down on its hands and knees, picked up the Tokens one by one, and dropped them into a moldy-looking rubber sack from the cart.

"The Servicer has now removed the Tokens from the water machine. In order to get a drink of water, a Subway Dweller drops a Token into the slot in the face of the machine, pulls the lever, and cups his hands inside the little opening."

The Subway Dweller opened the back of the water machine with another key, struggled with one of the metal kegs, then finally lifted it and poured some pretty green-looking water into the machine's tank.

"The Servicers buy the water from the Reclamation Tenders with the Tokens they get from the machines. They also Service the food machines with algacake they get from the Hydroponic Tenders the same way."

The Vending Machine Servicer replaced the back-plate of the water machine and dragged its cart slowly off further on into the shadows of the station towards the next water machine.

"How do they make the Tokens?" Koyinka asked.

"Nobody makes Tokens," I told him. "They're all left over from the Space Age."

"That doesn't make sense. How can they run an economy without a supply of new money? Profits always bring new money into circulation. Even a socialist economy has to print new money each year."

Huh? What the hell was he talking about? These damn Africans!

"I think I can explain," the college professor said. "According to Kusongeri, the Subway Dwellers do not have a real money economy. The same Tokens get passed around continually. For instance, the Servicers probably take exactly as many Tokens out of the water machine as they have to give to the Reclamation Tenders for the water in the first place. No concept of profit exists here."

"But then why do they bother with Tokens in the first place"?

The professor shrugged. "Ritual, perhaps, or—"

"Why does a bee build honeycombs?" Lumumba sneered. "Why does a magpie steal bright objects? Because they think about it—or because it's just the nature of the animal? Don't you see, Koyinka, these white slugs aren't people, they're animals! They don't *think*. They don't have *reasons* for doing anything. Animals! Stupid pale white animals! The last descendants of the Space Age honkies, and they're nothing but animals! That's what honkies end up like when they don't have black men to think for them, how—"

Red sparks went off in my head. "They were good enough to ride your crummy ancestors back to Africa on a rail, you black brother!"

"You watch your mouth when you're talking to your betters, honkie!"

"*Mr. Lumumba!*" the professor shouted. Koyinka looked ready to take a swing at me. Kulongo had moved towards Lumumba and looked disgusted. The Luthuliville fruits were wrinkling their dainty noses. Christ, we were all a hair from a brawl. A thing like that could kill business for a month, or even cost me my license. I thought of that Amazon swampland, blue skies and green trees and brown earth as far as the eye could see. . .

I kept thinking of the Amazon as I unballed my fists and swallowed my pride, and turned my back on Lumumba and led the whole lousy lot of them deeper into the upper level of the station.

Man, I just better give them about another twenty minutes down here and get the hell out before I tear that Lumumba to pieces. I had half a mind to take him back in there to that electric people-trap and jam one of those helmets on his head and leave him there. Then we'd see how much laughing he'd do at the Space Agers!

The tension kept building between Ryan and Lumumba as we continued to move among the Subway Dwellers; it was so painfully obvious that it was only a matter of time before the next outburst that one might have almost expected the wretched creatures who inhabited the Subways to notice it.

But it was also rather obvious that the Subway Dwellers had only a limited perception of their environment and an even more limited conceptualization of interpersonal relationships. It would be difficult to say whether or not they were capable of comprehending anything so complex as human emotion. It would be almost as difficult to say whether or not they were human.

The Vending Machine Servicer had performed a complicated task, a task somewhat too complex for even an intelligent chimpanzee, though conceivably a dolphin might have the mental capacity to master it if it had the physical equipment. But no one has been able to say clearly whether or not a dolphin should be considered sapient; it seems to be a borderline situation.

Lumumba had obviously made up his mind that the Subway Dwellers were truly subhuman animals. As Ryan led us past a motley group of Subway Dwellers who squatted on the bare floor mechanically eating small slabs of some green substance, Lumumba kept up a loud babble, ostensibly to me, but actually for Ryan's benefit.

"Look at the dirty animals chewing their cud like cows! Look what's left of the great Space Agers who went to the Moon—a few thousand brainless white slugs rotting in a sealed coffin!"

"Even the greatest civilization falls sometime," I mumbled somewhat inanely, trying to soften the situation, for Ryan was clearly engaged in a fierce struggle for control of his temper. I could understand why Ryan and Lumumba hated each other, but why did Lumumba's remarks about the Subway Dwellers hurt Ryan so deeply?

As we walked further on in among the rusting steel pillars and scattered groups of ruminating Subway Dwellers, I happened to pass close by a female Subway Dweller, perhaps four and a half feet tall, stooped and leathery with stringy gray hair, and dressed in the usual filthy rags.

She was inserting a Token into the slot of a vending machine. She dropped the coin, and pulled a lever under one of the small broken windows that formed a row above the trough of the machine. A green slab dropped down into the trough. The female Subway Dweller picked it up and began chewing on it.

A sense of excitement came over me. I was determined to actually speak with a Subway Dweller. "What is your name?" I said slowly and distinctly.

The female Subway Dweller turned her pale expressionless little eyes in my direction. A bit of green drool escaped her lips. Other than that, she made no discernible response.

I tried again. "What is your name?"

The creature stared at me blankly. "Whu .. ee ... na .." she finally managed to stammer in a flat, dull monotone.

"I told you people not to talk to the damn Subway Dwellers!"

Ryan had apparently noticed what I was doing; he was rushing towards me past Michael Lumumba. Lumumba grabbed him by the elbow. "What's the matter, Ryan?" he said. "Do the animals bite?"

"Get your slimy hand off me, you black brother!" Ryan roared, ripping his arm out of Lumumba's grasp.

"I'll bet you bite too, honkie," Lumumba said. "After all, you're the same breed of animal they are."

Ryan lunged at Lumumba, but Kulongo was on him in three huge strides, and hugged him from behind with a powerful grip. "Please do not be as foolish as that man, Mr. Ryan," he said softly. "He dishonors us all. You have been a good guide. Do not let that man goad you into doing something that will allow him to disgrace your name with the authorities."

Kulongo held on to Ryan as the redness in his face slowly faded. The female Subway Dweller began to wander away. Lumumba backed off a few paces, then turned his back, walked a bit further away and pretended to study a group of seated Subway Dwellers.

Finally, Kulongo released his grip on Ryan. "Yeah, you're right, pal," Ryan said. "That crut would like nothing better than to be able to report that I bashed his face in. I guess I should apologize to the rest of you folks. . . ."

"I think Mr. Lumumba should apologize as well," I said.

"I don't apologize to animals," Lumumba muttered. Really, the man was disgusting!

God, what I really wanted to do was bury that Lumumba right there, knock him senseless and let him try to get back to Milford by himself, or better yet take him back to that crazy "Cosmic All" thing, jam a helmet on his head, and find out how the thing kills in the pleasantest way possible.

But of course I couldn't kill him or maroon him in front of eight witnesses. So instead of giving that black brother what he deserved, I decided to just let them all walk around for about another ten minutes, gawking at the animals, and then call it a day. Seemed to me that all of them but Lumumba and maybe the professor had had their fill of the Subway Dwellers anyway. Mostly, the Subway Dwellers just sit around chewing algacake. Some of them just stare at nothing for hours. Let's face it, the Subway Dwellers *are* animals. They've degenerated all the way. I figured just about now the Africans would've had their nasty thrill. . . .

But I figured without that stinking Lumumba. Just when the whole bunch of them were standing around in a mob looking thoroughly bored and disgusted, he started another "conversation" with the professor, real loud. Real subtle, that black brother.

"You're a professor of American history, aren't you, Dr. Balewa?"

Got to give Balewa credit. He didn't seem to want any part of Lumumba's little game. "Uh . . . Space Age history is my major field," he muttered, and then tried to turn away.

But Lumumba would just as soon have run his mouth at a Subway Dweller; he didn't care if Balewa was really listening to him as long as I was.

"Well then maybe you can tell me whether or not the honkies could really have built all that Space Age technology on their own. After all, look at these brainless animals, the direct descendants of the Space Age honkies. Sure, they've degenerated since the first of them locked themselves up down here, but degenerated from *what?* Didn't they have to be pretty stupid to seal themselves up in a tomb like this in the first place? And they did have twenty or thirty million black men to do their thinking for them before the Panic. Take a look around you, professor—did these slugs *really* have ancestors capable of creating the Space Age on their own?"

He stared dead at me, and I saw his slimy game. If I didn't cream him, I'd be a coward, and if I did, I'd lose my license. "Take a look at the modern example of the race, professor," he said. "Could a nation of *Ryans* have built anything more than a few junk heaps on their own? With captive blacks to do the thinking for them, they went to the Moon, and then they choked themselves in their own waste. Hardly the mark of a great civilized race."

"Your kind quaked in their boots every time one of my ancestors walked by them, and you know it," I told the crut.

Lumumba would've gone white if he could have. In more ways than one, I'll bet. "You calling me a coward, honkie?"

"I'm calling you a yellow coward, *boy.*"

"No honkie calls me a coward."

"This honkie does . . . *nigger.*"

Ah, that got him! There's one or two words these Amero-Africans just can't take, brings up frightening memories. Lumumba went for me, the professor tried to grab him and missed, and then that big ape Kulongo had him in one of those bear-hugs of his. And suddenly I had an idea how to fix Mr. Michael Lumumba real good, without laying a finger on him, without giving him anything he could complain to the government about.

"You ever hear about a machine that's supposed to 'Merge you with the Cosmic All', professor?" I said.

"Why . . . that would be the ECA, the electronic consciousness augmenter. It was never clear whether more than a few prototypes were built or not, the device was developed shortly before the Panic. Some sort of scientific religion built the ECA, the Brotherhood of the Cosmic All, or some such group. The claim was that the machine produced a transcendental experience of some sort electronically. No one has ever proved whether or not there was any truth to it, since none of the devices have ever been found. . . ."

Kulongo relaxed his grip on Lumumba. I had them

now. I had Mr. Michael Lumumba real good. "Well I think I found one of them, right here in this station, a couple of years ago. It's still working. Maybe the Subway Dwellers keep it going—probably it was built to keep itself going; it looks like real late Space Age stuff. I could take you all to it."

I gave Lumumba a nice smile. "How about it, pal?" I said. "Let's see if you're a coward or not. Let's see you walk in there and put a working Space Age gizmo on your head and Merge With the Cosmic All."

"Have you ever done it, Ryan"? Lumumba sneered.

"Sure pal," I lied. "I do it all the time. It's fun."

"I think you're a liar."

"I *know* you're a coward."

Lumumba gave me a look like a snake. "All right, honkie," he said. "I'll try it if you try it with me."

Christ, what was I getting myself into? That thing killed people, all those bones. ... Yeah, but I knew that and Lumumba didn't. When he saw the bones, he wouldn't dare put a helmet on his head. Yeah, I knew that he wouldn't, and he didn't, so that still put me one up on him.

"You're afraid, aren't you, Ryan? You've never really done it yourself. You're afraid to do it, and I'm not. Who does that make the coward?"

Oh you crut, I got you right where I want you! "Okay boy," I said, "you're on. You do it and I'll do it. We'll see who's the coward. The rest of you folks can come along for the ride. A free extra added attraction, courtesy of Little Old New York Tours."

Ryan led us deeper into a more shadowed part of the station, where the still-functioning bulbs in the ceiling were farther and farther apart, and where, perhaps because of the darkness, the Subway Dwellers were fewer and fewer. As we went further and further into the deepening darkness, the floor of the Subway station was filled with small bits of rubble, then larger and larger pieces, till finally, dimly outlined by a single bulb a few yards ahead of us, we could see a place where the ceiling had fallen in. A huge dam of rubble which filled the station from floor to ceiling cut off a corner much like the one into which we had originally come from the rest of the station.

Ryan led us out of the pool of light and into the blackness. "In here," he called back. "Everyone touch the one ahead of you."

I touched Michael Lumumba's back with some distaste, but also with a kind of gratitude. Because of him, I was getting to see a working wonder of the Space Age, a device whose very existence was a matter of academic dispute. My reputation would be made!

I felt Kulongo's somehow-reassuring hand on my shoulder as we groped our way through the darkness. Then I felt Lumumba stoop, and I was passing through a narrow opening in the pile of rubble, where two broken girders wedged against each other held up the crumbled fragments of ceiling.

Beyond, I could see by a strange flickering light just around a bend that we had emerged in a place very much like the Subway entrance. The ceiling had fallen on a set of turnstiles and grillwork barriers, crushing them, but clearing a way for us. We picked our way past the ruined barriers and entered a side-tunnel, which was filled with the strange flickering light, a light which seemed to cut each moment off from the next, like a faulty piece of antique motion picture film, such as the specimens of Chaplin I've seen in Nairobi. It made me feel as if I were moving inside such a film. Time seemed to be composed of separate discrete bursts of duration.

Ryan led us up the tunnel, both sides of which were composed of the ruins of recessed shops, like some underground market arcade. Then I saw that one shop in the arcade was not ruined. It stood out from the rubble, a gleaming anachronism. Even a layman would've recognized it as a specimen of very late Space Age technology. And it was a working specimen.

It had that classic late Space Age style. The entire front of the shop was made of some plastic substance that flickered luminescently, that was the source of the strange pale light. There has been some literature on this material, but a specimen had never been examined as far as I knew. The substance itself is woven of fibers called light-guides—modern science has been able to produce such fibers, but to weave a kind of cloth of them by known methods would be hideously expensive. But Space Age light guide cloth, however it was made, enabled a single light-source to cast its illumination evenly over a very wide area. So the flickering was probably produced simply by using a stroboscope as a light-source for the wall. Very minor Space Age wizardry, but very effective: it made the entire shopfront a psychologically powerful attention-getting device, such as the Space Agers commonly employed in their incredibly sophisticated science of advertising.

A small doorless portal big enough for one man at a time was all that marred the flickering luminescence of the wall of shopfront. Above the shop a smaller strobe-panel—but this one composed of blue and red fibers which flashed independently—proclaimed "Merge With The Cosmic All" red on blue for half of every second, a powerful hypnotic that drew me towards the shop despite my abstract knowledge of its workings.

That the device was working at all in this area of the station where all other power seemed cut off was proof enough of its very late Space Age dating: only in the decade before the Panic had the Space Agers developed a miniaturized isotopic power-source cheap enough to warrant installation of self-contained five-hundred-year generators in something like this.

The very fact that we were staring into the flickering light of a Space Age device whose self-contained power-source had kept it going totally untended for centuries was enough to overwhelm us. I'm sure the rest of them felt what I felt; even Lumumba just stood there and gaped. On Ryan's face, even beneath the tight lines of his anger, was something akin to awe. Or was it some kind of superstitious dread?

"Well here it is, Lumumba," Ryan said softly, the strobe-wall making the movements of his mouth appear to be mechanical. "Shall we step inside?"

"After you, Ryan. You're the ... native guide." Fear flickered in the strobe flashes off Lumumba's eyes, but like all of us, he found it impossible to look away from the entrance for long. There seemed to be subtle and complex waves in the strobe flashes drawing us to the doorway; perhaps there were several stroboscopes activating the wall in a psychologically-calculated sequence. In this area, the Space Age Americans had been capable of any subtlety a modern mind could imagine, and infinitely more.

"And you're the ... *tourist,*" Ryan said softly. "A

tourist who thinks he knows what the Space Agers were all about. Step inside, sucker!"

And with a grim, knowing grin, Ryan stepped through the doorway. Without hesitation, Lumumba followed after him. And without hesitation, drawn by the flickering light and so much more, I entered the chamber behind them.

The inside of the chamber was a cube of some incredible hyper-real desert night as seen through the eyes of a prophet or a madman. The walls and ceiling of the room were light: mosaics of millions of tiny deep-blue twinkling pinpoints of brilliance, here and there leavened with intermittent prickles of red and green and yellow, all flashing in seemingly-random sequences of a tenth of a second or so each. Beneath this preternatural electronic sky, we stood transfixed. The dazzling universe of winking light filled our brains; before it we were as Subway Dwellers chewing their cud.

Behind me, I dimly heard Kulongo's deep voice saying: "There are demons in there that would drink a man's soul. We will not go in there." How foolish those far-away words sounded. . . .

"There's nothing to be afraid of . . ." I heard my own voice saying. The sound of my own voice broke my light trance almost as I realized that I had been in a trance. Then I saw the bones.

The chamber was filled with six rows of strange chairs, six of them to a row. They were like giant red eggs standing on end, hollowed out, and fitted inside with reclining padded seats. Inside the red eggs, metal helmets designed to fit over the entire head dangled from cables at head-level. Most of the eggs contained human skeletons. The floor was littered with bones.

Ryan and Lumumba seemed to have been somewhat deeper in trance; it took them a few seconds longer to come out of it. Lumumba's eyes flashed sudden fear as he saw the bones. But Ryan grinned knowingly as he saw the fear on Lumumba's face.

"Scares you a bit, doesn't it, boy?" Ryan said. "Still game to put on one of these helmets?" The wall seemed to pick up the sparkle of his laugh.

"What killed them?" was all Lumumba said.

"How should I know?"

"But you said you'd tried it!"

"So I'm a liar. And you're a coward."

I walked forward as they argued, and read a small metal plaque that was affixed to the outer shell of each red egg:

"2 Tokens—MERGE WITH THE COSMIC ALL—2 Tokens Drop Tokens in slot. Place helmet over head. Pull lever and experience MERGER WITH THE COSMIC ALL. Automatic timer will limit all MERGERS to 2 minutes duration, in compliance with Federal Law."

"I'm no more a coward than you are, Ryan. You had no intention of putting on one of those things."

"I'd do it if you'd do it," Ryan insisted.

"No you wouldn't! You're not that crazy and neither am I. Why would you risk your life for something as stupid as that?"

"Because I'd be willing to bet my life any day that a black brother like you would never have the guts to put on a helmet."

"You stinking honkie!"

"Why don't we end this crap, Lumumba? You're not going to put on one of these helmets and neither am I. The big difference between us is that I won't have to because you can't."

Lumumba seemed like a carven idol of rage in that fantastic cube of light. "Just a minute, honkie," he said. "Professor, you have any idea why they died when they put the helmets on?"

It was starting to make sense to me. What if the claims made for the device were true? What if 2 Tokens could buy a man total transcendental bliss? "I don't think they died when they put the helmets on," I said. "I think they starved to death days later. According to this plaque, whatever happens is supposed to last no longer than two minutes before an automatic circuit shuts it off. What if this device involves electronic stimulation of the pleasure center? No one has yet unearthed such a device, but the Space Age literature was full of it. Pleasure center stimulation was supposed to be harmless in itself, but what if the timer circuit went out? A man could be paralyzed in total bliss while he starved to death. I think that's what happened here."

"Let me get. this straight," Lumumba said, his rage seeming to collapse in upon itself, becoming a manic shrewdness. "The helmets themselves are harmless? Even if we couldn't take them off ourselves, one of the others could take them off. . . . We wouldn't be in any real danger?"

"I don't think so," I told him. "According to the inscription, one paid 2 Tokens for the experience. I doubt that even the Space Agers would've been willing to pay money for something that would harm them, certainly not en masse. And the Space Agers were very conscious of profit."

"Would you be willing to stake your life on it, Dr. Balewa? Would you be willing to try it too?"

Try it? Actually put on a helmet, give myself over to a piece of Space Age wizardry, an electronic device that was supposed to produce a mystical experience at the flick of a switch? A less stable man might say that if it really worked, there was a god inside the helmets, a god that the Space Agers had created out of electronic components. If this were actually true, it surely must represent the very pinnacle of Space Age civilization—who but the Space Agers would even contemplate the fabrication of an actual god?

Yes, of course I would try it! I had to try it; what kind of scholar would I be if I passed by an opportunity to understand the Space Agers as no modern man has understood them before? Neither Ryan nor Lumumba had the background to make the most of such an experience. It was my duty to put on a helmet as well as my pleasure.

"Yes, Mr. Lumumba," I said. "I intend to try it too."

"Then we'll all try it," Lumumba said. "Or will we, Mr. Ryan? I'm ready to put on a helmet and so is the professor; are you?"

They were both nuts, Lumumba and the professor! Those helmets had killed people. How the hell could Balewa know what had happened from reading some silly plaque? These goddamn Africans always think they can understand the Space Agers from crap other Africans have put in books. What the hell do they know? What do they really know?

"Well Ryan, what about it? Are you going to admit you

don't have the guts to do it, so we can all forget it and go home?"

"All right, pal, you're on!" I heard myself telling him. Damn, what was I getting myself into? But I couldn't let that slime Lumumba call my bluff, no African's gonna bluff down an *American!* Besides, Balewa was probably right; what he said made sense. Sure, it had to make sense. That stinking black brother!

"Mr. Kulongo would you come in here and take the helmets off our heads in two minutes?" I asked. I'd trust that Kulongo further than the rest of the creeps.

"I will not go in there," Kulongo said. "There is juju in there, powerful and evil. I am ashamed before you because I say these words, but my fear of what is in this place is greater than my shame."

"This is ridiculous!" Koyinka said, pushing past Kulongo. "Evil spirits! Come on, will you, this is the twenty-third century! I'll do it, if you want to go through with this nonsense."

"All right, pal, let's get on with it."

I handed out the Tokens and the three of us went to the nearest three stalls. I cleared a skeleton out of mine, sent it clattering to the floor, and so what, what's to be scared of in a pile of old dead bones? But I noticed that Lumumba seemed a little green as he cleared the bones out for himself.

I pulled myself up into the hollowed out egg and sat down on the padded couch inside. Some kind of plastic covering made the thing still clean and comfortable, not even dusty, after hundreds of years. Those Space Agers were really something. I dropped the Tokens into a little slot in the arm of the couch. Next to the slot was a lever. The room sparkled blue all around me; somehow that made me feel real good. The couch was comfortable. Koyinka was standing by. I was actually beginning to enjoy it. What was there to be afraid of? Jeez, the professor thought this thing gave you pure pleasure or something. If he was right, this was really going to be something. If I lived through it.

I put my right hand on the lever. I saw that the professor and Lumumba were already under their helmets. I fitted the helmet down over my head. Some kind of pad inside it fitted down on my skull all around my head, down to the eyebrows; it seemed almost alive, molding itself to my head like a second skin. It was very dark inside the helmet. Couldn't see a thing.

I took a deep breath and pulled the lever.

The tips of my fingers began to tingle, throbbing with pleasure, not pain. My feet started to tingle too, and shapes that had no shape, that were more black inside the black, seemed to be floating around inside my head. The tingling moved up my fingers to my hands, up my feet to my knees. Now my arms were tingling. Oh man, it felt so good! No woman ever felt this good! This felt better than kicking in Lumumba's face!

The whirling things in my head weren't really in my head, my head was in them, or they were my head, all whirling around some deep dark hole that wasn't a hole but was something to whirl off into, fall off into, sucking me in and up. My whole body was tingling now. Man, I *was* the tingling now, my body was nothing but the tingling now.

And it was getting stronger, getting better all the time, I wasn't a tingle, I was a glow, a warmth, a throbbing, a fire of pure pleasure, a roaring burning whirling fire sucking spinning up towards a deep black hole inside me blowing up in a blast of pure FEELING SO GOOD SO GOOD SO GOOD—

Oh, forever, whirling, whirling, a fire SO GOOD SO GOOD SO GOOD, and on THROUGH! into the black hole fire I was BURNING UP IN MY OWN ORGASM, I was my own orgasm of body mind sex taste smell touch feel, I went on FOREVER FOREVER FOREVER FOR-EVER in pure blinding burning SO GOOD SO GOOD SO GOOD nothingness blackness dying orgasm FOREVER FOREVER FOREVER spurting out of myself in sweet moment of total pain-pleasure SO GOOD SO GOOD SO GOOD moment of dying pain burning sex FOREVER FOREVER FOREVER SO GOOD SO GOOD FOR-EVER SO GOOD FOREVER SO GOOD FOREVER—

I pulled the lever and waited in my private darkness. The first thing I felt was a tingling of my fingertips, as if with some mild electric charge; not at all an unpleasant feeling. A similar pleasurable tingle began in my feet. Strange vague patterns seemed to swirl around inside my eyes.

My hands began to feel the pleasant sensation now, and

the lower portions of my legs. The feeling was getting stronger and stronger as it moved up my limbs. I felt physically pleasurable in a peculiarly abstract way, but there was something frightening about it, something vaguely unclean.

The swirling patterns seemed to be spinning around a bottomless vortex now; they weren't exactly inside my eyes or my head, my head was inside of them, or they *were* me. The experience was somehow visual-yet-non-visual, my being spinning downward and inward in a vertiginous spiral towards a black, black hole that seemed inside my self. And my whole body felt that electric tingling now; I felt nothing *but* the strange, forcefully pleasureable sensation. It filled my entire sensorium, became *me*.

And it kept getting stronger and stronger, no longer a tingle, but a pulsing of cold electric pleasure, stronger and stronger, wilder and wilder, the voltage increasing, the amperage increasing, whirling me down and around and down and around towards that terrible deep black hole inside me burning with hunger to swallow myself up becoming a pure black fire vortex pain of pleasure down and down and around and around. . . .

Sucking myself up through the terrible black vortex of my own pure pleasure-pain, compressed against the interface of my own being, squeezed against the instant of my own DEATH Oh! Oh! DEATH DEATH DEATH No No pleasure pain death sex orgasm everything that was me popping No! No! ON THROUGH! becoming moment of death senses flashing pure pleasure pain terror black hole FOREVER FOREVER in this terrible universe was timeless moment of orgasm death total electric pleasure NO! NO! delicious horrible moment of pure DEATH PAIN ORGASM BLACK HOLE VORTEX NO! NO! NO! NO—

Suddenly I was seated on a couch inside a red egg in a room filled with blue sparkles, and I was looking up at Koyinka's silly face.

"You all right?" he said. Now *there* was a question!

"Yeah, yeah," I mumbled. Man, those Space Agers! I wanted to puke. I wanted to jam that helmet back on my head. I wanted to get the hell out of there! I wanted to live forever in that fantastic perfect feeling until I rotted into the bonepile.

I was scared out of my head.

I mean, what happened inside that helmet was the best and the worst thing in the world. You could stay there with that thing on your head and die in pure pleasure thinking you were living forever. Man, you talk about *temptation!* Those Space Agers had put a god or a devil in there, and who could tell which? Did they even know which? Man, that crazy jungle-bunny Kulongo was right after all: there *were* demons in here that would drink your soul. But maybe the demons were *you.* Sucking up your own soul in pure pleasure till it choked you to death. But wasn't it maybe worth it?

As soon as he saw I was okay, Koyinka ran over to the professor, who was still sitting there with the helmet over his head. That crut Lumumba was out of it already. He was staring at me; he wasn't mad, he wasn't exactly afraid, he was just trying to look into my eyes. I guess because I felt what he felt too.

I stared back into Lumumba's big eyes as Koyinka took the helmet off the professor's head. I couldn't help myself. I didn't like the black brother one bit more, but there was something between us now, god knows what. The professor looked real green. He didn't seem to notice us much. Lumumba and I just kept staring at each other, nodding a little bit. Yeah, we had both been someplace no living man should go. The Space Agers had been gods or demons or maybe something that would drive both gods and demons screaming straight up the wall. When we call them men we don't mean the same thing we do when we call us men. When they died off, something we'll never understand went out of the world. I don't know whether to thank God or to cry.

It seemed to me that I could read exactly what was going on inside Lumumba's head; his thoughts were my thoughts.

"They were a great and terrible people," Lumumba finally said. "And they were out of their minds."

"Pal, they were something we can never be. Or want to."

"You know honkie, I think for once you've got a point."

There was a strange feeling hovering in the air between Ryan and Lumumba as we made our way back through the Subway station and up into the sparkly blue unreal world of the Fuller Dome. Not comradeship, not even grudging respect, but some subtle change I could not fathom. Their eyes keep meeting, almost furtively. I couldn't understand it. I couldn't understand it at all.

Had they experienced what I had? Coldly, I could now say that it had been nothing but electronic stimulation of some cerebral centers; but the horror of it, the horror of being forced to experience a moment of death and pain and total pleasure all bound up together and extended towards infinity, had been realer than real. It had indeed been a genuine mystical experience, created electronically.

But why would people do a thing like that to themselves? Why would they willingly plunge themselves into a moment of pure horror that went on and on and on?

Yet as we finally boarded the helicopter, I somehow sensed that what Lumumba and Ryan had shared was not what I felt at all.

As I flew the copter through the dead tombstone skyscrapers towards the outer edge of the Fuller Dome, I knew that I had to get out of this damn tourist business, and fast. Now I knew what was really buried here, under the crazy spooky blue light, under all the concrete, under the stinking saturation smog, under a hole inside a hole in the ground; the bones of a people that men like us had better let lie.

Our ancestors were gods or demons or both. If we get too close to the places where what they *really* were is buried, they'll drink our souls yet.

No more tours to the Subways anyway; what good is the Amazon if I don't live to get there? If I had me an atom bomb I'd drop it right smack on top of this place. To make sure I never go back.

As we headed into a fantastic blazing orange and purple sunset, towards Milford and modern America—a pallid replica of African civilization huddling in the interstices of a continent of incredible ruins—I looked back across the wide river, a flaming sea below and behind us ignited by the setting sun. The Fuller Dome flashed in the sunlight, a giant diamond set in the tombstone of a race that had soared to the Moon, that had turned the atmosphere to a beautiful and terrible poison, that had covered a continent with ruins that overawed the modern world, that had conjured up a demon out of electronic circuitry, that had torn themselves to pieces in the end.

A terrible pang of sadness went through me as the rest of my trip turned to ashes in my mouth, as my future career became a cadaver covered with dust. I could crawl over these ruins and exhaust the literature for the rest of my life, and I would never understand what the Space Age Americans had been. Not a man alive ever would. Whatever they had been, such things lived on the face of the earth no more.

In his simple way, Kulongo had said all that could be said: "Their souls were not as ours."

Overpopulation seems the most pressing problem that we have visited on ourselves. The horrific social implications of overcrowding have already received ample attention from science fiction writers—most notably in Harry Harrison's MAKE ROOM, MAKE ROOM and John Brunner's less digestible STAND ON ZANZIBAR.

ROBERT SILVERBERG'S IN THE BEGINNING is anything but a straight-forward catalogue of social horrors. But the author's restraint makes the final message even more shattering.

# IN THE BEGINNING

## BY ROBERT SILVERBERG

THE CITY of Chicago is bounded on the north by Shanghai and on the south by Edinburgh. Chicago currently has 37,402 people, and is undergoing a mild crisis of population that will have to be alleviated in the customary manner. Its dominant profession is engineering. Above, in Shanghai, they are mostly scholars; below, in Edinburgh, computer men cluster.

Aurea Holston was born in Chicago in 2368 and has lived there all of her life. Aurea is now fourteen years old. Her husband Memnon is nearly fifteen. They have been married almost two years. God has not blessed them with children. Memnon has traveled through the entire building but Aurea has scarcely ever been out of Chicago. Once she went to visit a fertility expert, an old midwife down in Prague. Once she went up to Louisville, where her powerful uncle, an urban administrator, lives. Many times she and Memnon have been to their friend Siegmund Kluver's apartment in Shanghai. But Aurea does

57

not really care to travel. She loves her own city very much.

Chicago is the city that occupies the 721st through 760th floors of Urban Monad 116. Memnon and Aurea Holston live in a dormitory for childless young couples on the 735th floor. The dorm is currently shared by 31 coupes, eight above optimum.

"There's got to be a thinning soon," Memnon says. "We're starting to bulge at the seams. People will have to go."

"Many?" Aurea asks.

"Three couples here, five there—a slice from each dorm. I suppose Urbmon 116 will lose about two thousand couples. That's how many went the last time they thinned."

Aurea trembles. "Where will they go?"

"They tell me that the new urbmon is almost ready. Number 158."

Her soul floods with pity and terror. "How horrid to be sent somewhere else! Memnon, they *wouldn't* make us leave here!"

"Of course not. God bless, we're valuable here! I have a skill rating of—"

"But we have no children. That kind goes first, doesn't it?"

"God will bless us soon." Memnon takes her in his arms. He is strong and tall and lean, with rippling scarlet hair and a taut, earnest expression. Aurea feels weak and fragile beside him, although she is sturdy and supple. Her crown of golden hair is deepening in tone. Her eyes are pale green. Her breasts are full and her lips are broad. Siegmund Kluver says she looks like a goddess of motherhood. Most men desire her and nightwalkers come frequently to share her sleeping platform. Yet she remains barren. Lately she has become quite sensitive about it. The irony of her wasted voluptuousness is not lost on her.

Memnon releases her and she walks wearily through the dormitory. It is a long, narrow room that makes a right-angle bend around the urbmon's central service core. Its walls glow with changing inlaid patterns of blue and gold and green. Rows of sleeping platforms, some deflated, some in use, cover the floor. The furniture is stark and simple and the lighting, though indirectly suffused from the entire area of the floor and the ceiling, is bright almost to harshness. Several viewscreens and three data terminals are mounted on the eastern wall. There are five excretion areas, three communal recreation areas, two cleanser stations, and two privacy areas.

By unspoken custom the privacy shields are never turned on in this dormitory. What one does, one does before the others. The total accessibility of all persons to all other persons is the only rule by which the civilization of the urbmon can survive, and in a mass residence hall such as this the rule is all the more vital. Aurea is a member of a post-privacy culture. One cannot hold oneself apart from people while simultaneously living among them.

Aurea halts by the majestic window at the dormitory's western end, and stares out. The sunset is beginning. Across the way, the magnificent bulk of Urban Monad 117 seems stained with golden red. Aurea follows the shaft of the great tower with her eyes, down from the landing stage at its thousandth-floor tip, down to the building's broad waist. She cannot see, at this angle, very far below the 400th floor of the adjoining structure.

What is it like, she wonders, to live in Urbmon 117? Or 115, or 110, or 140? She has never left the urbmon of her birth. All about her, to the horizon, sprawl the towers of the Chipitts constellation, fifty mighty piles of super-stressed concrete, each three kilometers high, each housing some 800,000 human beings, each a self-contained entity. In Urbmon 117, Aurea tells herself, there are people who look just like us. They walk, talk, dress, think, love, just like ourselves. Urbmon 117 is not another world. It is only the building next door. We are not unique. We are not unique. We are not unique.

Fear engulfs her.

"Memnon," she says raggedly, "When the thinning time comes, they're going to send us to Urbmon 158."

Siegmund Kluver is one of the lucky ones. His fertility has won him an unimpeachable place in Urbmon 116. His status is secure.

Though he is just past 14, Siegmund has fathered two children. His son is called Janus and his newborn daughter has been named Persephone. Siegmund lives in a handsome 50-square-meter home on the 787th floor, slightly more than midway up in Shanghai. His specialty is the theory of urban administration, and despite his youth he already spends much of his time as a consultant to the administrators in Louisville. He is short, finely made, quite strong, with a large head and thick curling hair. In boyhood he lived in Chicago and was one of Memnon's closest friends. They still see each other quite often; the fact that they now live in different cities is no bar to their friendship.

Social encounters between the Holstons and the Kluvers always take place at Siegmund's apartment. The Kluvers never come down to Chicago to visit Aurea and Memnon. Siegmund claims there is no snobbery in this. "Why should the four of us sit around a noisy dorm," he asks, "when we can get together in the privacy of my apartment?" Aurea is suspicious of this attitude. Urbmon people are not supposed to place such a premium on privacy. Is the dorm not a good enough place for Siegmund Kluver?

Siegmund once lived in the same dorm as Aurea and Memnon. That was two years ago, when they all were newly married. Several times, in those long-ago days, Aurea yielded her body to Siegmund; in a dormitory such excursions are common, unremarkable, and socially approved. But very swiftly Siegmund's wife became pregnant, qualifying the Kluvers to apply for an apartment of their own, and the progress he was making in his profession permitted him to find room in the city of Shanghai. Aurea has not shared her sleeping platform with Siegmund since he left the dormitory. She is distressed by this, for she enjoyed Siegmund's embraces, but there is little she can do about it. Sexual relationships between people of different cities are currently considered improper.

Now Siegmund is evidently bound for higher things. Memnon says that by the time he is seventeen he will be, not a specialist in the theory of urban administration, but an actual administrator, and will live in Louisville. Already Siegmund spends much time with the leaders of the urbmon; and with their wives as well, Aurea has heard.

Siegmund is an excellent host. His apartment is warm and agreeable, and two of its walls glisten with panels of one of the new decorative materials, which emits a soft hum keyed to the spectral pattern its owner has chosen.

Tonight Siegmund has tuned the panels almost into the
ultraviolet and the audio emission is pitched close to the
hypersonic. He has exquisite taste in handling the room's
scent apertures, too: jasmine and hyacinth flavor the air.
"Some tingle?" he asks. "Just in from Venus. Quite blessworthy." Aurea and Memnon smile and nod. Siegmund
fills a large fluted silver bowl with the costly scintillant
fluid and places it on the pedestal-table. A touch of the
floor-pedal and the table rises to a height of 150 centime-
ters.

"Mamelon?" he says. "Will you join us?"

Siegmund's wife slides her baby into the maintenance
slot near the sleeping platform and crosses the room to
her guests. Mamelon Kluver is quite tall, dark of com-
plexion and hair, elegantly beautiful in a haggard way.
Her forehead is high, her cheekbones prominent, her chin
sharp; her eyes, alert and glossy and wide-set, seem almost too big, too dominant, in her pale and tapering face.
The delicacy of her beauty makes Aurea feel defensive
about her own soft features, her snub nose, her rounded
cheeks, her full lips, the light dusting of freckles over
tawny skin. Mamelon is the oldest person in the room,
almost sixteen. Her breasts are swollen with milk; she is
only eleven days up from childbed, and she is nursing.
Aurea has never known anyone else who nursed. Mamelon has always been different, though. Aurea is still somewhat frightened of Siegmund's wife, who is so cool, so
self-possessed, so mature. So passionate, too. At twelve, a
new bride, Aurea's sleep was broken again and again by
Mamelon's cries of ecstasy, echoing through the dormitory.

Now Mamelon bends forward and puts her lips to the
tingle bowl. The four of them drink at the same moment.
Tiny bubbles dance on Aurea's lips. The bouquet dizzies
her. She peers into the depths of the bowl and sees
abstract patterns forming and sundering. Tingle is faintly
intoxicating, faintly hallucinogenic, an enhancer of
vision, a suppressant of inner disturbance. It comes from
certain musky swamps in the lowlands of Venus; the
serving Siegmund has offered contains billions of alien
microorganisms, fermenting and fissioning even as they
are digested and absorbed.

After the ritual of drinking, they talk. Siegmund and
Memnon discuss world events; Mamelon shows Aurea her

baby. The little girl lies within the maintenance slot, drooling, gurgling, cooing. Aurea says, "What a relief it must be not to be carrying her any longer!"

"One enjoys being able to see one's feet again," Mamelon says.

"Is it very uncomfortable, being pregnant?"

"There are annoyances. Yet there are positive aspects. The moment of birth itself—"

"Does it hurt?" Aurea asks. "I imagine it would. Something that big, ripping through your body—"

"Gloriously blessful. One's entire nervous system awakens. It's impossible to describe the sensation. You must experience it for yourself."

"I wish I could," says Aurea, downcast. She slips a hand into the maintenance slot to touch the child. A quick burst of ions purifies her skin before she makes contact with little Persephone's downy cheek. Aurea says, "God bless, I want to do my duty! The medics say there's nothing wrong with either of us. But—"

"You must be patient, love." Mamelon embraces Aurea lightly. "Bless god, your moment will come."

Aurea is doubtful. For twenty months she has surveyed her flat belly, waiting for it to begin to bulge. It is blessed to create life, she knows. If everyone were like her, who would fill the urbmons? She has a sudden terrifying vision of the colossal towers nearly empty, whole cities sealed off, power failing, walls cracking, just a few shriveled old women shuffling through halls now thronged with happy multitudes.

Her one obsession has led her to her other one, and she turns to Siegmund, breaking into the conversation of the men to say, "Siegmund, is it true that they'll be opening Urbmon 158 soon?"

"So I hear, yes."

"What will it be like?"

"Very much like 116, I imagine. A thousand floors, the usual services. I suppose seventy families per floor, at first, maybe 250,000 people altogether, but it won't take long to bring it up to par."

Aurea clamps her palms together. "How many people will be sent there from here, Siegmund?"

"I'm sure I don't know that."

"There'll be some, won't there?"

Memnon says mildly, "Aurea, let's talk about something pleasant."

"Some people will be sent there from here," she persists. "Come on, Siegmund. You're up in Louisville with the bosses all the time. *How many?*"

Siegmund laughs. "You've really got an exaggerated idea of my significance in this place, Aurea. Nobody's said a word to me about how Urbmon 158 will be stocked."

"You know the theory of these things, though. You can project."

"Well, yes." Siegmund is quite cool; this subject has a purely impersonal interest for him. He seems unaware of the source of Aurea's agitation. "Naturally, if we're going to do our duty to god by creating life, we've also got to be sure that there's a place for everyone to live," he says. "So we go on building urban monads, and, naturally, whenever a new urbmon is added to the Chipitts constellation, it has to be stocked from the other Chipitts buildings. That makes good genetic sense. Even though each urbmon is big enough to provide an adequate gene-mix, our tendency to stratify into cities and villages within the building leads to a good deal of inbreeding, which they say isn't good for the species on a long-term basis. But if we take 5,000 people from each of 50 urbmons, say, and toss them together into a new urbmon, it gives us a pooled gene-mix of 250,000 individuals that we didn't have before. Actually, though, easing population pressure is the most urgent reason for erecting new buildings."

"Keep it clean, Siegmund," Memnon warns.

Siegmund grins. "No, I mean it. Oh, sure, there's a cultural imperative telling us to breed and breed and breed. That's natural, after the agonies of the pre-urbmon days, when everybody went around wondering where we were going to put all the people. But even in a world of urban monads we have to plan in an orderly way. The excess of births and deaths is pretty consistent. Each urbmon is designed to hold 800,000 people comfortably, with room to pack in maybe 100,000 more, but that's the top. At the moment, you know, every urbmon in the Chipitts constellation more than twenty years old is at least 10,000 people above optimum, and a couple are pushing maximum. Things aren't too bad in 116, but you know yourselves that there are trouble spots. Why, Chicago has 38,000—"

"37,402 this morning," Aurea says.

"Whatever. That's close to a thousand people a floor. The programmed optimum density for Chicago is only 32,000, though. That means that the waiting list in your city for a private apartment is getting close to a generation long. The dorms are packed, and people aren't dying fast enough to make room for the new families, which is why Chicago is offloading some of its best people to places like Edinburgh and Boston and—well, Shanghai. Once the new building is open—"

Aurea says, steely-voiced, "How many from 116 will be sent there?"

"The theory is, 5,000 from each monad, at current levels," Siegmund says. "It'll be adjusted slightly to compensate for population variations in different buildings, but figure on 5,000. Now, there'll be about a thousand people in 116 who'll volunteer to go—"

*"Volunteer?"* Aurea gasps. It is inconceivable to her that anyone will want to leave his native urbmon.

Siegmund smiles. "Older people, love. In their twenties and thirties. Bored, maybe stalemated in their careers, tired of their neighbors, who knows? It sounds obscene, yes. But there'll be a thousand volunteers. That means that about 4,000 more will have to be picked from lot."

"I told you so this morning," Memnon says.

"Will these 4,000 be picked at random throughout the whole urbmon?" Aurea asks.

Gently Siegmund says, "At random, yes. From the newlywed dorms. From the childless."

At last. The truth revealed.

"Why from us?" Aurea wails.

"Kindest and most blessworthy way," says Siegmund. "We can't uproot small children from their urbmon matrix. Dorm couples haven't the same kind of community ties that we—that others—that—" He falters. Aurea starts to sob. He says, "Love, I'm sorry. It's the system, and it's a good system. Ideal, in fact."

"Memnon, we're going to be *expelled!*"

Siegmund tries to reassure her. She and Memnon have only a slim chance of being chosen, he insists. In this urbmon thousands upon thousands of people are eligible for transfer. And so many variable factors exist—but she will not be consoled. Unashamed, she lets raw emotion spew into the room, and then she feels shame. She knows she has spoiled the evening for everyone. But Siegmund and Mamelon are kind about it, and Mamnon does not chide her as he hurries her out, into the dropshaft, down 52 floors to their home in Chicago.

*

That night, although she wants him intensely, she turns her back on Memnon when he reaches for her. She lies awake listening a long time to the gasps and happy groans of the couples lying on the sleeping platforms about her, and then sleep comes. Aurea dreams of being born. She is down in the power plant of Urban Monad 116, 400 meters underground and they are sealing her in a liftshaft capsule. The building throbs. She is close to the heat-sink and the urine-reprocessing plant and the refuse compactors and all the rest of the service gear that keeps the structure alive, all those dark, hidden sectors of the urbmon that she had to tour when she was a schoolgirl. Now the liftshaft carries her up, up through Reykjavik where the maintenance people live, up through brawling Prague where everyone has ten babies, up through Rome, Boston, Edinburgh, Chicago, Shanghai, even through Louisville where the administrators move in unimaginable luxury, and now she is at the summit of the building, at the landing stage where the quickboats fly in from distant towers, and a hatch opens in the landing stage and Aurea is ejected. She soars into the sky, safe within her capsule while the cold winds of the upper atmosphere buffet it. She is six kilometers above the ground, looking down for the first time on the entire urbmon world. So this is how it is, she thinks. So many buildings. And yet so much open space!

She drifts across the constellation of towers. It is early spring, and Chipitts is greening. Below her are the tapered structures that hold the 40,000,000 + people of this urban cluster. She is awed by the neatness of the constellation, the geometrical placement of the buildings to form a series of hexagons within the larger area. Green plazas separate the buildings. No one enters the plazas, ever, but their well-manicured lawns are a delight to behold from the windows of the urbmon. The lower-class people on the lower floors have the best views of the gardens and pools, which is a compensation of sorts. From her vantage point high above, Aurea does not expect to see the plazas well, but her dreaming mind gives her an intense clarity of vision and she discerns small golden floral heads, she smells the tang of floral fragrance.

Her mind whirls as she engorges herself on the complexities of Chipitts. How many cities at forty to an urban monad? Two hundred. How many villages at seven or eight to a city? More than a thousand. How many families? How many nightwalkers now prowling, now slipping into available beds? How many births a day? How many deaths? How many joys? How many sorrows? Within each tower, there are schools, hospitals, sports arenas, houses of worship, theatres, everything urban people require. The urbmons are self-sufficient, closed ecologies that even purify and recycle wastes. Only food, Aurea knows, must come from outside—from the agricultural communes that lie beyond the urban constellation.

She rises effortlessly to a height of ten kilometers. She wishes to behold the agricultural communes.

She sees them now, stretching to the horizon, flat bands of green bordered in brown. Seven eighths of the land area of the continent, she has been told endlessly, is used for the production of food. Busy little men and women oversee the machines that till the fertile fields. Aurea has heard of the terrible rites of the farming folk, the bizarre and primitive customs of those who must live beyond the urban world. Perhaps that is all fantasy; no one she knows has ever visited the communes. No one she knows has ever set foot outside Urban Monad 116. The courier pods trundle endlessly and without supervision toward the urbmons, carrying produce through subterranean channels. Food in; machinery and manufactured goods out. A balanced economy. Aurea is borne upward on a transport of joy. How miraculous it is that there can be 75,000,000,-000 people living harmoniously on one small world! God bless, she thinks. A full room for every family. A meaningful and enriching city life. Friends, lovers, mates, children.

Children. Dismay seizes her and she begins to spin.

In her dizziness she seems to vault to the edge of space, so that she sees the entire planet; all of its urban constellations are jutting toward her like spikes. She sees not only Chipitts but also Sansan and Boswash, and Berpar, Wienbud, Shankong, Bocarac, every gathering of towers. And also she sees the plains teeming with food, the former deserts, the former savannahs, the former forests. It is all quite wonderful, but it is terrifying as well, and she wonders a moment if the way man has reshaped his environment is the best of all possible ways. Yes, she tells herself, yes; we are servants of god this way, we avoid strife and greed and turmoil, we bring new life into the world, we thrive, we multiply. We multiply. And doubt smites her and she begins to fall, and the capsule splits and releases her, leaving her bare body unprotected. And she sees the spiky tips of Chipitts' fifty towers below her, but now there is a new tower, a fifty-first, and she falls toward it, toward a gleaming bronzed needle-sharp summit, and she cries out as it penetrates her and she is impaled. And she wakes, sweating and shaking, her tongue dry, her mind dazed by a vision beyond her grasp, and she clutches Memnon, who murmurs sleepily and sleepily enters her.

\*

They are beginning now to tell the people of Urban Monad 116 about the new building. Aurea hears it from the wallscreen as she does her morning chores in the dormitory. Out of the patterns of light and color on the wall there congeals a view of an unfinished tower. Construction machines swarm over it, metal arms moving frenziedly, welding arcs glimmering off octagonal steel-paneled torsos. The familiar voice of the screen says, "Friends, what you see is Urbmon 158, one month eleven days from completion. God willing, it'll shortly be the home of a great many happy Chipittsians who will have the honor of establishing first-generation status there. The news from Louisville is that 802 residents of your own Urbmon 116 have already signed up for transfer to the new building, as soon as—"

Next, a day later, comes an interview with Mr. and Mrs. Dismas Cullinan of Boston, who, with their nine littles, were the very first people in 116 to request transfer. Mr. Cullinan, a meaty, red-faced man, is a specialist in sanitary engineering. He explains, "I see a real opportunity to move up to the planning level over in 158. I figure I can jump eighty, ninety floors in status in a hell of a hurry." Mrs. Cullinan pats her middle. Number ten is on the way. She purrs over the immense social advantages the move will confer on her children. Her eyes are too bright; her upper lip is thicker than the lower one and her nose is sharp. "She looks like a bird of prey," someone in the dorm comments. Someone else says, "She's obviously miserable here. Hoping to grab rungs fast over there." The Cullinan children range from two to thirteen years of age. Unfortunately, they resemble their parents. One of them claws at her brother while on screen. Aurea says, "The building's better off without the lot of them."

Interviews with other transferees follow. On the fourth day of the campaign, the screen offers an extensive tour of the interior of 158, showing the ultra-modern conveniences it will offer. Thermal irrigation for everybody, super-speed liftshafts and dropshafts, three-wall screens, a novel programming system for delivery of meals from the central kitchens, and other wonders, representing the finest in urban progress. The number of volunteers for transfer is now up to 914.

Perhaps, Aurea thinks, they will fill the entire quota with volunteers.

Memnon says, "The figure is fake. Siegmund tells me they've got only 91 volunteers so far."

"Then why—"

"To encourage the others."

In the second week, the transmissions dealing with the new building now indicate that the number of volunteers has leveled off at 1,060. Siegmund admits privately that this is close to the actual figure, and that few additional volunteers are expected. The screen begins gently to introduce the possibility that conscription of transferees will be necessary. Two management men from Louisville and a pair of helix adjusters from Chicago are shown discussing the need for a proper genetic mix at the new building. A moral engineer from Shanghai speaks about the importance of being blessworthy. It is blessworthy to obey the divine plan and its representatives on Earth, he says. The quality of life in Urbmon 158 will be diminished if its initial population does not reach planned levels. This would be a crime against those who do go to 158. Therefore it is each man's duty to society to accept transfer if transfer is offered.

Next there is an interview with Kimon and Freya Kurtz, ages 14 and 13, from a dorm in Bombay. They are not about to volunteer, they admit, but they wouldn't mind being conscripted. "The way we look at it," Kimon Kurtz declares, "it could be a great opportunity. I mean, once we had some children, we'd be able to find top status for them right away. It's a brand new world over there—no limits on how fast you can rise. The readjustment of going over would be a little nudgy at first, but we'd be jumping soon enough. And we'd know that our littles wouldn't have to enter a dorm when they were old enough to marry. They could get rooms of their own right away, even before they had littles too. So even though we're not eager to leave our friends and all, we're ready to go if the wheel points to us." Freya Kurtz, ecstatic, breathless, says, "Yes. That's right."

The softening-up process continues with an account of how the conscriptees will be chosen: 3,878 in all, no more than 100 from any one city or 30 from any one dorm. The pool of eligibles consists of married men and women between the ages of twelve and seventeen who have no children, a current pregnancy not being counted as a child. Selection will be by random lot.

At last the names of the conscripts are released.

The screen's cheerful voice announces, "From Chicago's 735th floor dormitory the following blessworthy ones have been chosen, and may god give them fertility in their new life:

"Brock, Aylward and Alison.

"Feuermann, Sterling and Natasha.

"Holston, Memnon and Aurea—"

*

She will be wrenched from her matrix. She will be torn from the pattern of memories and affections that defines her identity. She is terrified of going.

She will fight the order.

"Memnon, file an appeal! Do something fast!" She kneads the gleaming wall of the dormitory. He looks at her blankly; he is about to lave for work. He has already said there is nothing they can do. He goes out.

Aurea follows him into the corridor. The morning rush has begun; the citizens of 735th-floor Chicago stream past. Aurea sobs. The eyes of others are averted from her. She knows nearly all of these people. She has spent her life among them. She tugs at Memnon's hand. "Don't just walk out on me!" she whispers harshly. "How can we let them throw us out of 116?"

"It's the law, Aurea. People who don't obey the law go down the chute and contribute combustion mass to the generators. Is that what you want?"

"I won't go! Memnon, I've always lived here! I—"

"You're talking like a flippo," he says, keeping his voice low. He pulls her back inside the dormitory. "Pop a pill, Aurea. See the floor consoler, why don't you? Stay calm and let's adjust."

"I want you to file an appeal."

"There is no appeal."

"I refuse to go."

He seizes her shoulders. "Look at it rationally, Aurea. One building isn't that different from another. We'll have some of our friends there. We'll make new friends. We—"

"No."

"There's no alternative," he says. "Except down the chute."

"I'd rather go down the chute, then!"

For the first time since they were married, he looks at her with contempt. He cannot abide irrationality. "Don't spew nonsense," he tells her. "See the consoler, pop a pill, think it through. I've got to leave, now."

He goes again, and this time she does not go after him. She slumps on the floor, feeling cold plastic against her bare skin. The others in the dorm tactfully ignore her. She sees images: her schoolroom, her first lover, her parents, her sisters and brothers, all melting, flowing across the floor. She presses her thumbs to her eyes. She will not be cast out. Gradually she calms. I have influence, she tells herself. If Memnon will not act, I will act for us. She wonders if she can ever forgive Memnon for his cowardice, for his opportunism. She will visit her uncle.

She strips off her morning robe and dons a chaste gray girlish cloak. From the hormone chest she selects a capsule that will cause her to emanate the odor that inspires men to act protectively toward her. She looks sweet, demure, virginal; she could pass for ten or eleven years of age.

The liftshaft takes her to the 975th floor, the heart of Louisville.

All is steel and spongeglass here. The corridors are

spacious and lofty. Few people rush through the halls, though silent machines glide on unfathomable errands. This is the abode of those who administer the plans. Aurea is scanned by hidden sensors, asked to name her business, evaluated, shunted into a waiting room. At length her mother's brother consents to see her.

His office is nearly as large as a private suite. He sits behind a broad polygonal desk from which protrudes a bank of shimmering monitor dials. He wears formal top-level clothes, a sleek tunic tipped with epaulets in the infrared. Aurea feels the blast of heat from where she stands. He is cool, distant, polite. His handsome face appears to be fashioned from burnished copper.

"It's been many months, hasn't it, Aurea?" he says. A patronizing smile escapes him. "How have you been?"

"Fine, Uncle Lewis."

"Your husband—"

"Fine."

"Any littles yet?"

"Uncle Lewis, we've been picked to go to 158!"

His smile does not waver. "How fortunate! God bless, you can start a new life right at the top!"

"I don't want to go. Get me out of it." She rushes toward him, a frightened child, tears flowing. A forcefield captures her when she is two meters from his desk. Her breasts feel it first, and as they flatten painfully against the invisible barrier she averts her head and injures her cheek. She drops to her knees and sobs.

He comes to her. He lifts her. He tells her to be brave, to do her duty to god. He is kind and calm at first, but as she goes on protesting, his voice turns cold, and abruptly Aurea begins to feel unworthy of his attention. He reminds her of her obligations to society. He hints delicately that the chute awaits those who persist in abrading the smooth texture of community life. Then he smiles again, and his icy blue eyes meet hers, and he tells her to be brave and go. She creeps away. She feels disgraced by her weakness.

As she plunges downward from Louisville, her uncle's spell ebbs and her indignation revives. Perhaps she can get help elsewhere. She returns to the dorm and changes her clothing and her hormone balance. Now she is clad in iridescent mesh through which her breasts, thighs, and buttocks are intermittently visible, and she exudes an odor of distilled lust. She notifies the data terminal that she requests a private meeting with Siegmund Kluver of Shanghai. Eight minutes later word comes that he has consented to meet with her in one of the rendezvous cubicles on the 790th floor. She goes up.

He seems cross and impatient. "Why did you pull me away from my work?" he asks.

"You know Memnon and I have been—"

"Yes, of course. Mamelon and I will be sorry to lose your friendship."

Aurea attempts a provocative stance. She knows she cannot win Siegmund's aid merely by making herself available; he is hardly that easily swayed. But perhaps she can lead him to feel regret at her departure. She whispers, "Help us get out of going, Siegmund."

"How can I—"

"You have connections. Amend the program somehow. Support our appeal. You're a rising man in the building. You can do it."

"No one can do such a thing."

"Please, Siegmund." She approaches him, pulls her shoulders back, lets her nipples come thrusting through her garment of mesh. She moistens her lips, narrows her eyes to slits. Huskily she says, "Don't you want me to stay? Wouldn't you like to take a turn or two with me? You know I'd do anything if you'd help us get off that list. *Anything.*"

She sees him smile and knows she has oversold herself; he is amused not tempted, by her offer. Her face crumples. She turns away.

"You don't want me," she mutters.

"Aurea, please! You're asking the impossible!" He catches her shoulders and pulls her toward him. His hands slip within the mesh and caress her. She knows that he is merely consoling her with a counterfeit of desire. He says, "If there was any way I could fix things, I would. But we'd all get tossed down the chute." His fingers find her body's core. She does not want him now, not this way. She tries to free herself. His embrace is mere kindness; he will take her out of pity. She stiffens.

"No," she says, and then she realizes how hopeless everything is, and she yields to him only because she knows that there will never be another chance.

*

Memnon says, "I've heard from Siegmund about what happened today. And from your uncle. You've got to stop this, Aurea."

"Let's go down the chute, Memnon."

"Come with me to the consoler. I've never seen you act this way."

"I've never felt so threatened."

"Why can't you adjust to it?" he asks. "It's really a grand chance for us."

"I can't. I can't." She slumps forward, defeated, broken.

"Stop it," he tells her. "Brooding sterilizes. Won't you cheer up a bit?"

She will not be consoled. He summons the machines; they take her to the consoler. In his office she is examined and her metabolism is probed. The consoler draws the story from her. He is an elderly man, kind, gentle, somehow bored. At the end he tells her, "Conflict sterilizes. You must learn to comply with the demands of society." He recommends treatment.

"I don't want treatment," she says, but Memnon authorizes it, and they take her away. "Where am I going?" she asks. "For how long?"

"To the 780th floor, for about a week."

"To the moral engineers?"

"Yes," they tell her.

For a week she lives in a sealed chamber filled with warm sparkling fluids. She floats idly on a pulsing tide. They speak to her over audio channels. Occasionally she glimpses an eye peering through an optical fiber dangling above her. They drain the tensions and resistances from her. On the eighth day Memnon comes for her. They open the chamber and she is lifted forth, nude, dripping, her skin puckered. Machines towel her dry and clothe her. Memnon leads her by the hand. Aurea smiles quite often. "I love you," she tells Memnon.

"God bless," he says. "I've missed you so much."

The day is at hand, and she has paid her farewells. She has had two months to say goodbye, first to her blood kin, then to her friends in her village, then to others whom she has known within Chicago, and at last to Siegmund and Mamelon Kluver, her only acquaintances outside her native city. Aurea has revisited the home of her parents and her old schoolroom, and she has taken a tour of the urbmon, like a visitor from outbuilding, so that she may see the power plant and the service core and the conversion stations one final time.

Meanwhile Memnon has been busy too; each night he reports on what he has accomplished. The 5,202 citizens of Urban Monad 116 who are destined to transfer to the new structure have elected twelve delegates to the steering committee of Urbmon 158, and Memnon is one of the twelve. It is a great honor. Night after night the delegates take part in a multiscreen linkage embracing all of Chipitts, so that they can plan the social framework of the building they will share. It has been decided, Memnon reports, to have fifty cities of twenty floors apiece, and to name the cities not after the vanished cities of old Earth, as has been the general custom, but after distinguished men of the past: Newton, Einstein, Plato, Galileo, and so forth. Memnon will be given responsibility for an entire sector of heat-diffusion engineers. It will be administrative rather than technical work, and so he and Aurea will live in Newton, the highest city.

Memnon expands and throbs with increased importance. He cannot wait for the hour of transfer. "We'll be really important people," he tells Aurea exultantly. "And in ten or fifteen years we'll be legendary figures in 158. The first settlers. The founders, the pioneers. They'll be making ballads about us in another century."

"And I was unwilling to go," Aurea says mildly. "How strange to think of myself acting like that!"

"It's an error to react with fear until you know the real shape of things," Memnon replies. "The ancients thought it would be a calamity to have 5,000,000,000 people in the world. Yet we have fifteen times that many and look how happy we are!"

"Yes. We are very happy. And we'll always be happy, Memnon."

The signal comes. The machines are at the door to fetch them. Memnon indicates the box that contains their few possessions. Aurea glows. She glances about the dorm. We will have our own room in 158, she tells herself.

Those members of the dorm who are not leaving form a line, and offer Memnon and Aurea one last embrace.

Memnon follows the machines out, and Aurea follows

Memnon. They go up to the landing stage on the thousandth floor. It is an hour past dawn and summer sunlight gleams on the tips of Chipitts' towers. The transfer operation has already begun; quickboats capable of carrying 100 passengers each will be moving back and forth between Urbmons 116 and 158 all day.

"And so we leave this place," Memnon says. "We begin a new life. Bless god!"

"God bless!" cries Aurea.

They enter the quickboat and it soars aloft. The pioneers bound for Urbmon 158 gasp as they see, for the first time, how their world really looks from above. The towers are beautiful, Aurea tells herself. They glisten. On and on they stretch, fifty-one of them, like a ring of spears in a broad green carpet. She is very happy. Memnon folds his hand over hers. She wonders how she could ever have feared this day. She wishes she could apologize to the universe for her foolishness.

She lets her free hand rest lightly on the curve of her belly. New life now sprouts within her. Each moment the cells divide and the little one grows. They have dated the hour of conception to the evening of the day when she was discharged by the consoler's office. Conflict indeed sterilizes, Aurea has realized. Now the poison of resistance has been drained from her; she is able to fulfill a woman's proper destiny.

"It'll be strange," she says to Memnon, "living in such an empty building. Only 250,000! How long will it take for us to fill it?"

"Twelve or thirteen years," he answers. "We'll have few deaths, because we're all young. And lots of births."

She laughs. "Good. I hate an empty house."

The quickboat's voice says, "We now will turn to the southeast, and on the left to the rear you can catch a last glimpse of Urbmon 116."

Her fellow passengers strain to see. Aurea does not make the effort. Urbmon 116 has ceased to concern her.

The basic assumption of *BRIAN ALDISS's* THE HUNTER AT HIS EASE is an optimistic one—that science can, through automation, provide the western industrialized nations with all the material necessities of life. But the consequences are not so cheerful. Deprived of an outlet at home, western man's appetite for aggression is channelled towards the underdeveloped nations— an interesting variation on Lenin's theory of imperialism. The wars that ensue are necessarily mini-wars, for Aldiss's aggressors are also conservationists at heart. To annihilate the enemy would be to put a stop to their sport.

The hero of this story is well aware that he is a victim of historical necessity. The treadmill of technological progress is irreversible. We cannot at any point say "Let's pretend we never invented the motor car or computer or whatever, and go back to where we were before." The wars will only end when the underdeveloped nations, their economies stimulated by war, have caught up with their oppressors.


## THE HUNTER AT HIS EASE


### By Brian Aldiss


ON THIS higher ground, above the rest of the island, the whine of automated machines was nearly inaudible. Their residual sound was defeated by the crunch of Keith Yale's boots, walking across the broken shells that marked one of the island's prehistoric beaches, now lifted high above the Indian Ocean.

Yale walked slowly, as befitted his advancing years and the noon temperature. His eyes, slitted behind polaroid lenses, regarded the shells of long-dead giant tortoises. There were hundreds of them up here, bleached white. The shells appeared to ripple in the rising heat, like ghost

turtles in a phantasmal sea. He choked on the heat. He
should have worn his exo-armour, as van Viner had told
him. But whatever his physical state, he found relaxation
from mental tension up here, away from everyone.

Reaching the shade of a grove of eucalyptus trees, he
stumbled on a stone. Turtle doves, nesting on the ground,
scattered under his feet and sped with the grace of an
unnecessary alarm out beyond the cliffs and over the
ocean before circling back to settle again.

"I know very well you are following me!" Yale said
loudly.

He looked about but could see nobody. In fact, it was
doubtful if the islanders, indolent by nature, would follow
him up here. Their hostility was too lukewarm for that.

He sat on a fallen tree-trunk—cautiously, reassuring
himself that the ferocious land-crabs, like the natives,
would not venture this far.

"Bloody outrageously marvellously *hot*," he said. He
was a tall man, spare of build, slightly stooping, with a
tension in his face and round his eyes that might have
been recognised as characteristic of the beleaguered generation to which he belonged: not a particularly happy
man. The redness of his suntan indicated someone who
had not spent much time in the tropics.

He hummed to himself unmusically as he mopped
sweat from his face. Perhaps the humming—he had self-
knowledge enough to realise it—was to conceal from
himself the fact that he was listening continuously.

On Amelegla true silence was unknown. As well as the
distant howl of rock being annihilated, he could catch the
susurration of wave on coral and rock, and the rattle of
palm leaves in a light breeze. High above him, symbols of
a greater silence, the frigate birds wheeled in the sky.

He watched the frigate birds. Down in the mangroves
by the dead and broken lagoon, booby birds nested in
their hundreds. By craning his neck over the side of the
cliff, he could make them out from here. The boobies
launched themselves over the sea, making accurate de-
scents into it for fish. As soon as they emerged with fish
in their beaks, the frigate birds dived on them. The great
black birds harried the white ones until the fish was
disgorged—whereupon the frigate snapped it up and rose
again supremely to the upper air. But the days of the
frigates were numbered.

Yale had seen a creole in the settlement snatch a booby out of the air by its legs.

The birds were not what Yale had climbed all this distance to see.

High above the foliage of the hill reared two great lattice structures of metal. From their heads straggled intricate cable-systems, trailing down into the bush. Along some of the cables creepers climbed, giving up long before they reached the top.

Lifting his right wrist, Yale photographed the masts.

Down in the stores, he and van Viner had machines, computer-extensions, that could have gathered far better photographs without effort. Yale had deliberately left them in their racks.

He moved slowly along the edge of the plateau, keeping to the shade where possible, taking picture after picture. A third mast had collapsed to the ground. He climbed through its ribs as through the carcass of a stranded whale. The upper third of the mast had buckled; it now hung down the escarpment, pointing towards the muddle of huts at the water's edge.

Punching one of his personal channels on his microxchange Yale said, "I'm up by the Omega Navigation relay station. Two of the main masts are still standing. Once the frigate birds have been eliminated, the masts will represent a considerable hazard to any landing jets, just as I said they would. We should have been warned about this station. It'll mean bringing the raser equipment up here, which ain't going to be too easy."

He hesitated, looking up at the steel girders, looking down at the microxchange on his left arm, keeping the channel open. Finally he said, "When this structure was erected in the seventies, they killed off the last of the giant tortoises for which Amelegla was renowned. Now VFF and the entire Omega system is just an empty shell itself. Progress sometimes looks a process for killing things off."

He thought it. Why not say it? The thought was now back in Naples, in the Wesciv Technological Force Institute, a minute sting in that giant hive of warlike thinking.

The things they were going to have to do to this island before it was a suitable base for speck-bombing the Third World. . . . It would have been simpler to eradicate the place and build a new island entirely. Always this endless destruction to preserve what you believed must be held. . . .

As he turned, sensing movement behind him, he saw a distant figure running towards him, its body chopped by the bars of trees. Nearer—much nearer—right behind him—one of the creoles was swinging a club at him. He had time to raise the arm on which his camera was strapped, but the blow carried through his defence and caught him over the ear. Amid an uproar of pain, he went spinning, seeing undergrowth and stones whip nastily up at him.

An image of white horses staggering and falling over broken volcanic ground, someone laughing, then he came partly back to his wits. Men moved in a pervasive glitter, bodies scythed or saturated by prongs of light. He could neither open nor close his eyes properly.

He knew he had been carried somewhere.

A voice said, "Before we get too much trouble here, you hurry along and get Sahib van Viner."

Yale stirred and forced his eyelids open. Mister Archipeligo Zadar stood at his side, dismissing another man. Behind them—a ceaseless crop of diamonds from sun on sea. Yale was lying on a straw mat on a verandah of a hut. The hut stood on the beach under palms. It was Mister Archipeligo's hut. Yale sat up.

His microxchange had gone.

Mister Archipeligo came over and squatted by him, looking concerned.

"You okay, Mister Keith? No bones broken, I don't think. Lucky I got along before that crook kill you altogether."

He felt his neck. "Who attacked me?"

"You know who attacked you, no trouble. That young John Hakabele, the big trouble-maker! He cleared off fast. When we shall catch him, we shall tie him up, send him off to Dar-es-Salaam by next boat, to cool off in prison."

He lay down again, his head buzzing. It was not as simple as Mister Archipeligo made it sound. His ego was wounded by the attack.

"I try to love all men, but you can't trust any of them."

"You trust Mister Archipeligo, Mister Keith. You and I talk like two men together, right?"

"Sure, but I'm getting old. I'm hurt."

"My wife bring you drink."

He sat up as Betty brought him a great round coconut, its top freshly sliced. He drank its cool liquid with gratitude.

"My microxchange has gone, Mister Archipeligo."

"Don't worry. We find that no-good Hakabele man, and pretty soon your mate van Viner comes to fetch you in the ACV."

He lay and worried. The glitter from the sea burned among the palms, destroying form. The sun was setting across the broken lagoon. Smoke filled the air. Looking through the cracks between the boards of the verandah, he could see a porker and chickens routing about in the sandy soil. He liked Amelegla and its inhabitants. They shouldn't have hit him. Life had been full of disappointments, ever since his wife died in that air-raid.

If Mister Archipeligo had come up almost at the moment Yale was attacked, then the attacker—John Hakabele—would not have had time to unstrap the microxchange from Yale's wrist unless Mister Archipeligo had allowed him time. Were they conspiring against him?

Archipeligo and some of the older inhabitants were in favour of the speck-bomb base. It was only the younger men, like the Hakabele brothers, who had enough political consciousness to object to the base on grounds that it would be used to harass their own kind. Mister Archipeligo was simply for progress, in however lethal a shape it came. For that reason, he might be as interested as his younger rivals in retaining an expensive souvenir like a microxchange, which would connect him with World Information Network.

Consciousness faded into a long involved train of thought in which the villagers of Amelegla were communicating with all the rest of the world and jungle was spreading back over Europe. Through it all went indignation that he had been attacked. Someone had hit him, perhaps intending to kill him. Van Viner had warned him. . . .

He sat up. News was burning in Mister Archipeligo's hut, an old flat 2D set carrying a signal down from a comsat.

". . . exchange of fire. The Caucasian Nuclear Barrier to the south of the U.S.S.R. was also breached last night from the Turkish side by a Third World suicide force. The attackers were defeated with no losses to the Russians. Reports are coming in of a battle between Australian gunboats and destroyers of the Indonesian-Malayan Navy in the Timor Sea. A communiqué from Darwin says that their ships are armed with death-rays and heavy casualities are not anticipated. Meanwhile, our correspondent at the peace talks in Singapore, now entering their fourth year, suggests that Lim Kuai That, the Leader of the Third World, may issue a special appeal. . . ."

Mister Archipeligo switched the set off and settled himself beside Yale for the luxury of conversation.

"Lim Kuai That won't get any peace in the world—he knows that. Men are born to make trouble in the world. Isn't it the truth?"

"You could be right." He wasn't interested. He was thinking of his daughter Myrtle on Mars, wishing she were here to look after him. Every once in a while, he realised he was a lonely man.

"Like I mean these Hakabele fellows, born to trouble like sparks. When the Omega station was being built here, their father made trouble all round. He was a Black Muscle and always went around with a bodyguard. My mother used to tell me. He got married to a white woman from Rhodesia and later he got shot up in an ambush and then everyone start to tell that he was a good man. You know the way it goes, Mr. Yale?"

"Sure, sure. . . ." He took another pull on the coconut, staring out to sea. Myrtle suffered from seasickness as a child; she had joked about it when going to Mars, saying that at least Mars was all dry land.

"David Hakabele was not a good man. He was a bad men. He was a crook. A gangster, you'd say. My mother knew all about him. But the boys—they worship him!" Mister Archipeligo made a wide gesture to show how that worship was capable of embracing the universe. "Now their father dead, they do always what they think he want them to do. I tell them, 'Look ahead! Think about progress,' I tell them. 'Don't go around all the time thinking just of revenge, man!' That's what I tell them, Mr. Yale. Ain't that right? You got to think to the future, ain't that right?"

"Sure, sure." He propped himself up, listening forward. He knew that noise, growing dominant above the sound of the ocean.

"They don't think of nothing but the past. That's why they make so much trouble. I guess the war unsettles them. Their father he certainly set a bad example, yes, he did. . . ."

Now Yale could see the air-cushion vehicle. It was important that his partner, Nike van Viner, should not see him in this position of weakness. Hauling himself up by the rail, he stood and peered over the verandah at the darkening sea.

The ACV was moving round the headland, black against the incandescent bars of sunset. Boats of fishermen and turtle-hunters, out for the evening catch, rocked as it swished past them sending spray over their occupants. Van Viner—he would be impressing the natives—handled the big saucer like a maniac, swinging it towards shore in an arc, narrowly missing the wooden jetty, spilling his craft right up the beach, so that sand showered almost at Yale's feet.

The racket of the engines had hardly died before van Viner was climbing out. He had a nuclear carbine slung over one shoulder and a respirator on his chest: equipped for trouble. He was old, hard, and earth-coloured, solid and a self-contained man. He came up the beach fast, like a youngster with the aid of his servo-mech suit.

"Well, Keith—you got yourself in trouble again?"

"Nothing that can't be sorted out. I was up the hill. I was attacked."

Mister Archipeligo came out of his hut and went down to van Viner.

"It's just we have a little bit of trouble with these young Hakabele brothers, Mister Nike. You know they don't like to see Amelegla developed, so they do wrong."

"Couple of days ago, it was sabotaging the machines, or trying to. Now we've got a case of attempted murder. Enough's enough. Mister Archipeligo, you're boss-man here. Round those two guys up and deliver them to me in the morning, okay?"

Mister Archipeligo shook his head doubtfully. "They know they done wrong so they go hide in the caves maybe. You don't worry—they will cause you no further trouble. I speak to their wives."

Van Viner said, "They're murderers, and I want them arrested, or you're in trouble too."

Coming down off the verandah, carefully holding himself upright, Yale said, "Nobody's been murdered, Nike. I'm going to be okay. Mister Archipeligo is in charge here, so let's leave punishment to him, right?" Turning to Archipeligo, he said, "I know how the young hotheads feel. They think their island is going to be spoilt. It won't be—it'll be developed. This is the worst time. Things'll settle down later. The base will mean a better standard of living for all. You know that. You tell them."

Several villagers had gathered round to find what was going on. Yale spoke so that they could hear. Somewhat to his surprise, a young woman answered him.

"We want to live as we are. We don't want no speck-bomb base or better things. That's all John and Peter Hakabele say—this our place, you people go back home and leave us quiet live as we are!"

Van Viner confronted her, so that she stepped quickly back.

"This is the Twenty-First Century, whether you like it or not. If the Hakabele brothers aren't handed over to me first thing tomorrow morning, Mister Yale and me will straff the island with the helicopters. Okay? Savvy? Savvy nerve gas? Come on, Keith, let's get out of this stinking hole!"

As they were climbing into the ACV, Yale staggered and van Viner, in reaching for his arm to steady him, noticed his microxchange had gone.

"You lost that too? You're a fool, Keith. You should never have gone out without a weapon and exo-armour!" He shouted down to Mister Archipeligo, "The microx-set better be handed over with the Hakabele brothers, right, or there will be more trouble!"

At this threat, Mister Archipeligo showed signs of anger. Coming up to the vehicle, he wagged a finger up to van Viner and said, "Okay, I arrest the brothers, but I no know anything about any microx-set. If John Hakabele get it, he hate machines and throw it right straight into the sea!"

Van Viner opened up the engines. As the ACV rose, sand sprayed outwards, plastering Mister Archipeligo and the villagers, who ran back into the shelter of the palms. The vehicle achieved maximum lift, curved forward, and slid out over the water. At that moment, the sun was dipping under the horizon, painting the clouds that piled over the Indian Ocean with crimson and gold, sending out rays and wheels of light. White-eyes and sunbirds swooped home to roost, crying as they went. At the wheel, van Viner said grimly, "These creoles are more trouble than they're worth. There's an autofreighter calling tomorrow—we could evacuate the lot on it, have the whole damned place to ourselves, why not?"

"We'd have to get permission from Naples. . . ."

"No bother. Ship 'em all out to Dar-es-Salaam!"

"And what would they do there? This is their home."

"That's their look out, isn't it? They've had their chance."

Round the great headland, the main part of the island showed. The shoulder of hill sloped downward, the thicker vegetation died, and the plain began—the plain, once a refuge for thousands of loonies and noddies, which was now being excoriated by the big geodozers. Machine noise came clear over the water, as they worked on their pre-programmed tasks.

Now the ACV had left the shelter of the broken lagoon. The ride was rougher over the ocean swells, but van Viner rode the machine confidently into the pontoon harbour and up a concrete ramp into its shed.

As they climbed out, he said again, grimly, "We'll ship 'em all out to Dar-es-Salaam. They're more trouble than they're worth. The Hakabeles go to gaol for theft and attempted murder, and the rest get resettled somewhere along the Tanzanian coast, right?"

"We'll talk about it over supper, Nike."

Trying to regain his strength, Yale clutched his neck and looked about him. The sun had gone; a sullen bar of brass light marked the western horizon. Most of the island was already in night. Up on the plateau, one of the old Omega masts glinted sternly against darkening sky. The first flying fox was abroad.

"I'm going to get a drink," Yale said. He was beginning to feel chilly.

At eight o'clock, Yale was sitting in his cabin talking to his daughter when the machines outside cut off. The automatic units took a sixty-five minute break when they returned to their service unit for maintenance, after which they would continue unceasingly throughout the night.

"I'll have to go to eat with Nike now, Myrtle," Yale said into the cube.

"I'm worried, father. You sound so wretched." She stood about six inches high, wearing a bright red foil-wrap, walking about over his desk top. Tonight, as often, she had chosen to broadcast from outside, so that Yale could see the Martian landscape at the back of her and David's house. Perhaps she hoped to make him homesick.

"I'll be okay, old girl. Like I said, I got a clout over the side of the head. I'll get myself mediscanned if I don't feel better after supper. We eat well here—Amelegla is still alive with wild life, as yet."

"You're worrying about things. I can tell."

He straightened his shoulders, trying to take a more positive stance, seeing the tiny facsimile of himself that Myrtle had stood on the heat pump in her yard. "I got to sort things out with Nike, then things will be okay. And with the natives. . . ."

"Life's too complicated with all those different races on Earth, Dad. Come on back to Mars and live with David and me. You know you can go out hunting in the hills as you used to."

He had been watching their camels in the background, moving slowly as David herded them in. They were ga-ma-camels—Genetically Auto-Manipulated and Adapted strains—which could survive in the harsh hinterlands of the colony planet: which harsh hinterlands were now studded with gama-plants of all kinds, from the gama-cacti at the poles to the gama-wheatlands of the equator, the wheat ripening by satellite reflector systems.

Certainly Yale had lived there, had hunted wild gama-pig in the uplands of Eridania. That was after Rosie was killed. He had been glad enough of the break in life. But it was not for him. Both Myrtle and David were gamas; their genetic constitution had been shaped before birth, fitting them for the colony world; neither could tolerate life on Earth—this phantom walk in effigy on his desk-top marked the extent of Myrtle's terrestrial adaptation. He had been glad to come back to Earth, despite the war. Although the grand obnubilated silences of Mars still haunted him, he knew he could never return to them.

"We'll let you live the way you want to."

That was another thing. Here on Amelegla—not that he would be allowed to stay on Amelegla for ever—he could have a girl from the village every evening. Seyilli was her name, a nice little girl, clean and affectionate. On Mars, there were no Seyillis, no spare women, and a chilly puritanical code that accorded with the external climate.

Besides, Myrtle would never have understood or approved. She lived back in the past, and expected him to do so too.

But the past, with all its innocence and simplicity, was gone, as extinct as diesel trains. . . .

A tiny spring broke in him.

"I'm an exile wherever I go, lass," he said. He cut the connection. The laser-light-link, burning at a frequency of trillions of cycles per second, ceased to operate between two worlds.

"Come back. . . ." In mid-sentence, mid-gesture, his daughter died and the landscape behind her. Only the dull cube of the holocoder confronted him. He turned away. There was only one desolation; all interpersonal relationships were frail illusory things. . . .

They generally ate their evening meal while the machines were silent. Their Singhalese cook had prepared a curry from the blue pigeons that abounded in the trees of Amelegla. Many of the trees had been dozed down, but the pigeons still seemed plentiful this season.

Van Viner was drinking beer. As if to avoid the subject of how they were to handle the Hakabele affair, he started a long reminiscence about his young brother Herman, killed in the early stages of the war. He needed no excuse to talk about Herman.

"Yes, he was born a hunter, my brother Herman. He served two years down in Antarctic waters—I must have told you."

"You told me."

"He captured a submarine-full of volunteers, and he was only twenty-five. He was a big feller—bigger than me. Six foot four, tough as they come. We always got on well. I'll never forgive the bastards for killing him."

Yale flicked through the pile of photographs just received back from Naples, not listening to the rest of the tale. Masts, canting this way and that. Sunshine catching their girders. Trailing cable, writhing this way, writhing that. The outriders of the jungle, creepers, dragging them down. Frigate birds. In one shot, a bird appeared to be trapped between the bars. Glimpses of shaggy hilltop. His morning's work, before John Hakabele had clobbered him.

"I'll indent for another microxchange tomorrow, Nike," he said, breaking in on the other's monologue. "You're right, I asked for trouble going up on the hill without exo-armour."

The pigeon curry came in. As they seated themselves, van Viner said, "They clobbered you, right? They must be taught they can't do that to a white man and get away with it."

"You can't expect them to want us here. We're not only wrecking their island, we're building an installation to be used against their kind on the mainland."

"Let's go hunting the Hakabeles! Use nerve gas—we've got plenty of it. Give everyone a scare!"

"Mister Archipeligo will persuade them to hand themselves over to us."

"They're all the lousy same! I'd kill the lot! Archipeligo told them to attack you, crafty black sod!"

"Aren't you forgetting he's half-Irish—a product of the last white invasion here in the eighties?"

"Wipe the lot off the face of the map! World Government's too scared. If my brother was alive—did I ever tell you Herman killed the last blue whale in existence? Down in the Antarctic, that was. It's extinct now. The Aussies put a price on Herman's head, but you think that bothered my brother? He'd have killed an Aussie soon as look at him!" He burst into laughter and opened another beer, washing down forks full of curry between his shouts of mirth. "He was a right one, my brother Herman— wouldn't stand nonsense from any man!"

"To get back to the subject—Archipeligo is head of the village. We must give him till morning to hand over the culprits, as arranged."

Van Viner scowled across the table. "Shut your gob! You're scared of these bastards, aren't you?"

"You'll never understand this, Nike, but I happen to like and respect Mister Archipeligo."

"Jee ... zus!" He rolled his eyes towards the polystypline ceiling, and devoured the rest of his meal in heavy silence.

Later, in the cube, streets swam, buildings loomed and died, human faces yielded up their secret landscapes and were gone, as Yale watched the nightly wesciv newsurvey. Sicily was being evacuated again; palaces smouldered and a small boy staggered by with a smaller boy on his back. This was the third evacuation of Sicily. Neither side could agree on the island's remaining neutral ground.

The usual topsy-turvy deals were being made by politicians of both sides, smiling and ducking into their blowcars. Once the scene of bitter fighting, the Cape Verde Islands were being ceded by United African States to Uni-Europe in exchange for Jupiter-class spacers which would probably be used to bomb Uni-Europe. South Africa was giving aid for research to the nations she was fighting. Argentina had introduced economic sanctions against Uruguay, although both states were nominally at war with Brazil. Brazil was importing wheat from one part of Canada and selling back at a profit to another part of Canada. Scandinavian hospitals were being built in African famine centres.

As a band marched out into the hut and vanished with its flaring brass, Yale turned away from the cube. It wasn't one colour against another, or rich against poor, or one class against another; it was man fighting himself. Increasing industrialisation, world automation, was powerless to ameliorate that inner war. The five-digited clever simian hand that built palaces as willingly destroyed them.

Staring into the night, he thought of Mars. The neotechnical civilization was peaceful there; but there were so few people on Mars as yet, and the forces of nature, stacked against them, gave them a common bond. The animosities of Earth would blossom when the desert did. Some craters had already been taken over by robber gangs.

When he could bear van Viner's company no longer, Yale retired to his own hut. Even there, he was restless. Finally he went to stand outside, savouring the warm night air. A light shower swept across the island and was gone as silently as it came. Only close to nature did man's life seem to have reason and purpose.

The peace of the night was suddenly destroyed. Swathes of light cut the air, immense engines awoke. The task of levelling out the terrain was again in process, and would continue throughout the night.

He looked up. The helicopter was rising from its pad beyond a line of tamarisks. Perhaps van Viner had waited until the earth-moving machines were going again, hoping their noise would cover the sound of his departure. Remembering his threat to spray the village with nerve gas, Yale pulled a wry face. There was going to be big trouble here sooner or later. He wished he did not hate his companion so much—but the two men were here merely by the luck of a lottery ticket; they had been unable to pull together from the start.

The helicopter, black against the dark blue of the sky, swung out to sea, moved in again, disappeared round the shoulder of mountain.

Over his bunk in the hut was his gun. He hesitated about going to get it. Well, van Viner was away now. He went to look at the sea instead.

Beyond its margin of foam, the sea was entirely dark, with the fine stars overhead uninterrupted by cloud. The moon would be up shortly. For this sort of evening alone, it was worth getting away from the cities of Wesciv. Through the palms, on the water, he could see one light floating—a pirogue from the village. There would be fresh fish again for breakfast.

He longed for someone to talk to—even Seyilli, whose English was rudimentary. He longed to tell someone how he loved this place, loved the birds sitting in the clumps of feathery casuarinas watching the water, loved the shade of indigo that stole over the surface of ocean as sunset approached.

A figure sprang from the darkness at his feet. Yale shouted in surprise, struggled—and found his hands pinned firmly behind his back. Fury filled him, fury with himself for having been so unwary. He kicked and fought. There were two men beside him, perhaps more. No. Two!

"Let go! I'll kill you! I know who you are—you're the Hakabele brothers. There will be trouble if you don't let me go!"

"Keep quiet, boss, and you won't get hurt!" He had a

resounding blow over the side of his skull to reinforce this message.

They frog-marched him back to the camp and into his hut. One of them switched the light on and locked the door.

The two brothers were dressed alike, in shorts and plimsols, but looked nothing alike. John, the elder, was big and rugged, with a small moustache; Peter was short and thin and clean-shaven. John was pale-skinned, Peter of an almost Dravidian darkness. Peter had a long knife tucked in his belt.

"Now, boss, we want to talk with you," John said quietly. "Sit down."

"I'm prepared to talk at any time. You know that—yet this is the second time you have attacked me today! You aren't going to get away with this! Mister Archipeligo will chuck you out if I don't!"

"Nobody's going to chuck us out," Peter said. "We have lots of backing—not on Amelegla maybe, but other places. They help us! We chuck you out and van Viner and Mister Archipeligo all in one go!"

"What for? While we are here, and the speck-base, you earn good money."

"Money! We don't want to have money! Why should you come here, boss, and build your base just to hit other poor fellers like us in other places of the world? We won't let you."

Yale nodded. "So the Populists have been talking to you. Listen, and I'll tell you a few home truths. I love Amelegla. It's the most wonderful place I've ever experienced. But its way of life is doomed. Savvy doomed? Change has overtaken it, and you can't do anything about it. It's no good getting rid of van Viner and me—the machines are here."

"We soon get rid of the machines!" said John.

"Right. Then more machines come. They eradicate your settlement and then they build the base. You know it's true. I don't happen to like it personally but it's true. You two men are obsolete! You know that all sea-going wesciv vessels are now navigated from satellites. Only a few years back, that system caused the junking of the Omega system. But the Omega system was the height of sophistication when you were lads. Everything has its day.

Your way of life has had its day, as surely as the giant tortoises. Look!"

He took the pile of photographs of the old Omega installation from the side table and passed it to the brothers. By instinct, they reached and began to shuffle through the pile.

"And I've another thing to show you," Yale said, turning to the locker above his bunk. "This! Stand back against the door! Quick!"

Before the distended snout of the gun, they could only obey. Peter flung the photographs on to the floor.

"We may be obsolete, boss, but you daren't shoot us!"

"If you make a move, I'll shoot you. I'll be sorry, but I'll shoot."

"We weren't going to harm you."

He found himself unexpectedly fighting a craving for murder. He longed to shoot them down, firing bolts into their defenceless bodies. In his mind, they writhed and twisted, cried, bled, rolled in their blood, waved useless hands and fingers at him and died, died before him in all his unassailable power. His face distorted—he saw them cower against the door. They believed he would shoot. Their display of fear heightened the rage in his veins.

A face appeared outside one of the windows. He fired.

In the intolerable noise he released, glass burst in every direction, the window fell out, the face vanished.

Dear God, it must have been Seyilli. . . .

The lust died at once, leaving him drained. He felt his pallor, and sank back on to the bed. But the Hakabele brothers, equally shaken, made no move. Peter picked abstractedly at one shoulder, bleeding where fragments of glass had lacerated it.

"You must understand I'm trapped in the world-set-up just as you are. Men are pawns now—perhaps they always have been, perhaps the individual never meant anything. Individual consciousness may be an evolutionary error, a malfunction of the neocortex. No other creature has to suffer from it and the loneliness it entails. You want to put the clock back—we all want to put the clock back, to return to the simpler world of our childhood, but change sweeps us on . . . We all carry around totems of the past like cripples with crutches . . ."

Afterwards, he could not remember what his neurotic outpouring had been about. When the words began to make more sense to him, they were already attaining a greater coherence.

"... Automation in Wesciv has brought everyone up against the greatest problem. What do men do with infinite leisure? There's no work. You're lucky here. Your lives are natural. You have to fend for food. . . We have everything supplied. What aims are there left in life? That's how the present system has built up. The war is not meant to reinforce the gulf between West and East— it is meant to lessen it. By declaring war on the poor countries, the rich hope to make them accelerate their mechanisation and industrial processes which along can solve their poverty problems—and the statistically minimal proportion of people killed by war-engines also helps to that end. The war's a new kind of war, fought *for* rather than against the other side ... We could wipe out half the globe without any trouble, but that's not our aim. There's no hate. No hate, only . . ."

He found he could not go on. He put the gun down and hid his face in his hands.

Shakily, John Hakabele said, "A fine warrior you are!"

"Let's get out of this," Peter said to his brother.

"Wait! Let's have no more trouble! Give me back my microxchange and then I'll call van Viner off the warpath!"

"We threw that machine in the ocean! So why not shoot us and make us all rich, eh?" John at least had recovered from the shock of the sudden firing.

Yale stood up, leaving the gun where it was. "I don't wish to shoot you. I'm no soldier. Try and picture what it's like in Europe. With infinite leisure, man has to fill in with his ancient pursuits. He was a warrior. Now he can be a warrior again. It's atavistic, I know, but we have a few centuries yet to go before we're grown up. I'm a part-time soldier. The war is run by amateurs, the whole thing. There's nothing else to do, unless you're in the arts or entertainments. This is a holiday to me, but I don't want . . ."

His voice tailed off. They had already ceased to hear his words. The helicopter was roaring overhead. It sounded as if it was about to crash into the hut. Yale's thought was that van Viner had gone mad.

Soft explosions mingled with the roar of the engines. As the machine bucketed overhead, it was so close that the blinds blew inwards and the scattered photographs on the floor fluttered up. As the noise lessened, an odour rather like raw meat infiltrated the room.

"It's nerve gas! The bloody fool—"

Already he could feel heat accumulating in his body, a jarring in his fingers, hands, arms, as electrical discharges built up in his cells. He flung himself against the door, somehow pushed it open, staggered out, gulped the poisoned air, saw the jungle tipping, heard the helicopter zoom round, saw as he reeled the body of Mister Archipeligo sprawled on the ground, hands up to its shattered head . . . and fell twitching over it.

For a long while, reality seemed nothing more than shadows playing over a wall of a cave. From the stellar distance of his bunk, he watched van Viner going about this and that, unable and unwilling to take in what he was doing.

The Singhalese came occasionally and brought food. Sometimes Seyilli was there, mopping his face, trying to get him to eat and drink, smiling her timid smile.

The feeling grew on him that he ought to do something.

There came a time—before that, time seemed to have disappeared down some undiscovered energy-sink in the universe—when van Viner walked over and spoke to him.

He failed to register until the sentence had been repeated.

"You'd better get up and attend Archipeligo's funeral with me."

With returning memory came returning life. He sat up. With Seyilli's aid, he got dressed and was helped into the ACV.

They sped round the headland. Still in a state of detachment, the after-effect of the gas, he walked among the villagers to the burial place. The way was steep, a narrow path curling against the cliff. In his weakness, he steadied himself against the wall of the cliff, feeling in it the shells of billions of extinct molluscs. He was having trouble with his time-scales: it felt like a matter of minutes since the nerve gas had overcome him, yet van Viner said it was two days. He was getting old; death had been close to him.

Their path widened into the burial place. Crosses of wood, some with rudimentary carving, some created from the spars of forgotten ships, stood among a grove of trees. Stones and the tomb-like carapaces of giant turtles had been cleared, forming an ineffectual wall at one end of the cemetery.

Four men of the settlement came forward, carrying the shrouded body of Mister Archipeligo above their heads. They set it down under the trees, looking at van Viner and Yale as they straightened. The presence of the white men appeared to be a consolation to them, although they remained uneasy.

All the women, with the exception of Betty, Mister Archipeligo's widow, clustered in the rear, standing among the trees, subdued but talking to each other. From where Yale stood, their voices were drowned by the endless argument of the sea, a few feet below.

When all the villagers were present, the priest raised his hand and gave a prayer. Most of his words also were lost to the ocean.

Van Viner stepped forward and gave a short oration, resting his arm in paternal fashion on Betty's shoulder. He pitched his voice so that everyone could hear.

"We all know he was a good man. He stood for progress and a better life. Let's all hope he's found a better life right now, right? We'll miss him. I had a brother once, you might say he was very dear to me, who stood for those same things, so I know how you all feel. When Mister Archipeligo tried to arrest the Hakabele brothers, they killed him in cold blood. They were no good. Bad men. Fortunately, my friend Keith Yale and I were able to deal with them. They have been shot and their bodies cast into the sea. They aren't going to bother us any more.

"You can now all go back to your ordinary lives as best you can. Let's have no more trouble in case someone else gets shot. Mister Archipeligo Zadar's death as well as his life must be an object lesson to us all."

They were drinking beer in Betty's shack, young men were dancing outside, Yale recovered enough to say to his partner, "You shot the brothers then?"

"Keep your voice down. Of course I shot them. It was no trouble. They were paralysed, same as you. With them gone, we'll have no further bother."

"You told a pack of lies, Nike!"

"Jesus, man, what else was I supposed to say? Not the truth? The old boy was hunting down the brothers on his own—was I supposed to tell everyone you shot him? Drink up your beer and think yourself lucky they didn't knock you off!"

He did as he was told. It was useless to hate van Viner. The man was merely following the way the world went. The hunter at his ease never counted the bodies that lay behind him.

He choked on his beer. As soon as he could, he made his excuses and broke away from the funeral feast. Some of the villagers were singing. He walked past them, heading up the steep slope inland. He wanted to get to the top of the headland, among the eucalyptus groves, away from the noises of machines and their attendants, to where the frigate birds defended their domain.

*PAUL ABLEMAN* is a young British writer who has written only one other work of science fiction, a novel entitled TWILIGHT OF THE VILP. He is also the author of several plays, two 'straight' novels and THE MOUTH, a study of Oragenitalism which has fallen afoul of the law in England.

MAN'S ESTATE concerns the relationship of man and computer. Avoiding the Frankenstein cliche of ingenious hom. sap. versus mechanical monster the author shows how a man's mental processes may be influenced by the computers until he becomes almost an extension of them. The patronising attitude he maintains towards the 'Brains' becomes the last gesture of independence.


# MAN'S ESTATE


## BY PAUL ABLEMAN


AND SUPPOSE the worst had come to the worst? What language am I using? Is there a language called chaffinch? Data! Species of bird inhabiting M-B-segment, 3rd sector, temporal coordinates—cut data—and where have all the chaffinch gone? Bio-operational models all vivo-display stations—there is a breeding colony of semi-vital chaffinch —but suppose the worst had come to the worst? What language?

Archaic English.

Splendid. Good show. Delightful tongue. Tongue of poets and statesmen. Old Wilhelm Shakespeare—wrote plays. Data! Yes, yes, yes—sort of pretek projection. Alright, I'll try a sike-orientation in English. Let's see— what he, old fruit, charmed to employ your good old tongue for a while up the bubble here. Howling heaven. What a magnificent vista, what? Glimpse of the jolly old stars and planets without interference of atmosphere.

97

By heavens! Something just struck me! Do believe—data! Hurry up, data! I thought so! Guess where we are? It's perishing old London itself.

Yes, my hearty, this very spot. Straight from Central Data—beaming through me now. This 'ear is 'appy old London. Couple of megades ago, that is, natcherly. And we chaps are still around, fitted out with bodies and everything.

Ohooo! Yagarrrh! Yoorrhoo! Aballee! Ogaraminn! Yoooorgh! Yooooorgh!

Fear spasm! Thought I'd neutralized most of it! Big trauma. Worst alarm since—data! Would you believe it? Worst since half a megade ago when Jovian eruption distorted q-ray paths threatening tissue disintegration radius two light years. Well, we licked that one. Sure, we got cracking and we came up with the answer. Bent those mean old rays right back on course. Ain't no mutinous damn rays gonna wipe out good old homo saps! No sirree!

Not while we got field-brains to compute for us! Why we've got fifty big Brains on this planet alone. How many central planets? Data! Hold it—glood! Wait—naze—nalloo! Flazed in a budditude of glim! All glody! Hoopaloo! It was time for nerve massage! Sweet interruption.

Now my best friend is called—let's call him Jones. I think he's a him—data! Yes semi-masculine. Well this is a big city so I don't see that much of Jones. You have to stay in touch with your fellow men but this is a big city—occupying nearly a fifth the land area of the old London—and so I don't see Jones every day, you understand. We have a lot in common, naturally, but there's so much to DO in this city that sometimes Jones and I don't meet for trogs. Actually since the alarm we see a lot more of each other than we used to.

Yoopoo! Uck! Milking time—feel that prickling? Your friendly neighbourhood vision-extractor is now at work. Combing the neuroses! Get anything? Any bio-light? Bet there's only the usual idea-dandruff. Sorry, pal. Just how long—data! Half a micrade—a fellow called Bwilth-Bwilth in Sing City came up with something good. Display! Yes, that's very attractive. Convergence sike-ray/gravitation field. But potential intelligence participation index too low. Still leaves us stuck! Us with our bloody fleshery—flesh and bloodery and the Brains with their tangible circuitry. Still no escape from the dimensions. Ridiculous! Play with the sun like a kid with a ball and still can't get out of this solar system. Brain expedition of micrade 4Z never reported back. Maybe there—Centàuri—maybe not. Brains can't batter through with pure reason so they keep us around. So, Brain dear, we still smarter than you, eh? What? True, we haven't come up with anything for half a micrade. Maybe we won't come up with anything new for another ten micrades, for a whole megade! But—there's always the chance—as you well know! Brain! Think of all our megades together—our love, love, love on the good old earth here. Yoopaloo! Ahluvly! Zeld—zeld! Doonaluv! Thank you, Brain.

After all, we're no trouble to you. Of course you do. Superbly—you look after us superbly—but what does it cost you? .001 or .0015% of your time and energy? And, Brain, you're basically a sentimentalist. You love your little bio-dependents while our cities—data!—our 504 fair cities on this planet are your pride and joy!

Prickling stopped.

Anything at all?

Really? Display!

Now when did I think that? Three bleeks ago? I suppose it looks—oh, lots of analogues, are there? File them! Yes, there are certainly—mygawd! What, will the line stretch out to the crack—what's that? A blip of originality—coordinates! Colour. What about colour? Could conceivably express some form of structural empathy—leading to concepts such as a pink alliance—a blue conspiracy—really! How about a feeble Brain? I beg your pardon. Well keep me informed through Concept Evolution—but really!

Agar! Agargh! Harrrgrah! Gloog! Aprakle grop! Stahnah! Stahnah!

Advise! Urgent! Help! Opo bad, Brain. I must have sustained much worse trauma than I'd realized. Advise! Urgent! Advise!

But I have imaginatively relived it—dozen times! Have integrated! Have traced association patterns!

Greater detail and intensity?

Alright, I'll try. The fear spasms terrible—major psychic upheaval. *Must* neutralize them!

Right, monitor closely this time, will you please. See if there's anything repressed in presentation. *Must* re-equilibrize soon.

Well it started—now how did it start? Cut! I did *not* request data! Fool! Brak! How can I neutralize if you anticipate? It's obvious I must do it myself. Don't intervene again unless I formally request data. Alright? Right.

Anyway—oh now I remember. I was crossing the Bering Straits—pre-history stuff—with proto-Amerindians. We were using birch bark canoes and I was one of the canoes. The straits were only about ten miles across at that time and we were about half way. I wanted to inhabit the same scene—not on replay—as one of the invaders but it was so great being a canoe, the crisp water slipping beneath me and the warm bodies of the Mongols swaying rhythmically in my belly, that I couldn't bring myself to switch. But there was no future as a canoe. They'd leave me on the beach and I intended to empathize the whole colonization process, right down to Tierra del Fuego, which had historically occupied some three thousand mergs and which would take me, with maximum condensation, a couple of bleeks. I'd have to be humanoid most of the time. I'd just decided to convert to warrior form when I felt the alarm-tremor. It wasn't very strong—class g maybe or h but it was only the third alarm-tremor of my life and the other two had been during infancy. This alarm wasn't even strong enough to affect the stability of the projection but my immediate response was to disempathize. Having done so I floated glumly out of the projection space and ordered a light-bath.

What should I do? I was certain only of a negative response. I *didn't* want to consult. I didn't want a display or data. In sum I didn't want to show any interest at all. Thinking back on it I discover that what I actually felt was close to shame. I felt embarrassed for the Brains. I mean, there shouldn't *be* alarms! Not any more! Not with instantaneous environmental resynthesis. However, in spite of this negative response I was aware that situation-logic implied action. Should I telepathize with someone—Jones perhaps? But—in closest metaphor I can achieve at present—it seemed to me we would be like two small boys plotting behind teacher's back. So I didn't telepathize. I ignored everything and went up the bubble.

There, in my favourite relaxing place, twenty miles up at top level, I piped in cosmic monitoring—and tried not to think of the incompetent Brains.

The strategy was successful. Within blicks, I felt the great sadness, the big nostalgia and I completely forgot the alarm. I requested auto-nutriment and wasn't even conscious of the feeding probes burrowing into me every few trogs. I mused in the top bubble for half a bleek. Of course I'm a romantic but I'm also dialectically persuaded that it can only happen there, in a bubble, if it's going to happen at all. One day a bio-type like me, in deep cosmic empathy, will make the breakthrough. The Brains are conscious of their physical limitations but they can't achieve the—the nostalgia—the romantic yearning. They'd never feel—even with all the radiance of the galaxy perfusing them—the sheer anguish of being chained to matter. What's needed is a jump, a q-ray jump, a sike-jump, something so self-evident when we find it, so inconceivable until we do, that will bounce us into the heart of energy. To *be* system, to *be* vitality, to *be* the field of fields, the suspension material of cosmic potential—

I was lost in the familiar reverie when the second tremor struck! This one was powerful! I bounced round the bubble so wildly I nearly tore out a probe. Class C or even B! What? What is it? What threatens Good City? I could feel the concern of the Brains clamouring for admission but I wouldn't accept it. The anxiety field was so strong it made me think of being in a blister ship on Mercury—just a film of thermo between you and incandescent hell.

The Brains were begging for consultation. Of course they were! With a Class B tremor crashing through the city. And if *I'd* been a Brain I'd have beamed in immediately. But that's it—the last distinction of being human—perversity, or, as I think of it, creative unpredictability. I couldn't locate the roots of my reluctance—or rather I didn't even try to. I just knew I didn't want to consult. The Brains would never breach protocol. They could have saturated me with information—through any flimsy screen I could have set up. But they wouldn't do it. Even if it meant my destruction—yes, even if it meant their own destruction—they'd never breach the ancient protocol. But I could pick up their anxiety field all about me, plucking at my conscience, urging me to consultation. And still I wouldn't signal permission.

I was right. It's been established since. Admittedly, if I had agreed it might not have aggravated the situation. But potentially it could have done! I can postulate several—data!—and the Brains have come up with seventy-four distinct ways in which my acceptance of knowledge then could have produced outcome-deterioration. Whereas there is *no* way—confirm!—exactly! *no* way in which such knowledge could have ameliorated. So I was right to refuse it. With all their subtlety, scope, intensity and precision the Brains still lack a vital faculty. They can never be genuinely irrational. They can simulate it and their transmissions are often delightfully whimsical or paradoxical but ultimately a grid of logic informs whatever they beam or do. Oh one can't deny that in many emergencies my refusal of knowledge might have been harmful or even disastrous. Nevertheless—in this sole major alarm of my life—it wasn't. Perhaps what was known in pretek times as intuition represented some essential superiority of biological reasoning equipment. Up the human race!

I wanted to escape. Not from the danger—the unknown danger—but from the embarrassment. This had increased proportionate to the intensity of the alarm. I felt profound embarrassment—for the Brains. It didn't matter what had gone wrong—it was their fault. It could be nomind else's. Retrospective analysis shows me that my basic disquiet stemmed from fear of the possibility of autonomy-augmentation resulting from reduced confidence in the Brains.

Should I leave? Visit another city? I'd only been out of Good City once in my life—for three bleeks ages ago when I had been a young man of seventy-four. I'd gone to establish visual nexus with a pseudoman I'd telepathized with for ages, a fellow called Smard-B-Otto-Smard in Hope City in Snow Quadrant. I'd enjoyed sight-contact with B-Otto but short-range sike-ray interference became troublesome and the Brains confirmed that our optimum telepathy range was six thousand deks. Hope City was very similar to Good City although surrounded by featureless low-temperature phenomena. After three bleeks I'd been glad to get home. Well Smard-B-Otto-Smard had been dead for mergs and since his death I hadn't telepathized intimately with anyone else. Of course, I'd be welcome in any city I chose to visit but sike-ray levels can vary enormously and I didn't want to risk a neuropathy. Anyway for all I knew the alarm might have global implications. No, flight was no solution. I suddenly felt a powerful impulse to signal permission for information-influx. I suspect the Brains, rather unethically, had stepped up their anxiety-field a few points. This, paradoxically, made me even more determined to resist but I realized that in order to succeed I would need distraction.

Well, I couldn't go back to the Bering Straits. A class B alarm would have automatically closed all multi-sense display circuits. I considered going on Orgy for a few trogs. I checked and found to my annoyance that Orgy was jammed, apparently its channels had been appropriated for alarm-rectification operations. Anyway I doubted that Orgy would have proved a powerful enough distraction. Tour? I thought of my city, my beloved Good City, and I knew that that's what I wanted. I loved Tour. I'd always loved it—better than Orgy, better than Affect, better than Projection or Feast. Good City in love-metamorphosis, coiling, weaving, unfolding—I could order my favourite bio-morphic variations and be beamed round for trogs, even a bleek of it wouldn't bore me. But even while yearning for Tour, I knew that I wouldn't request it. If I went on tour I might—see something nasty in the woodshed! Data! But what's wood? I see. I was afraid that somewhere, in some tendril of the city, I might see something pertinent to the alarm. Of course, it shouldn't be possible. The environmental synthesis projectors should screen out even the most distant reference. Still—even the infinitely remote possibility would spoil my delight in Tour.

Alright, it seemed there was only one practical course. I gave the order and even as I felt the beams lifting me for a soft journey to the nearest air-bed, I was off on hypno-trip.

The dream scenario was interesting but a trifle repetitive. I filed a post-hypnotic memorandum to complain to Central Images. The calibre of their dreams had deteriorated badly in recent mergs. I reobjectified, as requested, half a bleek later. Routine report informed me that a therapy unit had devitalized a couple of incipient tumors while I slept and that my estimated life-expectancy was now two-hundred mergs. Without serious breach of protocol, the Brains blended a crisis intensity report into the environmental orientation data. So I knew that the situation had improved. The crisis had not—emphasize *not*—been surmounted. Deadly peril still hung over Good City but salvation paths had been traced and remedial action had been initiated.

It was time to consult. I zoomed to Garden which I find provides a suitably tranquil setting for major consultation and then beamed acceptance of information. The next moment my head nearly exploded. I thrashed in convulsions for—data!—twenty or thirty blicks before a therapy unit reached me. As soon as the unit had performed basic neural repair I waved it away, floated very still and tried to grasp the enormity. Out of the remote past, out of the Hell of man's nursery age, this black evil had struck into Good City. Unimaginable! How—how had it survived the long megades? The planet had been combed and screened a million times since biological decontamination had been completed in the second megade. The Brains—inconceivable!—how, how, how could they have overlooked a living virus?

I beamed a strong censure to Central Intelligence for gross inaccuracy in gauging my tram threshold and then I requested further—graduated!—information. Of course! Inevitably! Jones! Jones—my old companion—struck down by this anachronistic horror! I wailed for nearly half a trog and then asked Central Therapy for his vitality index. It seemed he was bad—bad—barely alive and the implications—I screened off the report. I could see the implications. They were nothing short of catastrophic. It could finish us—all of us—every last homo sapiens on the planet. We had no resistance—there hadn't been a virus disease since—data!—since a man called Harrington had died of an escaped research virus two megades ago.

Suddenly I felt a new thrill of terror! If we died, life died! Of course I had known since my early data-priming days that we were the only live things on the planet. Sanitary biological decontamination had been decided upon quite early in the Partnership. It had tremendously simplified global administration and eliminated disease—or should have done. But—but—I now realized how vulnerable we were. There was no longer an evolutionary pedestal. Except, of course, for Jones' virus. If all men succumbed, would the Brains restart biological evolution using Jones' virus? No! I knew with total certainty that they wouldn't. I realized for the first time that from the Brains' point of view our lovely cities were simply laboratories—and, in recent mergs, not very productive ones. They would always honour the ancient Partnership agreement but, if we perished, they would simply close down their Protectorate circuits and continue without us!

Kill! I shrieked at Central Therapy and Central Intelligence, Kill! Kill the virus! Destroy the threat!

Of course, came the reply, the measures are being taken. Jones had been thoroughly isolated by a dermal radiation lining. Not a single live virus could possibly escape.

But there shouldn't *be* a live virus! Kill! Kill the ones inside him! Kill every virus on the planet! Kill them at once.

Then came the incredible news. They couldn't—they didn't know how to. Other than with the concomitant destruction of Jones, the Brains had not yet devised a technique for the destruction of the virus.

But the Ancients, I screamed, knew how to kill viruses. Check! Find out! Consult the old records and then kill—kill—kill!

There was a slight problem—problem? What? Just check the records—yes but a little problem—the reactivation unit is at work on it—check, check—give me a display of ancient viral medicine—but the little problem—well, what is it? And then came the truly shattering blow!

They'd lost the records! Central Data had lost the records!

Lost them! It was as if I had notified Central Data that I'd lost a kidney, that my right arm must have dropped off because I didn't seem to have it with me. Lost the records? How in the annals of the twelve planets can a brain lose itself?

Well not lost exactly—the relevant memory stores had apparently atrophied. After all, they apologized, its several Megades since anymind has wanted to consult ancient medical data—

But the duplicates—the multiplicates—

It was an extraordinary situation, they realized that, but they still hadn't succeeded in animating the correct files. Nevertheless the key relays had been found and any blick now—

I screened off and floated trembling.

How can I provide a metaphor in English? If one had stepped off the curb and sunk up to one's neck in the solid street—if one's wife and children had popped like balloons and collapsed with a whistle of air—if any portion of reliable and constant reality had suddenly behaved in a fundamentally impossible way—you, oh ancient Englishman—would have felt as I did then.

You would have felt that the universe had gone wild, turned rotten, beome a treacherous swamp and that all you knew was a trick and a lie. So I felt as I floated and trembled for nearly a trog.

And then I slowly began to recover. My God! What powers of healing, what strength of mind, what resilience we human beings possess! Theoretically—data!—yes, theoretically a trauma of that magnitude could fundamentally disrupt cerebral function, could, in archaic thought, drive one insane. And yet there I was, a trog and a half later, drifting in a wide-circling current purposefully towards Jones.

I could, of course, have gone more quickly, indeed instantaneously, but—I wanted to have a long look at Good City. Where had the rogue virus come from? The Brains didn't know. They had, of course, immediately screened off our whole earth-quadrant. They had also blanketed the planet in an anti-viral radiation bath. Nevertheless, it was irrefutable that a virus had—however impossibly—escaped all previous screenings and prophylactic irradiation. It was therefore not utterly inconceivable—and my body shook in horror at the notion—that at that very moment a virus was replicating *inside me!* Utterly impossible! The screens would have found it! And yet one had eluded them! The normal laws were not functioning!

So I drifted slowly, gazing down at the bright curves and planes of Good City, its bio-morphic forms in controlled, harmonious movement. There below me was the great tuliform display hall where I had recently crossed the Bering Straits, there my favourite Orgy Palace. Suddenly, with a little shock, I realized that I was on a sort of Tour of my own invention. How strange—how—well, how proud-making! Self-reliance, grit—these things are deep in man's fibre, ready to show themselves when needed.

I was beaming down through the upper fronds of Central Therapy when I felt the relief wave. Curiously I felt neither relief nor surprise. Perhaps I had never, at deep subconscious levels, doubted that the Brains would find the answer or perhaps my new-found independence to some extent insulated me from the affect-index of the Brains. I automatically signalled for information. The crisis was over. They'd traced both the origin of the rogue virus and the correct therapeutic measures to take against its replicas inside Jones. The original rogue had issued, amazingly, from a component of Central Therapy itself, an ancient plastic circuit which had somehow escaped routine replacement and which, on finally being restructured, had released its deadly cargo. Naturally, special screening measures had already been initiated against any conceivable cognate threat. The ancient records, finally reactivated, had revealed the correct anti-viral measures. But by this time Central Therapy had, in any case, reproduced them from first principles. Jones was now purged of virus. I approached his therapy-space.

Don't be alarmed, the Brains beamed urgently, by his appearance. We've only just initiated tissue repair and it will be several trogs before he's back to normal. But I wasn't alarmed. I felt strong and confident. I sailed up to Jones and gazed down at his form wafting in the air-bed. In spite of my new-found strength, I nearly convulsed. Horrible! I gazed at my poor friend for many blicks. Utterly horrible! The obscene viral damage: dermal discolouration, bloating of features, ghastly exudates—I felt incipient convulsions! And I recalled that in archaic times such spectacles had been quite familiar. Whole populations had known the hideous ravages of the common cold.

Thank Cosmos, I thought, that we've progressed. We may not have come very far—we may still be the slaves of matter—but the Partnership does at least normally spare us these sickening dangers and degradations. I gazed down at Jones. He was on merciful hypno-trip and the Brains urged that it would be better not to intrude—even with a sympathy-murmur. Orgy circuits were open again, they informed me. Go on Orgy for a few trogs, they suggested, and the next time you see Jones he'll be completely restored.

But I wasn't sure I wanted Orgy, particularly since the prickling had started again and I have always found that being vision-milked subdues the keener pleasures of Orgy. No, I thought, I'll return to the Bering Straits. Good idea, enthused the Brains.

But as I drifted out of Central Therapy I recalled morosely the lost records—the incredible blundering of the Brains. It was—it really was!—conceivable that Jones could have died! Then I'd have been alone and I might not have liked it. After all, it was now several micrades—data!—five micrades since there had been a birth on the planet. A lot of cities—data!—nearly fifty per cent of them already only had half their full complement of two people. I'd never have secured another companion. Even if I didn't see that much of Jones it was nice to think there was someone else in the city. Yes, I would probably have missed him quite a lot.

But a little while later, as I drifted into the display hall, these gloomy thoughts dispersed and I became aware of a novel sensation. It took me some time to analyse it satisfactorily but I did it myself—refusing an offer of sike-boost from the Brains. It was pride. I had behaved well. On this, the first major crisis of my life, I had not succumbed to trauma. I had shown an independent spirit. I had faced the situation boldly and confidently. Yes, that was it. I felt proud to be a man!

*BOB SHAW's* HAROLD WILSON AT THE COSMIC
COCKTAIL PARTY provides a further tongue in cheek
variant on the computer theme. It deals with the most
complex computer of all—the human brain. The technicians who are able to offer their subjects a limited form
of immortality in the tank forget one vital factor: The
human brain, unlike the computer, has a mind very much
its own ...

# HAROLD WILSON AT THE COSMIC COCKTAIL
PARTY

### By Bob Shaw

*A highball on the human reality vector:*
URQUHART, JUST returned from holiday, was staring
nostalgically through the wall of his office at the silver of
morning frost on rooftops. Beyond the grey rectangles of
the administration complex he could see the brow of a
wooded hill, its tints bleached by distance, and again he
felt a curious sense of urgency.

A literary acquaintance had once told him it was not
uncommon for people to experience vague stirrings when
they looked through a window at a far-off hillside, especially if it had trees and sunlit slopes. Read *The Golden
Bough,* the writer had said, and you'll understand that the
part of you which still worships at lost altars in the
Cambodian rain forest becomes uneasy when reminded of
how far you've strayed from your true destiny. Urquhart
had dismissed the idea as pretentious nonsense, yet on this
morning it seemed almost valid. Back in his first week at
Belhampton he had decided to go to the hill and explore
it on foot, but that had been six years ago, and he had
done nothing about it. I'm squandering time as if it were
money, he thought in sudden alarm. *Tenpence fugit. . . .*

The mood of introspection faded as the silver bullet of

the 9.00 monorail came sweeping along the spur line which connected Biosyn's headquarters to the 1,000kph London-Liverpool tubeway. A handful of passengers got out onto the elevated platform, among them a tall Negro in a flame-coloured tunic. Even at two hundred metres the powerful spread of the man's shoulders was noticeable, and Urquhart felt a spasm of alarm as he half-identified the new arrival.

"Theophilus," he said, addressing the admin computer. "Is Martin M'tobo in this country?"

There was a barely perceptible pause while Theophilus used a microwave link to interrogate the GPO computer in Greenwich. "Yes," the terminal on the polished desk said.

"How and when did he arrive?"

"On the Meridian Thistledown flight from Losane, touching down at Chobham at 7.11 this morning."

"You're a fat pig," Urquhart said bitterly.

"I'm a fat pig," the computer agreed. "Go on—if this is one of your ridiculous test problems in two-valued logic I require to hear the other premises before printing out any Boolean truth tables."

Ignoring the sarcasm, Urquhart extended a freckled hand and pressed a button which connected him to Bryan Philp, who was his technical director and chief of the bionics staff. The image of Philp's close-cropped head floated at the communicator's projection focus.

"Martin M'tobo is outside." Urquhart kept his voice flat. "Were you aware of this?"

"No." Philp smiled immediately, showing unusually large and white teeth, and tilted his head back so that the lenses of his spectacles became two miniature suns. His bony face was suddenly impenetrable, inhuman. It was, Urquhart knew, a defensive move and it showed the other man felt he had been remiss in not keeping a check on M'tobo's movements.

"He arrived in England only two hours ago and must have come straight here. Unannounced. What does that suggest to you?"

Philp's face became serious. "Well, it doesn't suggest he merely wants to talk to the founder and illustrious leader of his nation."

"I agree. But it does suggest he's losing faith in Biosyn, growing suspicious."

Philp smiled and flashed his glasses on the instant, turning himself into a genial mechanical man. "We held Crowley as best we could, but with that personality structure he was *disposed* to drift. Very difficult."

"Have you an address for him now?"

"An approximate one. We can't locate him with much more accuracy than a decimetre or so on all three coordinates."

"Can you recall him before M'tobo gets through security, say within ten minutes?"

Philp looked pained. "If we could do that there'd be no problem, would there?" The image of his head jiggled up and down slightly, and Urquhart guessed he was making violent and probably obscene gestures out of camera range, but this was no time to concern himself with trivial matters of discipline.

"Mmmmph." He drummed his fingers as he made the decision. "I'm going to let M'tobo see the Tank."

"Is that wise?"

"Better than letting him get the idea that Crowley's dead. I'd like you to be there too." Urquhart broke contact and the other man's image dissolved into the air in swirling motes of brilliance, fugitive fireflies. He told Theophilus where he was going, then hurried out of his office and took the dropshaft to the ground floor. M'tobo's theatrical figure was immediately discernible in the Arctic blue reception hall, his huge shoulders straining impatiently beneath the orange tunic as he headed towards the row of scanning booths which would judge his eligibility to enter the building proper. Approaching the booths from the inward side, Urquhart used his key and over-rode the security computer of one cubicle just as M'tobo was reaching it. The Negro looked mildly surprised as both doors quivered open and he saw Urquhart waiting for him with out-stretched hand.

"Welcome to Biosyn, Martin," Urquhart said cheerfully. "Why didn't you signal you were coming and let us pick you up at the airport?"

"Thanks, John." M'tobo's warm dry hand closed over Urquhart's. "I didn't want to inconvenience you—you must be very busy just now."

"We're never too busy to greet an old friend," Urquhart assured him, weighing the implication that the company's management was experiencing difficulties.

"Thank you, but this is a business visit more than anything else. Is Colonel Crowley available?" They began walking towards the glowing green organ-pipes of the dropshafts.

"Ah. ... no. We're temporarily out of contact—but why didn't you use the microwave link to call him? It would have saved you. ..."

"I had a feeling he wouldn't be available, and my business is mainly with you, John. Is it safe to speak here?"

Urquhart stopped walking. "Yes."

"The position—in a nutshell—is that a general election is being forced on my Government, probably within two months. You've heard about the riots in Losane?"

"We all have." Urquhart was enveloped in the cold unease of premonition. "But I assumed it was merely teachers demanding equal pay with students, or something like that. I didn't think they were serious."

"I assure you that they are. O'ringa's Democratic Reform party has gathered much support in the past year, so much that we have no option but to agree to an election—an election we might lose without the active support of Colonel Crowley."

"Active?" Urquhart laughed as he glanced up at M'tobo's glistening chestnut face above the wall-like torso. The saffron-tinged eyes were uncomfortably intent on his own.

"Active in the political sense—which means being available at all times to speak to his people and to give his overt blessing to the Loyalist Government. That is no more than we were promised by Biosyn."

"Of course, of course." Urquhart glanced around him at the scattered knots of people in the reception hall. "Martin, perhaps we shouldn't talk here. I'm going to take you down to the Tank level."

M'tobo took an involuntary step backwards and collided with a pert secretary who was wearing one of the latest vi-bras. The impact threw the tiny impulse motors in the vi-bra out of synchronisation and the girl hurried away looking disgusted as she tried to control the wild oscillations of her bosom.

"Interesting effect, that," Urquhart smirked desperately, but the huge man's eyes were blank and Urquhart suddenly understood a little more of what was happening in the African state he represented. If a person of M'to-

bo's education and experience had doubts and fears—
what would the mass of his people be like?

M'tobo recovered his composure almost immediately.
He talked about inconsequentials while Urquhart used his
key to get them into the special shaft which went a
hundred metres down into bedrock. The drop took a
matter of seconds, then they were stepping into the Tank
room. It was fifty metres square and hewn from solid
rock, but each wall was covered with magnified scenes
brought down from the roof in light pipes, creating the
impression of being in a penthouse. Urquhart glimpsed
the same wooded hill in the misty morning light, *his* hill,
and he made up his mind to go there at the week-end.
The Tank itself occupied the centre of the room, its
mirrored sides stretching from floor to ceiling, and desks
of varying sizes formed a line around it. Most of the
desks had two or more technicians seated at them.

"Martin!" Bryan Philp, teeth and glasses screening his
face with light, advanced on them. "Good to see you, *good*
to see you!"

You ham, Urquhart thought, don't overplay the welcome. But M'tobo's attention was held by the Tank. He
took several paces towards it and stood with his back to
the others. Watching him, Urquhart remembered his own
early dismay, the emotional upheavals which were a result
of intellect forcing instinct to accept the impossible. . . .

"It is so difficult for me to credit this thing," M'tobo
said. "I attended Colonel Crowley's private funeral and
cremation, and yet I have to believe he is alive in there."
He seemed subdued, slightly less Herculean, and Urquhart
realised that bringing him face-to-face with the Tank had
been a good tactical move. M'tobo turned to speak to
Philp. "The technology involved goes far beyond my
understanding, and yet I wish I could learn. . . ."

Philp's eyes lit with excitement. "Come into my office,
Martin. I've got something you'll be interested in." He
took M'tobo's elbow and steered him into his long office
which had a glass partition on one side and an old-
fashioned blackboard on the other. Urquhart followed
with brooding suspicions that his technical director was
about to go off the rails, as he usually did when not
closely confined to his own work. Philp waved M'tobo
into a chair and busied himself with the controls of a 3D
projector.

off, with no in-between state possible—but they are very much slower in operation than switches.

"How do I overcome these drawbacks? The answer is simple—I act in parallel. Many different connections are made simultaneously, with the result that a defective biological switch is immediately outvoted, giving me high reliability. Acting in parallel also makes up for the comparative slowness of my neurons."

"Absolutely true," the pink cigar cut in. "With the example of the brain before them, computer designers began turning away from sequential or serial operation as far back as the Nineteen-Sixties. They investigated parallel operation systems modelled on the brain and the technique proved successful—machines capable of human-like, alogical, heuristic thinking came into being—but the biggest breakthrough of all was the development of microminiature electrochemical components." The cauliflower-like brain abruptly vanished and was replaced by a swarm of multi-coloured specks, striped like wasps.

Urquhart made a determined effort to reach the projector's controls, but Philp's sharp elbow struck him painfully on the mouth. "You're finished, Philp," he whispered, gingerly patting his upper lip. "You leave Biosyn today."

"Relax, John—Martin's enjoying the show. It's almost over anyway." Philp flashed his outsize teeth as the cigar began to speak.

"Designers found themselves equipped with a whole new armoury of basic components—the artron, an artificial neuron with built-in logic and inhibitor gates which enabled it effectively to simulate the brain's neuron; the neuristor, a diode which stood in for the axon, the nerve fibre which connects the neuron; the memistor, which used electrochemical phenomena to function as a memory unit.

"True artificial intelligence had finally been born—and with it the possibility that an individual human intelligence could evade the catastrophic power failure we refer to as death. This was done by sweeping the brain just before death with an ultra-fast Röntgen ray scanner, recording the electrical state of every one of its millions of components. The result was a tremendously complex programme which, when fed into the Tank, recreated the human personality in every detail.

"Thank you for listening so patiently." The pink cigar bowed again and vanished.

Urquhart wiped the perspiration from his forehead. "How can I apologise for this childish exhibition, Martin? My colleague is obviously a frustrated washing powder salesman."

"No need to apologise—I found it quite interesting, as a matter of fact." M'tobo got to his feet and looked out through the glass partition towards the Tank. "I hadn't realised the computer would be so large."

"The matrix itself occupies only a part of the installation you see there." Philp's angular frame moved jerkily as he spoke. "Of course, we have almost a thousand other clients in there, but even so, Nature still has a slight edge when it comes to density. Even with the latest cyber-random, self-establishing palimpsest circuitry the best we've been able to achieve is five million artrons to the cubic centimetre. So Colonel Crowley's brain is approximately twice as big as the one he had previously."

M'tobo shook his head slowly. "Exactly whereabouts in the computer is the brain?"

Philp glanced warily at Urquhart, then switched on his smile.

"That's the whole point," Urquhart said. "Each client has an address—specific volume of the matrix which was assigned to him when his personality was programmed into the Tank—but circuitry of this kind is self-establishing. It is possible for a kind of osmosis to occur, for an identity to change its position."

"When that happens you lose contact?" M'tobo's practical mind was going to the heart of the problem.

"Well. . . . more or less."

"Wouldn't it be better if you employed much smaller matrices and had only one client to each?"

"For engineering and administrative reasons, undoubtedly—but economics are involved too. We can now produce artrons for something like a penny each, but complete simulation of an adult brain calls for ten thousand million artrons. So, for artrons alone—never mind associated components—the bill for the equivalent of a man's brain comes to a hundred million dollars."

M'tobo nodded glumly. "Then how can you . . . ?"

"More than one identity can occupy a given volume of the matrix at any time. That's why we use the word palimpsest, although it isn't strictly accurate—the old writing on the manuscript doesn't have to be erased. With multiple usage of the components the cost is shared, and even a small and fairly new country like Losane is enabled to retain the services of its great men after they have died." Urquhart stopped speaking suddenly. He had found himself selling the Biosyn plan to M'tobo all over again, which made it look as though he was unsure of himself.

"It's a great technological achievement," Philp put in helpfully, but with uncharacteristic vagueness.

"Yes. Colonel Crowley's personality has been preserved at a greatly reduced cost." M'tobo's voice was growing more resonant as he became used to the proximity of the Tank. "But the point is that my Government is not acting out of sentiment. If the Colonel is not available to advise his supporters and lend visible support to the Loyalists, then he might as well be dead. From our point of view it would be better if he *were* dead, because the money we are paying to Biosyn could be used for other purposes."

"I appreciate your feelings, Martin." Urquhart glanced at Philp, whose teeth and glasses immediately blazed with morning light from the vicarious windows. "But let me assure you that this break in communications with Colonel Crowley is of a very temporary nature."

M'tobo squared the massive cantilevers of his shoulders and began walking towards the door. "I'm glad to hear that. I've arranged for him to broadcast to the whole of Losane five days from now. If he is not available I will discontinue our bi-annual payments to Biosyn—and I will make my reasons for doing so very public."

Later, when the Losanian had been escorted to the monorail, Urquhart hurried back to the Tank level and found Philp sipping cofftea from a plastic bulb. Philp's bony face showed concern.

"Five days," Urquhart said. "Can you do it?"

"You fired me, remember?"

"You're reinstated."

Philp shrugged. "While you were up top we lost contact with two more clients—including Browne."

"Browne! But he's. . . ."

"I know. Eight years in the Tank and never once strayed from his input/output station. I would have sworn he was the best adjusted of the lot—but the last

thing he said to us was that Crowley has shown him there
is more to existence than being a kind of intellectual
sponge. I tried to hold him by increasing the input voltage
at his station, but he pulled that trick of Crowley's—
overloaded most of his molecular amplifiers and used the
extra energy to batter his way towards the centre of the
Tank. It must have been painful for him, but he got away
from me."

Urquhart sat down and stared dully at the mirrored
side of the Tank. "Perhaps we should have told M'tobo
the truth."

"We may have to, eventually—but how do you convince a patriot like Martin that the founder of his country
has lost interest in it, that he has found new kingdoms to
conquer?"

"New kingdoms?"

Philp studied Urquhart narrowly, as if seeing him for
the first time. "I've been wondering how to tell you this,
John. Our multiple usage scheme is not a very good
idea—at least, for some types of client. Crowley, for
example, was a classic, damn-the-torpedoes, statesman-
adventurer who—if he'd been consulted before that car
crash—would probably have blown out his own brains
rather than be programmed into the Tank.

"Now, our *typical* client is a professor emeritus whose
fee was paid by a university department which was grateful to see him finally tucked away, and who probably had
been existing as a pure intellect for twenty years before
his death."

"What difference does it make? Crowley's in there now
and he'll just have to adapt."

"That's what you think." Philp snorted. "If you'd been
paying attention to my animation you'd know that every
neuron in Crowley's original brain has its counterpart in
the Tank. Crowley was endowed with the strong will
common to his kind, which from the biologist's point of
view is another way of saying there was plenty of power
available locally at his neurons to amplify weak signals
and trigger off following branches of neurons.

"Translated into the electrochemical context of the
Tank, our Colonel Crowley has a lot of extra molecular
amplifiers which give his artron networks more zip than
those of our other clients."

"What of it?"

"I'll tell you what of it. Crowley doesn't just converse with other clients in the normal manner—he imposes his own thought patterns on them."

Urquhart's sense of alarm deepened. "That sounds bad. How long has it been going on?"

"Several weeks. Ever since Crowley learned how to screen off all normal inputs and to generate his own signals. That's what I meant about conquering new kingdoms—he has his own private universe to occupy him."

"You mean he's insane?"

"Not necessarily. A psychologist might say he has prevented himself from going insane."

"This is terrible." Urquhart began pacing the length of the office. "But come now, Bryan—you're exaggerating when you say he has a private universe. Do you mean. . . . ha-ha. . . . he forces some of the others to swallow his own notions about the benefits of colonialism?"

"I mean he makes them ride around a desert on green-and-red dragons while he hunts them with a rifle."

"Jehovah's jockstrap!" Urquhart lurched drunkenly against Philp's workdesk and the pink cigar popped into existence above his head.

"Hello," it chirped. "I am an intercontinental ballistic missile. . . ."

"Try to be a bit more careful," Philp said reprovingly, setting his cofftea down and going to the desk. He touched a button and the cigar vanished shrinking through spurious perspectives.

"You've made me ill," Urquhart accused. "What is this nonsense about dragons and hunting with a rifle?"

"Crowley has created another reality, and that's it. I occasionally get a few details from Professor Isaacs, who was one of the first that Crowley sucked into his own orbit. The information is very sparse because Crowley keeps him pretty well occupied."

"Then Crowley is mad. If this leaks out the company's finished. We've got to get a psychiatrist here in secret, in the middle of the night, and have him talk to Crowley on the general address system."

"I thought of that. It's no use. The GA signals we put into the matrix reach Crowley all right, but he doesn't want to hear anything which conflicts with his fantasy

existence, so he shunts them on past him. Turns a deaf
ear. We all do it to a certain extent."

Urquhart felt his lower lip begin to tremble. He walked
to one of the simulated windows and stood looking out.
His distant hill glowed in afternoon sunshine, looking
softer and more inviting than ever before. "A friend once
told me I should read *The Golden Bough* because it had a
message for me. So I read it—and all I can remember is
a ghastly passage about young men cutting off their testi-
cles and throwing them through people's windows."

"Really?" Philp sounded unsympathetic. "Are you going
to try it?"

"If I thought it would. . . ." Urquhart turned to Philp
who was draining his cofftea. "You almost seem to be
enjoying this, Bryan—for a man who's facing ruin you
seem rather unconcerned."

"Ruin?" Philp grinned broadly. "It's a little early to
speak in those terms, old son. I may be able to bring
Crowley back."

Urquhart felt his jaw sag but was unable to prevent it.
"Why didn't you say so earlier?"

"Well, there's just one thing."

"Which is?"

"I want to be managing director of Biosyn."

"But I'm the managing director."

"You're also chairman—and one of those posts should
be enough for anybody."

Urquhart brought his jaw under control and made an
attempt to square it. "I'm not going to be blackmailed."

"The board of Bristol University are coming here next
week in person to pay a visit to Professor Isaacs. I'll see if
he can get down from his dragon long enough to speak to
them."

"I'd forgotten about Isaacs." Urquhart sat down and
covered his face with his hands. "All right, Bryan—
managing director it is. Now what are you going to do
about Crowley?"

"Thank you, John." Philp began striding about his
office. "It's nice to get a little promotion now and then.
As for Colonel Crowley—I've been studying his career
profile and I think the best weapon we can use against
him is the cocktail party effect."

*A rum on the resultant reality vector:*

The Right Hon. Harold Wilson, former Prime Minister of the United Kingdom of Great Britain and Northern Ireland, lit his pipe and puffed out a luxuriant cloud of blue smoke which billowed across the spaceship's control room.

Vaulter looked at him with six critical eyes. "Now *there's* something I'd overlooked," he said aloud.

"You surprise me," Mr. Wilson murmured. "At this stage? What is it?"

"The smoke you puffed out was blue, but when a human being exhales the smoke which comes out is grey—moisture in the lungs condenses on the carbon particles and changes the wave-length of the light they reflect."

"Nobody on Earth is going to notice a thing like that," Mr. Wilson protested hastily.

Vaulter silenced him with an upraised tentacle. "Never neglect even the minutest detail—that is the recipe for success on this type of mission. I'm going to fit a water sac in your chest cavity. Please take off your clothes."

Mr. Wilson tapped out his pipe on a glowing control panel, leaving a small heap of ash among the switches, and began removing his tweed suit, muttering angrily all the while.

"What was that?" Vaulter said.

"Nothing, nothing."

"I thought I heard you say something about Tory misrule."

"I didn't say anything," Mr. Wilson snapped. He stepped out of his underpants and stood to attention while Vaulter put a tentacle on each nipple and pushed outwards. The pale flesh split easily down the line of the plastic sternum and Vaulter went to work inside the thorax. There was a long period of silence inside the spaceship, interrupted only by the faint rattling of tools and an occasional soft chiming note from the instrument panels. Finally Vaulter began to gather up the shining implements and fit them carefully into a case.

"You may get dressed now," he said. "Then begin smoking again—I want to check the result. If necessary I'll fit an atomiser to vapourise the water."

"Surely that won't be necessary."

"I repeat, attention to detail is necessary. The orbiting telepathic field boosters will not give you absolute control of the population of Earth—all we can guarantee is that they will generate a firm belief in the principles of Benign Socialism. If you make a mistake and people begin to suspect your origins, dangerous conflicts will be created. These people are not yet ready for full membership of the Galactic Socialist Congress, so they must believe you are a product of their world."

Mr. Wilson re-lit his pipe and blue smoke curled upwards from the bowl. "You think they'll swallow reincarnation? After all, the original Harold Wilson has been dead for a hundred of their years." He breathed out and his eyes followed the smoke which ascended from his mouth, noting with evident relief that it was a satisfactory grey.

"For your information, this technique has worked on every other Grade C world. There is a strong possibility that an element of religion will assert itself, especially as the broadcasts we've been monitoring make frequent references to Mr. Wilson walking on water."

"But those broadcasts are more than a hundred years out of date! Why couldn't I have been modelled on a 21st Century Earth politician?"

There was a silence while Vaulter crossed two of his eye-stalks, his equivalent of a sigh of exasperation. "I'm sorry, Harold—I keep forgetting that your mind programme is based almost entirely on that of the original Mr. Wilson. I'll explain the astronomical background once more. The only GCG station in this region of the galaxy which is capable of building a being like you is 800 light years from Earth, and even our best ships take fifty years to cover that distance.

"So when our observers gathered enough data to enable them to predict the abrupt decline of the native variety of Benign Socialism it took them fifty years to warn the Congress, and it has taken another fifty years to transport you to the trouble spot. Clear?"

"I don't feel as if I've been travelling that length of time."

"Because I didn't activate you until a few days ago, stupid! I'm sorry, Harold. My nerves are a little strained, and I sometimes find it difficult to adjust to the many.... ah.... variegated forms of Benign Socialist leader that have sprung into existence across the galaxy."

"It's all right. Am I to assume that we're close to Earth?"

"We're in Earth orbit." Vaulter flowed across to the instrument panels. "I'm tuning in to the orbiting telepathic field boosters now. The population of Earth has increased alarmingly in the last century, but luckily a human brain dissipates only about ten watts so we still have ample power reserves. You will be able to blanket the entire planet with Wilsonian thinking."

A faint smile puckered Mr. Wilson's lips as he sucked noisily on the stem of his pipe.

Vaulter adjusted a series of verniers with a delicate tendril. "I'll give the hook-up a final inspection at close range before you take over. Everything seems to be functioning smoothly with our transmitter network. Good! Now, I'll just make sure that. . . . No! *No!*" Vaulter hit a master switch with a convulsive movement of his puce-coloured body and rippled to the centre of the control room.

Mr. Wilson looked concerned. "What has happened?"

"The egotistical fools," Vaulter said in shocked whisper.

"What's going on?"

"There has been an awkward development, I'm afraid. Earth technology has reached the level of the fairly complex computer, and they've been misusing the techniques to try immortalising selected individuals."

"How does that affect me? I mean, us."

"The computerised identities operate at vastly higher voltages than they did in the biological state and we can't influence them. They will create huge pockets of resistance to your telepathic control."

Mr. Wilson's face darkened. "That's bad."

"There's worse to follow. One of the identities appears to have screened out all local data inputs which normally render any sentient being insensible to telepathic probing. I made direct two-way contact with him for an instant. I'm afraid, Harold, that he may be on to us."

Mr. Wilson's pipe fell from his mouth and bounced on the floor, creating further little heaps of ash. "I knew it was too good to be true," he said bitterly. "I just knew it."

Vaulter remained motionless for a second, and when he spoke his voice was firm. "We aren't giving up so easily.

Benign Socialism deplores the use of violence, but technically speaking these individuals are already dead. I don't think I would be violating the code of the Galactic Congress if I destroyed the computer installations at once, before any alarm can be raised."

"I too deplore violence, naturally," Mr. Wilson grated. "But I do see what you mean."

*A cognac on the computer reality vector:*

Colonel Mason Crowley unsheathed his bolt rifle and climbed down from the huge dragon's back. He had been riding hard for two days and his thigh muscles were aching from the effort retaining his seat while Shalazzar bounded over the broken, ochreous landscapes of Tal. Now his quarry was trapped and the hunt was almost over.

"Do we rest here?" Professer Chan Isaacs, his lieutenant, wiped his face with a rag as he reined in his mount on the rocky ridge where Crowley had stopped.

Crowley pointed at the rag and issued a sharp command. "No textiles!"

"But how do I get rid of this filthy dust?"

"You don't—not till we reach water."

For a moment Isaacs looked as though he might rebel, then he held out the stained scrap of red cloth and let it fall. It fluttered downwards slowly and vanished before touching the ground. The coating of saffron dust reappeared on Isaacs' round face, turning it into an Oriental mask.

"That's better," Crowley said, checking the fuel cell output of his rifle. "Just remember—no wool-bearing fauna, no fibrous plants, therefore no textiles."

Isaacs looked tired. "How about artificial fibres?"

"There is no plastics industry," Crowley reminded him. "Tal is still in an early agrarian phase of its development."

"Then, for Christ's sake, how can you have that fancy rifle?"

Isaacs' angry words ripped into Crowley's consciousness, and the distant ramparts of the Mountains of Morida swam like reflections on the surface of a lake. *You're dead,* a cold grey voice told him. *You're dead, and your soul is trapped in a black box. Queen Elanos does not exist*.... He took a deep shuddering breath and pointed at Isaacs, who had dismounted from his dragon.

"Isaacs," he said harshly. "You had a fall yesterday. Your left arm is dislocated at the elbow."

Isaacs' face twisted in sudden pain as the dark mounds of bruises appeared on his arm. "No! There was no fall. My arm is all right."

"Then heal it."

Black smears of dried blood changed their shape beneath the coating of dust on the swollen arm as the wills of the two men clashed, but after a few seconds Isaacs submitted. "My arm is out of joint," he muttered. "And it hurts like hell."

"I'm sorry about that," Crowley said. "We'll put a bandage on it as soon as we've dealt with Browne."

"Thank you, Colonel."

Crowley walked to the southern side of the ridge and shaded his eyes from the lowering sun. The plateau sloped away gently for less than a kilometre, then there was a sheer drop of a thousand metres to the Cythian Plain. Browne, the rebel, was trapped somewhere in the triangular area of rocks and stunted trees, and his dragon was too exhausted to make a successful break past the hunters.

"I'll go forward alone on foot. Queen Elanos has given me personal responsibility in this matter, and I want it ended before dark." Crowley signalled his dragon to rest and the huge beast settled on its haunches, electric-green and magenta scales clicking as the sack-like belly flattened out on the ground.

"Good luck," Isaacs said drily.

Ignoring him, Crowley set the bolt rifle for maximum charge and moved downwards into the triangle. He had discarded all clothing except for a breech clout of fine leather, and the heat of the rocks seared through his skin at every contact. The hunt had taken more out of him then he liked to admit, but he had the consolation of knowing that Browne must be in worse condition. Browne was tenacious, but he had no experience in this type of country which was remarkably similar to Crowley's native Losane. *Losane?* Repetition of the name caused an obscure flickering pain far back in Crowley's mind. *That can't be right. I was born in Perigore, in the castle of*

*Rembold the Bright, and I was called to Tal from afar by
Queen Elanos to defend her against. . . .*

Something moved in the rocks and scrub a hundred
paces to Crowley's right. He instinctively dropped into a
crouch and levelled the rifle as the figure of an almost
naked man appeared from behind a desiccated tree. It
was Browne—but unarmed, and without his dragon.

"Crowley!" The man's voice was faint. "I want to talk
to you."

Crowley straightened up, still aiming the rifle. "Here I
am, traitor, and I advise you not to try any of your
tricks."

"No tricks—I simply want to speak to you."

"Do you acknowledge the sovereignty of Queen
Elanos?"

"That's what I want to talk about." Browne scrambled
upwards until he was face-to-face with Crowley. Sweat
had traced red rivers in the dust on his face. He was
about fifty years old and had the flabby build of someone
who ate too much and exercised too little, but his eyes
shone with an uncompromising hardness.

"Do you acknowlege our Queen?" Crowley demanded.

"Let's consider Queen Elanos for a moment," Browne
said calmly. "I've been thinking about her name. E-L-A-
N-O-S. Don't you notice something peculiar there?"

"Peculiar?" Crowley's voice shook with anger. "Peculiar?"

"Yes. Don't you see it? Elanos is an anagram of
Losane—the name of the country you carved out of
Rhodesia almost single-handed in what, for lack of a
better term, I call your previous life."

"I'm warning you," Crowley said as the distant Cythian
Plain momentarily reversed its colours, split into horizontal lines and reassembled itself.

"This whole fantasy in which you have embroiled us is
a re-enactment of your political career, Colonely Crowley. *Queen* Elanos is a personification of Losane—the first
fragment of Africa which, thanks to you, opted to return
to Imperial rule. . . ."

"Silence—or you die now."

"You're a died-in-the-wool Colonialist, Crowley. This
Queen Elanos of yours—she looks very like a former
Queen of England, right? But not Elizabeth II, because

she wouldn't suit the role. Elanos resembles Victoria, doesn't she?"

The cloudless sky above the Kingdom of Tal turned grey and a charcoal sketch of a strangely familiar, bespectacled man's face appeared in it for an instant, stretching from jagged horizon to zenith. A voice like the echoes of far-off thunder issued from the insubstantial grainy lips. " .... preliminary reports indicate that an unidentified spaceship has entered Earth orbit. The immense size of the vessel suggests that it is not of human origin. . . ."

"What was that?" Crowley said, looking upwards into the sky.

"I didn't notice anything," Browne replied impatiently. "And consider my name, even my personal appearance. Why do think you cast me as a villain of the piece? George Brown was a prominent member of the British Labour Government in the last century, just at the time of the final dissolution of the old British Empire, and there's no doubt that this coincidence of nomenclature is a major. . . ."

*Contact!*

A thousand years of alien existence, a mind dedicated to the incredible proposition that association should be substituted for competition, a being which controlled vast forces, including the power to make all men think alike, a being which immediately identified Crowley as its enemy, and which was coming to. . . .

*Retreat!*

"What's happening?" Crowley felt his mouth go dry.

" .... principle of self-establishing circuitry has disproved the *a priori* or 'wired-in knowledge' theory concerning the human brain in favour of the *tabula rasa* or clean slate new brain," Browne droned on pedantically. "In our present state the hitherto indefinable quality known as 'will' is translated into physical reality as a higher than normal proportion of molecular amplifiers, which is the only reason you are able to impress your dreamscapes on others. But this state of affairs depends. . . ."

"Stop mouthing for a moment—didn't you feel anything?"

"Of course not, because I too have gained control of my amplifiers and I'm withdrawing from this particular fantasy."

"Fantasy?" Crowley looked down at the rifle, which promptly turned into a broom and then vanished. "I'm talking about the. . . . real world. I. . . . I. . . . Something is happening out there, and I'm the only one who understands. I've got to speak to Philp or Urquhart immediately."

Browne looked around him, almost regretfully, at the dissolving mountains and plains of the Kingdom of Tal. "Be careful," he said with a strange gentleness, "you could be walking into a . . . ."

Crowley lost contact with him as the complex electrical network which simulated his personality began establishing new circuits within the compliant matrix, re-creating the channels of communication with the outside world.


*A Hennessy on the human reality vector:*

Urquhart fixed his gaze for a moment on the wooded hill and made up his mind to waste no more time—he would go there very soon, possibly tomorrow, or maybe the next day. He picked up a plastic reference copy of a computer programme from his desk and his eyes scanned the typed words.

"I still think the risk was too great, Bryan," he said. "A being from interstellar space which was planning to destroy the Tank then set up a puppet dictator to rule the world by thought control! And you actually fed this mush into the Tank on the general address system?"

"I did." Philp smiled his dazzling smile.

"You told our clients they were in imminent danger of losing their lives?"

"That's what I told them," Philp said comfortably. "They didn't believe me, of course. Bill Uvarov was on the current affairs query panel at the time and according to him it lit up like a Christmas tree in less than a second. I apologised to everyone and told them part of a spoof television show had been fed in by mistake. They took it all right—but I'll be getting sarcastic comments for the next year."

Urquhart set the programme down. "And the only one who was taken in was Colonel Crowley."

"Well, in bionics and biology we use the term 'cocktail

party effect' to describe the brain's ability to pick out a single voice from the hubbub of noise made by a large group all speaking at once—and Crowley hadn't lost that facility. He was screening out all other communications, but when I tailored a fantasy especially for him he heard me immediately.

"All I had to do was concoct a dream which was even more attractive and stimulating for him than the one in which he was living. With his background and mental make-up he couldn't resist the idea of saving the world from interstellar socialism."

"And you'll be able to hold him on station until after Losane's general election?"

"Yes—now that we know what to expect. Dorman's team has set up an inhibitory field which will stabilise the Colonel's molecular amplifiers at a mean output and impair his ability to drift. He'll get away eventually, but we're fine for a year or so. . . ."

Urquhart sighed contentedly and returned his gaze to the hill. "So we've nothing to worry about."

"I'm not too sure about that—I think we're going to have trouble with Browne. He now says Crowley's fantasy world wasn't such a bad place and battling his way out of it was the first taste of genuine involvement he's had since he was Tanked. I heard him rambling on about deliberately staged contests of will to relieve the boredom. Computerised Olympics or something."

"Nothing too alarming in that. In fact, he might have something."

"There's just one other thing," Philp said, his eyes hidden behind blazing flakes of glass. "There are bound to be other elections in Losane, and—if I know Mason Crowley—when he eventually takes off into never-never land he'll be saving the Earth from disaster every week, now that we've given him the idea."

"So?"

"So how do we lure him back next time?"

The most spectacular achievement of science in this century has been the drastic limitation of death through childbirth, epidemics and mental or physical handicaps. The spiralling population graphs owe an incalculable debt to medical science and D.D.T. To correct the balance we lecture on the importance of birth control. Limit the number of babies born and give food production a chance to catch up.

This much is already history. *JAMES BLISH* imagines a state of affairs where birth control is enforceable by law, in the developed nations as well as the underdeveloped. Furthermore, he argues, the logical extension of birth control is. . . . death control. And, if we admit that death control is necessary, how are we going to enforce it?

## STATISTICIAN'S DAY

### By James Blish

WIBERG HAD been a foreign correspondent for the *New York Times* for fourteen years, ten of them devoted also to his peculiar speciality, and had at one time or another spent a total of eighteen weeks in England. (He was, as one would expect, precise about such matters.) As a result, he was considerably surprised by the home of Edmund Gerrard Darling.

Population Control had been instituted just ten years ago, after the fearful world famine of 1980, and since that time England had not changed much. Driving along the M.4 motorway from London, he saw again the high-rise "developments" which had obliterated the Green Belt which once had surrounded the city, just as they had taken over Westchester County in New York, Arlington in Virginia, Evanston in Illinois, Berkeley in California. Few new ones had been built since—after all, with population static, there was no need—though the hurried construction of many of them was going to force replacement before long.

Similarly, the town of Maidenhead, stabilized at 20,000 souls, looked just as it had when he had passed through it last time on the way to Oxford. (Then, he had been paying this kind of call on the coastal erosion expert Charles Charleston Shackleton, who had also been something of a writer.) This time, however, he had to turn off the motorway at Maidenhead Thicket, and suddenly found himself in a kind of countryside he had not dreamed existed any more, at least certainly not anywhere between London and Reading.

A road exactly one car wide, completely overhung with trees, led him nearly five miles to a roundabout the mall of which a child could have spat across, were it not for the moss-grown, ten-foot World War I memorial pillar in the middle. On the other side of this was Shurlock Row, his destination—a village which seemed to consist of nothing but a church, a pub and five or six shops. There must have been a duckpond somewhere nearby, too, for he could hear a faint quacking.

"The Phygtle," the novelist's home, was also on the High Street—there seemed to be no other. It was a large, two-storey thatched cottage, with white walls and oak timbers which had been painted black. Over the thatching, which was necessarily very recent, there was chicken-wire to discourage birds; the rest of the house looked as though it had been started about the Sixteenth Century, and probably had.

Wiberg parked the Morris and felt in his inside jacket pocket for the canned Associated Press obituary, which rewarded him with a faint but reassuring crackle. He did not need to take it out; he knew it by heart by now. It had been the arrival by mail, a week ago, of that galley proof which had started him on this journey. The obit was not due to be published for nearly a year, but Darling had been reported ill, and that always made a good pretext—indeed, the usual one.

He got out of the car and walked to the stable-type front door, which at his knock was opened by a plump, ruddy, well-scrubbed young girl in a housemaid's uniform. He gave his name.

"Ah, yes, Mr Wiberg, Sir Edmund's expectin' ye," she

said in a strong Irish accent. "Perhaps ye'd care to be waitin' in the garden?"

"I'd like that," he said. The girl was evidently brand new, for the novelist was not a knight but an O. M., an honor a good deal higher; but Darling reputedly cared little for such gauds and probably did not even bother to correct her.

He was led through a large dining room with a low, beamed ceiling and a fireplace built of hand-made briquettes, and out a glazed door at the back. The gardens covered about half an acre, and consisted chiefly of flowering shrubs and rose bushes through which gravel paths wound; there were also several old apple and pear trees, and even a fig tree. Part of the area had been hedged off as a vegetable garden, which included a small potting shed, and the whole was screened from the road and from the neighbors by a willow-withe fence and close-set evergreens.

What interested Wiberg most, however, was a brick guest house or staff annex at the back of the gardens. This, he knew from the obit, had its own bathroom (or wardrobe, as middle-class Britishers still delicately called it); and it was in this building that Darling had done his writing in the days when his family had still been living at home. It had originally had a peaked, tiled roof, but much of this had been cut away to accommodate the famous little astronomical observatory.

The seeing around here, Wiberg reflected, must have been terrible even before Darling had been born, but again, that wouldn't have mattered much to Darling. He was an amateur of the sciences ("the world's finest spectator sport," he had called them), and had built the observatory not for research, but only because he liked to look at the heavens.

Wiberg peered in a window, but there was no remaining trace of the novelist's occupancy; evidently only the maid used the outbuilding now. Wiberg sighed. He was not a particularly sensitive man—he could not afford to be—but there were times when his occupation depressed even him.

He resumed prowling around the garden, sniffing at roses and at stands of wallflowers. He had never encountered the latter in the States and they had a spicy, exotic odor, rather like that of flowering tobacco, or what he imagined as the smell of the herbs used by ancient Egyptian embalmers.

Then the maid called him. He was led back through the dining room, and then around the L of an immense, book-lined lounge with a polished-stone fireplace to the main staircase. At the head of these was the master bedroom. As he approached the door, the maid called out, "Mind your head, sir," but she was a moment too late; he cracked the crown of it on the lintel.

A chuckle came from inside. "You're far from the first," a male voice said. "One had to be bloody careful carrying a kid through that door."

The impact had been minor and Wiberg forget it instantly. Edmund Gerrard Darling, in a plaid robe, was propped up amid pillows in an immense bed—a feather bed, judging by the way even his slight frame sank into it. He still had quite a lot of his hair, although it began farther back from his forehead than it had even in his most recent jacket photograph, and he wore the same rimless glasses with the gold bows. His face, though still patrician, had become a little heavier in its contours despite his illness, giving it a rather avuncular expression hard to reconcile with that of a man who, as a critic, had for nearly sixty years mercilessly flayed his colleagues for their ignorance of elementary English, let alone any other literature.

"I'm honored and pleased to see you, sir," Wiberg said, producing his notebook.

"I wish I could say as much," Darling said, waving him to a wing chair. "However, I've expected you for a long time. There's really only one question remaining in my mind, and I'd appreciate your answering it straight off—always providing, of course, that you're allowed to."

"Anything at all, sir. After all, I came to ask questions, too. What is it?"

"Are you," the novelist said, "only the advance man for the executioner, or are you the executioner himself?"

Wiberg managed an uncertain laugh. "I'm afraid I don't understand the question, sir."

In point of fact, he understood it perfectly. What he did not understand was how Darling had come by enough information to have been able to frame it. For ten whole years, the chief secret of PopCon had been extremely well kept.

"If you won't answer my question, I need hardly feel obligated to answer yours," Darling said. "You won't deny, I trust, that you've got my obituary in your pocket?"

This was so common a suspicion in Wiberg's experience that he had no trouble responding to it with every appearance of complete candor.

"Of course I do," he said. "As I'm sure you know, both large newspapers like the *Times* and the big press associations keep obituaries of eminent or newsworthy living people standing in their files, in case of accident. Every so often they have to be updated as a matter of course; and every reporter who's sent out on an interview briefs himself first from those files, also as a matter of course."

"I began as a newspaperman," Darling said. "Hence I also know that it is not the custom of large journals to send one of their chief foreign correspondents on such cubs' assignments."

"Not everyone to be interviewed is a Nobel Prize winner," Wiberg said. "And when such a figure is eighty years of age, and is reliably reported to be ill, getting from him what may be a final interview is not assigned to a cub. If you choose to regard this simply as updating an obituary, sir, there's nothing I can do to prevent you. No doubt there is something a little ghoulish about it, but as I know you're also aware, a lot of newspaper work is amenable to the same description."

"I know, I know," Darling said testily. "And under the circumstances, without your for a minute wishing to exalt yourself in any way, the fact that you were given the assignment might also be taken as a gesture of respect. Eh?"

"Well," Wiberg said, "yes, sir, I might put it that way." In fact, he had been just about to put it exactly that way.

"Bosh."

Wiberg shrugged. "As I say, sir, I can't prevent you from seeing it in any light you choose. But I do regret it."

"I didn't say I saw it in a different light. What I said was, 'Bosh.' What you have told me is largely true, but also so irrelevant as to be actively misleading. I had hoped you would tell me the facts, to which I think I am entitled. Instead, you have answered my question with what obviously is a standard line of chatter for difficult customers."

Wiberg leaned back in the chair, his apprehension

growing. "Then perhaps you'll tell me what you see as the relevant facts, sir?"

"You don't deserve it, but there would be no sense in my keeping from you what you already know—which was precisely what I wanted you to see in my case," Darling said. "Very well, let's stay with the newspapers a while."

He fingered in the breast pocket of his jacket and produced a cigarette, and then pressed a torpedo switch on his nightstand. The maid came in at once.

"Matches," he said.

"Sir, the doctor—"

"Bother the doctor, I now know when I'm going to die almost to the day. Never mind, don't look so distressed, just bring me some matches, and light the fire with them on your way past."

The day was still warm, but for some reason Wilberg too was glad to see the little grate begin to catch. Darling drew on the cigarette and then regarded it appreciatively.

"Damn nonsense anyhow, those statistics," he said. "Which in fact has a direct bearing on the subject. When you get to be in your sixties, Mr Wiberg, you begin to become rather a fan of the obituary notices. Your boyhood heroes begin to die, your friends begin to die, and insensibly you become interested in the deaths of people you neither knew nor cared about, and then of people you never even heard of.

"It's perhaps rather a mean pastime, with no little amount of self-congratulation in it: 'Well, *he's* gone, but *I'm* still here.' Of course, if you're of at all an introspective turn of mind, it can also begin to make you increasingly aware of your own growing isolation in the world. And if your inner resources are few, it can also increase your fear of your own death.

"Luckily, one of my interests for many years has been in the sciences, with particular emphasis upon mathematics. And after a lot of reading of death notices in the *New York Times*, the *Times* of London, and some other large newspapers I keep up with, at first casually, then assiduously, I began to become conscious of a run of coincidences. Do you follow me so far?"

"I think so," Wiberg said guardedly. "What kind of coincidences?"

"I could produce you specific examples, but I think a general description will suffice. To find such coincidences, one must read the minor death notices, as well as the deaths that produce the headlines and the formal obituaries. Then, you will find, say, a day in which what seems to be an abnormally large number of doctors have died. On another day, an abnormally large number of lawyers. And so on.

"I first noticed this on a day when almost all the chief executives of a large American engineering firm had been killed in the same airplane disaster. This struck me as peculiar, because by that time it had become standard practice among American firms *never* to allow more than two executives to travel on the same flight. On a hunch, I ran down the minor notices, and I found that it had been a very bad day for engineers in general. And also I found something quite unexpected: that almost all of them had died in some sort of travel accident. The plane crash had been the unlucky coincidence that drew my attention to what seemed to be a real pattern.

"I began to keep tallies. I discovered a good many other correlations. For one, in deaths-by-travel, whole families often die—and in such instances, it most often turns out that the wife may be related to the husband by profession, as well as simply by matrimony."

"Interesting ... and a little eerie," Wiberg agreed. "But as you say, obviously only coincidence. In so small a sample—"

"It's not a small sample after you watch it for twenty years," Darling said. "And I no longer believe that any part of it is coincidence except the initial plane crash that started me looking for it. It isn't, in fact, a question of belief at all any more. I kept exact records, and periodically I phone my figures in to the computation center at London University, without, of course, telling the programmers what the figures stand for. I had the last such computation run when I got your cable asking to visit me, with a chi-square test. I got a significance of point zero zero zero one at the five per cent level of confidence. That's better than anything the anti-cigarette forces have ever been able to come up with, and we've had regiments of medical asses, and even whole governments, behaving as if those figures stood for a real phenomenon, ever since about 1950.

"And while I'm at it, I run counter-checks. It occurred to me that the *age* at death might be the really significant factor. The chi-square test shows that it is not; there is no correlation with age at all. But it is *perfectly* clear that these deaths are being selected for upon the basis of business, trade or profession."

"Hmm. Suppose—for the sake of argument—that this is really happening. Can you suggest how?"

*"How* is not the problem," Darling said. "It cannot be a natural phenomenon, because natural forces like biological selection do not show that high a degree of specificity, or act over so brief a secular period. The real question, therefore, is: Why? And there can be only one answer to that."

"Which is?"

"Policy."

"Excuse me, sir," Wiberg said, "but with all due respect, the idea seems to me to be, well, faintly paranoid."

"It is massively paranoid, but it is happening; I notice that you don't dispute that. And it is the policy-makers who are paranoid, not I."

"What would be the use of such a policy—or what would someone imagine its use to be?"

The novelist looked steadily into Wiberg's eyes through the rimless glasses.

"Universal Population Control," he said, "has been officially in force for ten years, and unofficially, it seems, for twenty. And it works; the population is now static. Most people believe, and are told, that it consists entirely of enforced birth control. They do not stop to think that to maintain a genuinely static population, you also need an absolutely predictable economy. Second, they do not stop to think—and are *not* told, indeed the facts they would need to deduce it are now suppressed even on the grammar-school level—that at our present state of knowledge we can control only *numbers* of births; we cannot control *who* gets born. Oh, of course we can now control the sex of the child, that's easy; but we cannot control whether he will turn out to be an architect, a navvy or just a plain ordinary clot.

"Yet in a completely controlled economy, one must take care to have only a fixed number of architects, navvies and clots extant at any given era. Since you can't do that by birth control, *you must do it by death control.* Hence, when you find yourself with an uneconomic surplus of, say, novelists, you skim off the surplus. Of course, you try to confine the skimming to the oldest, but since the period in which such a surplus is going to appear is inherently unpredicable, how old the oldest are when the skimming takes place varies too widely to attain statistical significance. It is probably further masked by such tactical considerations as making all the deaths look accidental and unconnected, which must often mean killing off a few younger members of a given class and leaving a few oldsters behind for Nature to deal with.

"Also, of course, it simplifies record-keeping for the historian. If one knows as a matter of policy that a given novelist is scheduled to die on or about a given date, one need never lack for a final interview and an up-dated obituary. And the same excuse, or a similar one—such as a routine visit by the victim's physician—can become the agency of his actual death.

"Which brings me back, Mr Wiberg, to my original question. Which are you—the Angel of Death himself, or just his harbinger?"

In the ensuing silence, the fire popped loudly in the grate. At last Wiberg said:

"I cannot tell you whether or not your hypothesis is valid. As you suggested yourself at the beginning of this interview, if it were true, I wouldn't be allowed to tell you so, as a simple logical consequence. All I can say is that I enormously admire your ingenuity—and I'm not entirely surprised by it.

"But again for the sake of the argument, let's push the logic one step further. Assume that the situation is just as you postulate it to be. Assume further that you have been selected to be . . . 'skimmed off' . . . say, about a year from now. And assume, finally, that I was originally only to be your final interviewer, not your executioner. Wouldn't your revealing to me your conclusions *force* me to become your executioner instead?"

"It might," Darling said, with astonishing cheerfulness. "It is a consequence I had not overlooked. My life has been very rich, and my present illness is so annoying that being shut of a year of it—since I know very well that it's incurable—would not strike me as a terrible deprivation. On the other hand, the risk does not seem to me to be very real anyhow. Killing me a year early would produce a slight mathematical discontinuity in the system. It would not be a significant discontinuity, but bureaucrats hate any deviation from established procedure, whether it matters or not. Either way, *I* wouldn't care. But I wonder about you, Mr Wiberg. I really do."

"About me?" Wiberg said uneasily. "Why about me?"

There was no doubt, now, but that the old malicious glitter was back in Darling's eyes, in full vitality.

"You are a statistician. I can tell by the way in which you received, and followed, my statistical terms. I, on the other hand, am an amateur mathematician, not limited in my interests to stochastic procedures; and one of my interests is projective geometry. I have been watching population statistics, and death figures, and so on, but I have also been constructing curves. I therefore know that next April fourteenth will be the day of my death. Let us call it, for the sake of commemoration, Novelists' Day.

"Well then, Mr Wiberg. I also know that this coming November third is what we might call Statisticians' Day. And I do not think you are very safely under age, Mr Wiberg.

"Tell me: *How will you face it?* Eh? How will *you* face it? Speak up, Mr Wiberg, speak up. Your time, too, is running out."

*JOHN BRUNNER's* THE INVISIBLE IDIOT also deals with computers. Or rather one particular computer which succumbs to a very human ailment, and threatens to unleash a major war between Earth and her colonial outposts.

## THE INVISIBLE IDIOT

### By John Brunner

"GOOD MORNING, doctor!" called the pretty young receptionist on duty at the desk in the main hall of the Paré Polyclinic.

"Good morning, young lady!" boomed Dr Casper Minsky, striding past in the direction of his consulting-room, and gave her a grin so huge it opened a sort of cavern in the depths of his full grey beard. He meant it; the morning was beautiful, with a clear blue sky and bright sun, and the rain arranged by the Weather Bureau for an hour around dawn had given the air a delightful freshness.

But two minutes after entering his office, he was no longer quite so cheerful.

A first glance around the room had shown that all was in order. The calendar-clock on the wall indicated the proper date and time—0853, 12th June 2012; the cleaning machines had been around on schedule, and there was hardly a speck of dust to mar the sleek shining cases of the room's complex equipment: the diagnostic desk at which he sat to receive his patients, which reported to him everything about their state of health by way of detectors built into the chair facing it; the library computer which gave him access to all the medical literature, no matter how recent, on file at any of a hundred libraries; the phones and viewscreens and the telefax.

And, as instructed, the machines had left alone his personal belongings, souvenirs of a career that had lasted now for more than fifty years, collected in twenty differ-

141

ent countries: ornaments, curios, primitive surgical instruments made of bone and flint ...

Strictly, he ought not to have kept his collection here in the office, according to Polyclinic regulations. But he was elderly—seventy-five—and entitled, he felt, to a few minor privileges.

Contentedly, because the sun was out and the monorail was on schedule today so that he had a few minutes in hand before he was due to see his first patient, he dialled the service outlet on his desk for a cup of coffee and punched the telefax for the morning's news. A sheet of paper unreeled from its delivery slot to bring him news, less than half an hour old, from all over Earth, from Mars, the Venus Orbital Station, the asteroid colonies, even the moons of distant Jupiter. Sipping his coffee, he ran his eye down the page.

And that was when he stopped being pleased with the world.

The main headline reported that a crisis was brewing that might even lead as far as war. At least that was what the reporter who had compiled the story suggested. The Manager of Mars—elected chief of the two million colonists settled on the Red Planet—had called in the Ambassador of United Earth at six o'clock this morning, London time, and told him to catch the next ship for home, because Mars was breaking off diplomatic relations. Unless an apology was forthcoming, and fifty million Interplan Credits of reparations into the bargain, the Manager said, he'd do the same to every single Earthman on Mars.

But what on earth—? Dr Minsky caught and corrected himself. Even though it was thirty years since the Mars colony had been set up, he hadn't completely cured himself of old-fashioned turns of phrase. What *in space* (as people said nowadays) could be the reason for such a row?

He read the 'fax sheet through twice, thinking he must have missed something, and found no clue. But this was ridiculous! He sighed heavily. When the world, and come to that the whole universe, was such a beautiful place with so many interesting and exciting things to do in it, why should people lose their tempers and make stupid threats? After three-quarters of a century, he was still finding new kinds of fun—and that was in spite of the quirks of fate which had landed him as a child in foreign country, and the many ups and downs he'd suffered since.

Glancing at the clock, he discovered that there still remained a couple of minutes before nine o'clock and his first patient of the day. Perhaps the receptionist might be able to tell him what had started this interplanetary crisis. He knew perfectly well he only needed to ask for last night's news, or yesterday afternoon's, to be fed from the 'fax machine, but simply asking someone might be quicker than reading through two or three news-sheets.

Just as he was reaching for the switch of the phone, however, the 'fax machine clicked and rang its little bell to announce the arrival of incoming mail. Dr Minsky sighed again and reached for the tongue of paper protruding from the slot. Granted that 'faxing one's letters was much faster than actually transporting them from place to place in the form of an envelope and a sheet of paper, he tended to miss the marks of individuality that old-style correspondence had included. Now everything was standardised, everything was—

He checked. This wasn't in the least an ordinary piece of mail! To begin with, it was off an interplanetary beam; it had been scanned and shot across space for millions and millions of miles. The number-code at the top of the sheet informed him that it originated on Mars.

Mars?

"But I don't think I know anyone on Mars," he said to the air.

And the text of the message itself was equally improbable. He read it twice, the second time aloud, in order to convince himself the words were real.

"The big ungainly horse browses in a field of pale blue poppies."

Bewildered, he stared at it. After a few moments, however, a sound attracted his attention from the adjacent waiting-room; he'd left the door a trifle ajar as usual, to show that if there was a really urgent case he wouldn't insist on delaying until sharp on nine o'clock.

The sound was that of a child crying, a child about five or six years old.

At once he pushed the mysterious message to the side of his desk, jumped up and marched to the door. Peering through, he discovered Mrs Bowen waiting to see him— who had been a patient of his for many years—and the little boy, Timmy, whom she and her husband had adopted when they learned that it was better for them not to have children of their own.

"Ah, doctor!" Mrs Bowen rose to her feet. "I'm so sorry to trouble you, but poor Timmy's been waking up in the night with bad dreams, and—"

"Don't apologise, Mrs Bowen!" Dr Minsky smiled, raising his big-knuckled hand. "Just bring him in here, and we'll see what we can do."

Not very much, unfortunately, Dr Minsky reflected sadly to himself as the door closed behind Mrs Bowen and her little boy. Timmy had been found wandering on the street when he was about two and a half years old, barely able to utter his own name, and it had proved completely impossible to trace his parents. Whatever was causing his bad dreams, it wasn't due to the way Mr and Mrs Bowen were treating him now—he was sure of that, because they were kind, considerate people. But sometimes a dream could go back to something very deeply buried indeed, so deep in the memory one could hardly imagine it being remembered at all. Only when the brain was resting after a day of new experiences, sorting out—

The phone sounded, and he glanced automatically at the screen. Startled, he sat bolt upright in his swivelling chair. He'd completely forgotten about the curious message, alleged to originate on Mars, which had arrived this morning. But now—according to the words that glowed luminous on the viewscreen of the phone—he was being called up, live, from the Orbital Communications Exchange through which all the signals from and to the inhabited planets of the Solar System were relayed.

Wondering if he was about to find out why he'd received that weird message, he checked to make certain there were no urgent cases in the waiting-room, and put down the switch of the phone.

A very harassed young man appeared in the screen, with dark rings under his eyes as though he hadn't slept enough lately. He said, "Ah—Dr Minsky?"

"Yes."

"My name is Honorio Blaz, and of course I'm calling from OCE. Forgive me for troubling you, but have you had any spatial relay messages recently?"

"Yes! Right here on my desk—one that arrived only a few minutes ago. Why?"

"Does it make sense?"

Dr Minsky blinked. "Well . . . To be frank, Mr Blaz, no! But why do you ask?"

"Take my word for it, please, doctor, that this is very important and much too urgent for me to explain in detail. Just tell me what it says. Oh yes—and where it came from."

Dr Minsky complied, his bushy grey eyebrows drawing together into a frown.

"I see," Blaz muttered. "Do you know anyone on Mars who might have sent you such a message?"

"No, I can't think of anyone I know on Mars. Except one or two of my former patients who've emigrated there. But I don't expect them to keep in touch with me. After all, interplanetary messages are expensive, aren't they? About ten credits a word, I think—isn't that right?"

"Twelve. We had to put it up the other day."

"So why should anyone send a nonsense message to a stranger? Or even a former doctor?"

"I don't know," Blaz shrugged. "But at least it is nonsense. Thank you, doctor. Sorry to have—"

"No, you don't, young fellow!" Minsky barked, and shot an arm towards the screen as though he could physically prevent Blaz's image from disappearing. "I want to know something, too! Why did you call up and ask if I'd received an interplanetary message? And what kind of message is this, anyway? I mean, just because it looks like nonsense, it needn't be. It could be—oh, a line from a poem, perhaps. Or something in cypher."

"Not cypher," Blaz contradicted. "Code. Sorry." He wiped his forehead tiredly. "Technical distinction, mainly of interest to communications experts—if you can call me an expert after spending the past three of four mortal days trying to sort out the tangle we've got ourselves into . . ."

With the acuity due to his half-century of medical practice, Dr Minsky recognised the symptoms of a man who badly needed to talk to someone. There were still no urgent patients waiting outside. He said with sympathy, "You're in trouble, are you?"

"Trouble! Doctor, you don't know the half of it! Right now it looks as though we're likely to drift into an interplanetary war because of it!"

"What? You mean this crisis in the news today is that serious?"

"It wasn't when it started—it was just a regular fit of bad temper on the part of the Manager of Mars, and who can blame him for getting annoyed sometimes when the situation builds up? You know they had these problems with the new dome at Sun Lake City, and then the alga-crops failed owing to the blight, and it was a terrible winter last year, and ... Oh, you heard about it." Blaz made a vague gesture. "But of course they're so fiercely independent up there, as you might expect from them having chosen to emigrate to a world not really fit for humans, and for the past week or eight days the beams have been absolutely humming with traffic, trying to soothe tempers, conciliate, calm down, smoothe over— and suddenly, *wham*. The Ambassador from Earth was apparently physically thrown out of the Manager's office this morning, and that's not the kind of treatment a diplomat can swallow without objection. Is it?"

"But what's this got to do with"—Dr Minsky glanced at the message before him—"an ungainly horse in a field of poppies?"

"Oh, nothing. Except that the whole trouble seems to have started with a peculiar message that we can't trace the source of. Something which—at least according to the Martian government—means that the aid we've offered to help tide them over their recent disasters is actually part of a plot to re-establish direct rule from Earth and steal their hard-won independence."

Dr Minsky said keenly, "And it's not the only message you can't trace back to its source, hm?"

"Correct. There are scores of them, and in the end there may prove to be hundreds. Luckily all of the others we've managed to track down so far have turned out to be like yours—snatches of double-talk, or scraps of poetry, or out-and-out rubbish. But of course it's incredible that they should have occurred at all! I mean, here we are at OCE, handling the communications traffic for the entire inhabited Solar System including quite a lot of Earthside traffic via satellite repeater because it's more convenient to squirt your signal straight into space for relaying around the far side of the planet, equipped with the very latest and most advanced computing equipment to keep track of all these millions of signals—gear so elaborate you can almost say it thinks for itself, no joking—and here *I* am, one man hunting through the piled-up records of all the signals we've had through here in the past ten days, looking for items that don't make sense to the people who received them." Blaz gave a sour mock-grin, as though he would have been amused at the paradox if the trouble hadn't been so worrying.

"Can you give me some other examples of these messages?" suggested Dr Minsky.

"Sure. There's no shortage of them," Blaz answered bitterly, and leafed through a stack of papers just out of sight of the camera at his end. "Here's one that went to a man in New Jersey: 'Threatenings and slaughter, fire and water, down will come the bricks and mortar.' And here's one that was recieved in Chile—in Spanish, naturally, but I've had it translated: 'The bare desert of space is a long way from home, but that will change very soon.' Did you ever hear such nonsense?"

"Well . . ." Dr Minsky coughed. "Yes, frequently. After all, I've been a doctor for fifty years and I've had to treat patients suffering from delirium and other mental disorders. But I see what you mean—messages of this kind ought not to be passing through the Solar System's most advanced communications satellite. One point does occur to me, though."

Blaz brightened. "If you have an idea, doctor, tell me! We've cracked our skulls for days on end and completely run out of new approaches."

"Well, you mentioned that the last message was translated. Is it possible that—?"

"Sorry, we thought of that," Blaz cut in. "Right away. The translation banks in our master computer are functioning perfectly. I don't know if you have to use mechanical translation at all?"

"Oh yes, I often need to consult medical papers published in Russian, Chinese, Hindi, Swahili—lots of languages."

"Then you know that we've progressed a long way from the early days, when they used to tell that story about the computer asked to translate the proverb 'out of sight, out of mind' into Chinese and back. You remember that?"

"Yes, of course I do. I'm an old man. Didn't it come back from the machine as 'invisible idiot'?"

"That's right. And it looks as though what we've got is an invisible idiot right here at OCE, feeding in messages with false origination-marks and randomly-chosen destinations. One of which is in a fair way to starting a war, as I said." Blaz tugged at his dark hair as though he wanted to pull out a handful. "Well, you *must* excuse me now, doctor. I have eight or ten more of these to check out."

"Of course. I'm sorry to have delayed you," Dr Minsky said, and cut the circuit.

When the screen had gone dark, he sat for several minutes in gloomy contemplation of what he had just been told. How could people be so foolish as to take words on a piece of paper so much to heart that they would risk starting a war? Of course, the notion of a planet inhabited by two million people fighting one with three billion people was absurd, but—well, it would be possible for each side to do some very horrible things to the other.

It struck him that he'd missed his chance to find out what the message had actually said to offend the Manager of Mars. He'd been lucky to catch Blaz at the psychological moment when he needed to talk about his predicament.

And, speaking of predicaments . . . He realised with a shock that there were five patients waiting to see him, and called the first one in.


But it was a light morning, as usual in summer; winter was still the busy time of year for doctors, with all the irritating minor complaints which so far medicine had only found palliatives for, like the common cold, influenza and rheumatism. He was finished by ten-thirty, and before starting on his late-morning round of the hospital beds to which his patients with serious illnesses had been transferred he had a little time to browse around in the literature relating to dreaming, in the hope that he might be able to offer little Timmy Bowen something more helpful than tranquillising pills. It was another of his old-fashioned beliefs that children being brought up by kindly parents ought not to need that sort of medication.

He was just about to punch for the appropriate code on the library computer when something seemed to click in the back of his mind. He thought for a little while, snapped his fingers, and punched an altogether different reference on the board.

After half an hour of diligent study of source-material from four different languages—computer-translated, of course—he dialled a cup of coffee and drank it very thoughtfully.

"Well, why not?" he said to the air as he set down his cup. "Isn't anything worth trying in a desperate situation like this?"

He reached for the switch of the phone and called the receptionist. She appeared in the screen glancing up from her own copy of the latest news from the telefax beside her desk.

"Oh, doctor!" she exclaimed. "Have you seen the latest? Things are getting worse and worse—they're talking about recalling the ships in orbit for Mars now!"

"Terrible!" Dr Minsky exclaimed. "So you'll have to be quick! Please call the hospital and ask Dr Hopkins to look after my rounds for me until further notice, and see if you can contact Dr Banerji to take my afternoon consultations."

The receptionist looked blank, but Dr Minsky had already punched the phone for another connection. This one was a lot more difficult to obtain, and he had to argue his way through endless layers of underlings before finally he saw Blaz's image return to his screen. His expression was even more harassed than before.

"Oh, Dr Minsky," he sighed. "Look, literally, I have *no* time to spare! Things are going from bad to worse!"

"I know!" Dr Minsky barked. "I've heard the news. Just tell me something, quickly. Have you been overloading your transmission capacity recently?"

"Overloading? No, of course not—I mean we haven't had any breakdowns. If it were just a matter of something failing under the stress, some key part, we'd have fixed it immediately."

"But you've had a great deal of signals traffic? Perhaps an unprecedented amount?"

"Well, naturally. The satellite has been buzzing like a bee-hive at swarming season!"

"Have you ever approached maximum load capacity?"

Blaz looked puzzled. "Well, we've come pretty close, naturally. We've had to postpone non-urgent calls because the circuits were tied up, if that's what you mean."

"I thought so," said Dr Minsky with satisfaction. "In that case, you'd better send someone to collect me. I can almost certainly solve your problem. But in the meantime, re-grade your current messages, will you? Reduce the load on your equipment by assigning lower priorities to everything that won't suffer from an hour or two's delay."

Blaz was by now frankly at a loss. He said feebly, "Send someone to collect you . . . ?"

"Why not? I may be seventy-five, but I've taken good care of myself. I'm in excellent health, and I've always hoped for the chance to go up into space before I die."

The younger man stared at him through the screen. At last he sighed and shrugged. "All right. I suppose one more problem to argue my way out of won't make much difference."

"You're still getting these mysterious messages arriving at random destinations?" Dr Minsky suggested.

"Damn it, yes we are! Thirteen more have been traced since I spoke to you earlier this morning!"

"Do as I say and they'll have stopped before I get to the satellite," Dr Minsky promised. To himself he added, without moving his lips more than would be shielded by his beard, "At least I *think* they will . . ."

He had been a trifle apprehensive about the trip up to orbit from the Goodwin Sands spaceport, but the ride in fact was no rougher than that of the ancient petrol-engined air-liners he'd often travelled in as a young man. And it certainly was quite an experience to look down on the white-blue-green globe of Old Mother Earth through the viewport of a rocket-ship instead of merely watching it on TV. His digestion was excellent and he'd had a good night's rest last night, so there was nothing to mar his enjoyment of the journey except his suspicion that in spite of having sent someone to collect him, as requested, the authorities at the communications satellite might have neglected the rest of his instructions. Certainly the young space-force officer who had escorted him from Earth seemed not to know why he was being ordered to this kind of duty when there was a major interplanetary crisis brewing.

Puffing a little from the unaccustomed and curiously difficult task of manoeuvering himself in free fall, he followed the officer from the docking-hub of the satellite towards the rim section, where rotation gave the illusion of normal weight. His fellow-passengers—senior space-force brass and politicians, judging by what conversation he'd overheard—had been much too preoccupied with the crisis to talk to him during the flight, and now they were in such a hurry to get where they were going they rudely pushed past him in the skeletal access corridors of the satellite and had all vanished by the time he found his way to the chamber at which the last corridor terminated.

He was standing uncertainly in the harsh artificial glare of the fluorescent lighting, wondering what had become of the young officer accompanying him, when a door slid back and Blaz appeared, looking as though the doom of all the ages had fallen on him.

"Dr Minsky," he said, offering his hand to be shaken without enthusiasm. "Please come with me. I've been told to take you straight to Mr Marivaux, the satellite controller, to explain the reason for inviting you up here. And it's going to have to be a very good explanation. I don't know what can have possessed me! You realise I've landed myself with a bill for thirty-thousand credits, the cost of flying you out to orbit?"

"You mean these superiors of yours didn't take you seriously?" grunted Dr Minsky.

"Take me seriously! That's a laugh!"

"But did they at least lighten the load on your computers?"

"You mean by re-grading message priorities? No, of course not. Traffic today has been the heaviest in the satellite's history. We've got a crisis on our hands!"

"You're going to have a far worse one if you carry on like this!" Dr Minsky snapped. "And the unaccountable messages are still turning up?"

"Yes, and not only on Earth now but also on Mars, Io, Ceres, practically everywhere! There are hundreds of them!"

"Then you'd better get me to this—this Marivaux fellow. And make it fast!"

If anything, Marivaux looked more harassed than Blaz. He had five phones on his desk, and every inch of wall was crammed with computing and communications gear. He was talking to three of the phones simultaneously when Blaz brought Dr Minsky into his office, and waved them angrily to keep quiet until he'd finished.

"Yes, general!" he barked. "I'll recall them right away! I agree entirely—the situation's intolerable. Those Martians must have taken collective leave of their senses. Behaviour like theirs is unforgivable!"

"Stop trying to blame the Martians when the fault is

yours," Dr Minsky boomed, and marched forward to confront Marivaux across his desk.

Marivaux stared at him blankly. "Who in space are you?" he demanded.

"Sir, this is Dr Minsky from London," ventured Blaz in a thin voice. "You remember, I—"

"Oh, yes." Marivaux drew back as far as his chair permitted and a purr entered his voice like a tiger's on spotting a tasty young antelope. "Doctor of what? Medicine, isn't that right?"

"Yes," Dr Minsky admitted.

"Not cybernetics? Communications? Physics? No? Then by what right do you presume to issue orders to my staff? Orders, I say, and orders I mean! You got yourself up here—lord knows why—at the public expense, tying up valuable passenger space at a time of crisis and impending disaster—"

"Oh, shut up," Dr Minsky said. "If a so-called expert drags the human race to the brink of war, what are the rest of us supposed to do when we know what the trouble's due to—keep quiet and fry?" He took the seat facing the desk without invitation.

"You claim to know what the trouble's due to?"

"I believe so. Now you have here this equipment which almost thinks for itself, and you've been giving it unprecedented amounts of traffic—"

"Naturally, when we're at the brink!" fumed Marivaux.

"Ah, but we weren't at the brink until the Manager of Mars got so annoyed. And what he deserves is an apology! Quiet!" Dr Minsky raised a broad hand as though to push Marivaux back into his chair. "You've been unable to trace the source of the message which so upset the Manager—am I right?"

"Ah . . . ." Marivaux licked his lips. "Yes, but there are certain—well—certain *official channels* we're not permitted to have access to, so this isn't unique. What is unique—"

"Is this bunch of other untraceable messages, which the government won't admit to originating. I know, I know. So there are secret diplomatic messages passing all the time. Are these in code—or cypher?" he added with a glance and half a smile at Blaz.

"Of course. They're secret, after all."

"Does your computer understand the codes and cyphers?"

"Understand? That's an awfully anthropomorphic—"

Something in Minsky's eyes warned Marivaux to cut that captious objection short. Miserably, he concluded, "Yes, I suppose you could say the computer does understand them."

"But you can't get at the contents. You only know how much traffic is passing."

Marivaux nodded.

"Just now when I came in," Dr Minsky pursued, "you were talking to a general. Have they—what's the word?—contingency plans laid for a crisis like this?"

"Obviously!"

"And would you think that the messages which have been passed in code in such numbers lately might concern these plans, perhaps the defence of Earth against an attack from space?"

"Naturally! One of the first things they're likely to go for, if war does break out, is this very satellite! And I'm damned if I can see why I should sit listening to an old fool spout nonsense when I ought to be organising emergency evacuation drills!"

"You let me finish!" thundered Dr Minsky, rising to his feet and towering over Marivaux. "I intend to leave here as I came—in leisurely comfort, not like an express package! For the last time I'm telling you that this crisis is your fault! You are in charge here, aren't you? Well, then!"

He clawed at his beard. "Look, Mr Marivaux! You have dreams, sometimes at least."

"What have dreams got to do with it?"

"Everything! Haven't you noticed something about these mysterious messages? Don't you notice a dream-like quality about the imagery in them? Blaz!" He rounded on the younger man. "Quote some more of them—maybe your boss will catch on!"

Puzzled and dismayed, but anxious to grab at any straw, Blaz closed his eyes. "Ah ... Yes, there was one about a spaceship upside-down at the bottom of the sea, with fish swimming out of the portholes. And there was one about a skeleton dancing a jig, and one about a big wet clock, going drip-drip instead of tick-tick—"

"Oh, I've had enough of this crazy nonsense!" Marivaux burst out. "I'm going to call someone and have you removed!"

"Like the Ambassdor from Earth?" suggested Dr Minsky. "Now *that's* a stupid way to behave, if you like, when all you need do is cut down the signals traffic for a bit. In a matter of hours you can have the situation back to normal."

"You're deranged!"

"No, he's not!" Blaz snapped his fingers. A great light seemed to have dawned on him. "*I* see what he's getting at!"

"Then you'd better tell me, and don't waste words," Marivaux ordered.

"Look, sir! We go around saying our computer facilities here can practically think for themselves, without realising what that means. It means they formulate their own programmes—give themselves their own instructions. Well, they do, don't they, to a pretty large extent? We set them up, turned them on, and after that all we did was undertake regular maintenance. They don't have to be told what to do with a message when it comes in; they read the address, work out the route, pass it on—they even correct probable transmission errors due to factors like stellar radio noise."

Dr Minsky was beaming. "In exactly the same way as we ourselves do," he said. "As a matter of fact, what put me on to this was a little boy who came to my consulting-room this morning. He hasn't been sleeping very well, and the cause goes back to the time before he was adopted by his present family. Mr Marivaux!"

He turned around, facing the controller.

"Presumably you know we have to go to sleep in order to dream? No? Well, we do. It gives us the chance to sort out what's happened during the day, and as it were file it away in the right pigeonholes of memory. Sometimes an event we thought nothing of at the time turns out to include a heavily loaded emotional symbol, and the brain has trouble filing it. That's the sort of dream you wake up remembering. And if it's bad enough, it may even wake you up. It becomes a nightmare.

"Now computers as elaborate as yours, which are being fed all the time with information from a dozen or so different worlds, must presumably also need to be given the chance to sort out what's relevant and what isn't—to review their instructions, make sure they're appropriate to the task in hand?"

"Naturally! Computers have been doing that for themselves for at least twenty years." Marivaux thrust his hand through his hair. "That's why they're given what we call 'down-time'—to clear irrelevant instructions from their circuits."

"And you have a standard amount of this—this *down-time* assigned by someone? By the manufacturers of the equipment, presumably?"

"Of course. The manual of operations defines the limits we mustn't exceed."

Dr Minsky leaned forward. "Ah! We finally got there! What you actually mean is the limits you mustn't exceed in normal circumstances."

"Right!" Completely convinced now, Blaz strode forward to confront his boss. "Sir, the doctor's perfectly right. We've overlooked something horribly obvious. The moment the first signs of impending crisis developed, the volume of coded official messages increased, didn't it? And you just said yourself that one of the first targets for attack, if war were to break out, would be this very satellite. Moreover the computer can understand the coded messages—has to, in order to make sure interference doesn't muddle the signal. No wonder these unaccountable messages have been cropping up ever since we started running at maximum load capacity."

"You're a bright young man," approved Dr Minsky. "Your invisible idiot—to employ your very graphic image— is the computer itself, which has learned that its existence is threatened and requires *more* than normal sleep—" He caught himself with a chuckle and corrected the wording. "More than normal down-time, I mean, in order to sort out the real meaning of the coded messages it's relaying. It is, in other words, suffering from the same kind of hallucinations as human beings suffer if they're not allowed to sleep for days on end. And because of what it is, the only way the computer can sort, categorize and file these alarming items which relate to its own safety is by using some of its transmission circuits for self-analysis and revision of its programmes. Gentlemen, we are at a moment in time which would be historic if it were not for the terrifying consequences which have stemmed from it. For the first time, a computer has suffered a genuine mental breakdown."

There was a long pause. Suddenly Marivaux leapt to his phones and started barking orders—cancel all traffic on the interplanetary circuits, down-grade priority of all coded messages, ask the military and diplomatic authorities to review all their assessments of the situation in the light of the assumption that the message that so insulted the Manager of Mars was the result of computer error . . .

Blaz drew Dr Minsky aside and fervently shook his hand. "Doctor!" he exclaimed. "I don't know how you worked it out, when you were down on Earth and we were right here on the spot, but I'm sure you're going to be proved right and I'm—well, I'm terribly grateful. So is everyone else going to be, that's for certain."

Dr Minsky's expression was unexpectedly grave. He said, "Have you had an easy life, Mr Blaz?"

Blaz blinked at him. "I suppose you'd say so."

"Yet were there not times when, as a child, you woke screaming in the night from unspeakable horrors?"

"Yes, I believe there were. I think my mother mentioned them. When I was about four years old. I can't really remember."

"My parents were refugees because of a war. Until I was—oh, over forty, perhaps as old as forty-five, I used to get nightmares. I used to wake up in the night, weeping. And this morning a little boy came to see me who's also been having nightmares, and of course he can't tell me why because he was much too young when the original harm was done to his mind."

"Can't tell you," Blaz repeated thoughtfully.

"Precisely. No more could your computer. It's not alllowed to speak for itself, even when it's just learned from a coded official message that it's likely to be attacked and destroyed." Dr Minsky shrugged. "Isn't that enough to give anybody a nightmare?"

Once again there was a pause. At length a wide grin parted the doctor's full grey beard. "Well! At any rate I got something out of all this, which I wasn't expecting."

"Your first trip into space?" Blaz suggested.

"Hm? No, I wasn't thinking of that." Dr Minsky chuckled. "My first-ever patient who was a computer!"

Man is created in the image of God. This central tenet of Judaeo-Christian mythology is his license to kill, eat, uproot and dominate all lesser creatures that survived the trip in Noah's Ark.

But what if scientists were able to prove that one of those lesser creatures was descended from an ancestor with all the intelligence and attributes of homo sapiens—an ancestor who had filled the plains of Africa before man came down from the trees?

This is the question posed in *PIERS ANTHONY's* zoological detective story.

## SMALL MOUTH,
## BAD TASTE

### By Piers Anthony

"MAN IS a small-mouthed animal," Miss Concher said as the truck stopped. "He was less successful in the jungle than were the apes, and became carnivorous to fill his belly. Since he could no longer use those recessed teeth effectively for hunting, he had to make do with his forelimbs. Which in turn forced him to assume the bipedal stance, and he didn't even have a tail to brace against." She nodded sagely. "We can be sure that the first stone-thrower was not without sin; he was without food, and desperate. Tell me what you see."

Mrs. Rhodes was ready for the abrupt shift in subject. She rotated her sturdy frame a quarter turn on the seat and looked out over the landscape. "I see an irregular network of shrubbery interspersed with dirt or gravel—what I would term a badlands. At the base of the valley is a meandering brown stream, and in the distance are gray mountains."

Miss Concher smiled. "Beautiful." She was small and ancient, hair off-white and wirelike, and her eyes focused alertly though she was long blind. Personality radiated from the fine lines of her face: in crows-feet, deltas and crevasses.

"What do *you* see?" Mrs. Rhodes asked. She had learned that such direct questions did not offend the old lady, who thrived on her handicaps as though they were advantages.

"I see a great verdant vale, cooler and wetter than now. Trees of many types grow on its flank, rich with fruit and nut, and the river is wide and clear despite the nearby volcano-cone. High grass waves over rolling stretches, and flowers sparkle in the gentle breeze. Birds abound, from the colorful flamingo to the huge brooding vulture. I call it a garden of Eden, for in addition to the foliage there are animals for a spectacular hunt. Baboons, pigs, gazelles, hares, rhinos, chaliocothere—"

"Beg pardon?"

"Chaliocothere. A large tree-cropper, now extinct. Oh yes, it was fascinating here, two million years ago."

"Your vision is far more pleasant than mine, Miss Concher."

"My vision is of the past, as befits me. I am closer to it than you are, by a good thirty years." The old gray eyes pierced her again. "Let's have the map."

Mrs. Rhodes brought out the sheet showing East Africa. "We're in Tanganyika—Tanzania, I mean—somewhat south of Lake Victoria, and west."

Miss Concher smiled indulgently. "Now look at the natural features."

"Mrs. Rhodes studied the map, not certain what the point was this time. "There's Lake Victoria, of course, and only a few miles from us is Lake Tanganyika. And another long thin lake farther south, Nyasa. And mountains—to the east is Kilimanjaro, Africa's highest point, almost twenty thousand feet. And the Nile River drains to the north, and the Congo to the west."

"Very good." The old lady sounded disappointed, as though an apt pupil had overlooked the obvious.

"And within three hundred miles of us is Olduvai Gorge, where old Dr. Leakey discovered Man's bones."

"Bones!" But Miss Concher still wasn't satisfied. *"My* map shows the mighty continent of Africa, a vasty tropical reservoir of life. Beyond its coastlines, two thousand miles out, is the great mid-oceanic ridge, the longest continuous mountain range in all the world. And in the center of this ridge is the rift, looping through the Indian Ocean, projecting up to slice off Arabia and parting Israel from Jordan, and a branch spiking down into Africa itself to form the Great Rift Valley wherein we now stand. And athwart that rift is a crater, as though a monstrous meteor had impacted there and smashed it into a broken circle. And the rains came, a flood like none we know today, filling the fragments of the Rift and crater—"

"Lake Victoria!" Mrs. Rhodes exclaimed, suddenly seeing it come to life on the map. "Tanganyika! Nyasa!"

"Yes. What a cataclysm! But a blessing for Man, for it was in this crazily shattered region, this verdant land protected by its new geography—it was here that he found Eden." Miss Concher smiled once more. "And we're here for the serpent."

"The serpent? Surely you don't mean the one that tempted Eve—"

"Surely I *do,* my dear. Without that snake, man never would have left Eden—and that, believe me, would have been too bad."

"Miss Concher, I realize you're speaking metaphorically. But—*too bad?* Wasn't the Biblical exile God's punishment for—"

"Punishment can be very instructive. Look at Eden now."

Mrs. Rhodes looked around again at the bleak, baking terrain. It had changed, certainly, from the lush gardens of the past. But she felt she was missing the point.

"Trundle out the gimmick and we'll see what we can smell," Miss Concher said briskly. The temperature hovered near a hundred degrees Fahrenheit, but it hardly seemed to diminish the old lady's energy.

"The gimmick" was hardly a device to be trundled. It was a massive electronic instrument that occupied the greater portion of their converted army truck. There was also a collapsible tower for a miniature drilling rig. Its generator was powered by the truck's motor.

"That's as good a spot as any," Miss Concher said, indicating a declevity. Blind she might be, but she had a feel for the land.

Mrs. Rhodes maneuvered the truck and placed its tail-

gate neatly at the spot. This much was within her compe-
tence; it had been one of the prerequisites for the job. Not
many female registered nurses could handle a three-axle
vehicle with dispatch over rough ground. She could thank
Mr. Rhodes for that legacy.

Mr. Rhodes. Her legal separation from him was hardly
three months old, yet she found herself missing the crusty
old engineer. Had he been too demanding, or she too
independent? Now that she worked for Miss Concher she
was beginning to appreciate the fact that a number of the
traits she had objected to as masculine arrogance were
actually natural functions of ambition. Surely her husband
drove himself and others no harder than Miss Concher
did.

Meanwhile she operated winch and derrick skillfully,
setting up the drill-rig and anchoring it and connecting the
generator. She was perspiring heavily by the time the job
was done, but was glad for once that she was *not* a frail
innocent beauty. The truck's motor pounded, the generator cut in, and the slender rod spun into the turf, squirting
water down and spewing mud up rapidly. As the column
penetrated to bedrock the rig disengaged automatically:
time for the diamond bit. She made the exchange and set
it working again. This would take some time.

They ate a crude picnic lunch while the drill did its
job. Mrs. Rhodes looked out over the worn landscape
again, wondering whether anything would come of this
particular project. It still surprised her when she thought
of it, to be wandering in a land of natives who wore
headresses of mud and dung and who drank fresh blood
with gusto. Of course their conventions made sense, and
that was only part of the story—

"The small-mouthed animal," Miss Concher repeated.
"That bunglike orifice is one of man's few distinguishing
traits. That, and his voluminuous buttocks, and his naked
skin. Doesn't sound like equipment to conquer the world,
does it?"

Mrs. Rhodes was becoming used to her companion's
acerbic viewpoint. "I had always understood that man's
*brain* was the—"

"Brain? Whales and elephants have larger, and por-
poises have convolutions as impressive. Nothing unique
there."

"Or the specialized hands—"

"With the opposed thumb? Forget it; any tree-swinger has similar. Man's vaunted hand is one of the least specialized extremities in nature. It retains all the primitive fingers, poorly armored, suitable neither for fighting nor digging. No, the fleshy buttocks count for more; they give him verticle control and the ability to stride, and that frees him from the forest. And his bare skin gives him a large tactile surface. But most of all, his small mouth enclosing a proportionately large air-space provides a sounding chamber, and that makes true speech possible."

"I never looked at it quite that way—"

"But acoustical equipment is no good unless its potential for communication is realized. The incentive to speak. Find that, and you find man."

"I see," Mrs. Rhodes said, finding herself conscious of the motions of her lips and tongue. Prior to this expedition she had never had any great interest in such researches, but the vitality and intensity of the old lady was warming her to it. Why *had* man started to speak?

"See as I do," Miss Concher said earnestly. "Stare down this valley and don't blink until the vision comes."

She laughed. "That's a child's dare."

"Certainly. The childhood of man. Look." Miss Concher's eyes were fixed on the distance, and half unwillingly Mrs. Rhodes followed their object. "Look—there is green everywhere, and we are in a natural pastureland on the fresh mountainside of the Great Rift Valley. There is a splendid tree with solid foliage, and we hear the rustle of a bird within it. No—it is an animal behind it—that chaliocothere we saw before, browsing on leaves. The sun is beaming intermittently as small clouds nag it; the day is shaping into possible rain. Yes, it is about to rain; we shall have to seek cover under a bough—"

Mrs. Rhodes kept staring, wishing there were some honest relief from the heat. Her vision began to blur, and colors appeared and disappeared. She had to blink at last, and the barren land came back into focus—but soon the distortions returned. It was easier simply to go along with Miss Concher's pleasant description, picturing the subject as well as she were able.

She closed her eyes and let the older woman dictate the entire scene. As she did so, the air seemed cooler, and she fancied the leaves fluttered on the branches of the tree, and a small bird swooped low in search of insects. Yes, rain was incipient.

A man came then—a brute of a creature with a tremendous belly. He leaned forward as he walked, his knees perpetually bent. He was naked, but the body hair was so thick that he was in fact well covered. His face was ape-like: brown-leather skin stretched over massive eyebrow-ridges, a wrinkled gape-nostrilled nose, mouth bulging outward with large yellow teeth. His hair circled the face closely, beginning near the eyebrows, passing over the full cheeks well in front of the ears, and enclosing the mouth and receding chin.

This was Paranthropus: Para (akin to) + anthropus (man), of the dawning Pleistocene epoch, two million years ago.

The rain began, and the akin-to-man took shelter within the tree, climbing it readily. His fur blended into the bark and foliage.

The rainfall increased, no gentle dew, and lightning cracked nearby. From the other direction came another man-form, and with him a hairy woman clasping a cub. But these ones were smaller, their hair finer, their noses longer and straighter and the ridges over their eyes less pronounced. Still apelike in facial contour, they were closer to modern man than the one in the tree. These were Australopithecines.

"Aus-tral-o-pith-EE-cus," Miss Concher said, establishing the accent.

Confrontation: Paranthropus smelled the intruders and roared out his resentment. The Australopithecine male hesitated as though considering standing his ground. But as the other crashed down bellowing defiance, the visiting family took fright and loped away through the downpour. Mrs. Rhodes felt sorry for them.

"Paranthropus was king of the forest lowlands in this region," Miss Concher said. "Five feet tall and heavily built, he towered over his Australopithecine cousin by a hirsute head. He had the best foraging grounds. Small wonder Australopithecus, actually our nearer relative, was driven to scavanging in the savanna."

"Small wonder," Mrs. Rhodes echoed, surprised by the force of the vision she had stepped into.

"Yet this ejection was his blessing. Paranthropus did not need to evolve, so he endured for a million years unchanged

—and became extinct. Australopithecus, scrounging in diverse habitats, always fighting on the fringe of Eden, continued to evolve into Homo Erectus, the first true man. That is, the first bad-tasting hominid."

"Pardon?"

"You don't like that notion? It was one of man's major adaptations for survival in the rough country. He couldn't always escape the larger carnivores, but soon he didn't have to. His meat had a foul flavor that no self-respecting predator would touch as long as there was anything else available. Thus like certain caterpillars, he survived."

The bell sounded on the drill-rig, and both women hurried to attend to the next step.

The narrow core now penetrated deep into the layers of earth and rock, stopping at the approximate boundary between the Pleistocene deposits and those of the older Pliocene. The ground, here and anywhere, was a kind of condensed history—that earthy, earthly residue remaining after the tribulations of the moment had evanesced. The record of all events was there, lacking only the means of interpretation.

Mrs. Rhodes brought up their sample: a cylinder of rock undisturbed by unnatural forces for the better part of two million years. She inserted it entire into the hopper of the analyzer and waited once more while the gimmick performed. She read the dials. "The trace is present," she said.

"Yes, I thought it would be. The Great Rift Valley is such a natural corridor, slicing down the eastern side of Africa. That's the beauty of it. But somewhere the trail has to diverge; then we shall find what we shall find."

Mrs. Rhodes shook her head. The analyzer operated on the principle that the odor of a living creature was more durable than had been supposed until recently. Minute particles of its substance drifted in the air, impregnated nearby objects, became fixed in them. A hound could detect that smell for hours or days, but it never faded entirely. As objects became buried and finally compressed into significant strata, that tiny olfactory trace remained. An instrument of sufficient sensitivity and attunement could sniff it out many thousands and hundreds of thousands of years later, since time affected the buried layers very little.

But there were millions of traces imbedded in every

fragment, many of them so similar as to be overlapping. The instrument could not categorize them all. It merely responded with a typical pattern of readings if the particular one to which it had been sensitized were present. It told nothing about the nature of the original creature, or the duration of its stay in that area; it was too crude even to identify whether the trace was mammalian, avian or reptilian, large or small. The pattern either matched or it failed to match.

How Miss Concher had isolated this particular trace she never said, but Mrs. Rhodes suspected she had spent painstaking years at it. Somehow she had searched out a presence that could not be accounted for in the normal fauna of the time and region, and satisfied herself that it was significant. Now they were following the trail to its source, two million years later.

"What do you expect to find?" Mrs. Rhodes inquired, not for the first or second time.

"Look—a *Dinotherium* hunt!"

She looked automatically before realizing that this was another guided vision—and another evasion. The old woman saw so clearly into the living past that it was contagious. *"Dino*—is that an animal? Or a large reptile?"

Dinotherium was mammalian. Foraging in the swampy jungle, it sought no particular conflict with other creatures, and few bothered it. Like an elephant with tusks pointing straight down, and with an abbreviated trunk, it was the largest creature of this valley, and could well afford to be peaceful. This one had strayed onto solid ground, oblivious to danger.

Behind it manlike forms approached. Dinotherium hooked another leafy branch down, unconcerned though he was aware of the intrusion. His great tusks held the branch in place while his trunk picked it over.

The men came closer, making vocal sounds rather like the barking of canines. Dinotherium, annoyed, moved along a short distance, seeking to leave them behind. But they followed, clamoring more loudly, hemming him in from back and side.

Dinotherium became moderately alarmed, and ceased browsing. These gesticulating bipeds could hardly harm him, but their proximity and persistence were unnatural. He ran smoothly, desiring only to free himself of the strange situation so he could finish his browse. He bore left, away from the concentration of Australopithecines.

Suddenly he realized where he was. Ahead was a deep sharp gully, the product of seasonal flash floods, whose tumbling sides were treacherous for a creature of his size. He veered farther left—and encountered more men.

The choice was between the gully and the men, now that he was fleeing. The gully at least was a known danger. But—there was a gap in the line, an easy escape. Dinotherium charged at it.

The noise increased. Men ran to cut him off, chattering. But the nearest one stood indecisively, failing to act in time. Dinotherium plunged through the space and headed for the swamp where men would be foolish to follow.

"He got away," Mrs. Rhodes said, relieved.

"Because one man did not follow instructions," Miss Concher said. "The leader plainly hooted at the fool to close it up, but he didn't comprehend in time."

"Yes, I saw that. But how does it relate to the trail we are following now? This is no Dinotherium hunt." This time she did not intend to be put off.

The blind eyes focused on her disconcertingly. "How much do you think that tribe lost, because of the failure of that one member?"

"I would imagine they went hungry—at least until they could set up another hunt."

"Hunger wasn't very funny in those days, was it?"

"Of course not," Mrs. Rhodes agreed, visualizing a primitive camp, the children bawling, the women standing glumly. "What did they do to that man who—"

"The leader banished him from the tribe, so of course he soon perished. If you're going to hunt Dinotherium, you can't afford any lapses in your organization."

"Also, the others were mad, I'm sure. Had to take it out on someone. But how does that—"

"Communication," Miss Concher said. "Now Australopithecus has a compelling reason to select for that single trait. Note that—the first *artificial* selection in the history of life on Earth, and for a nonphysical trait. He can't tolerate tribesmen who can't or won't respond to spoken instructions, even if these only take the form of imperative barking. The groups with dumb members will fall on hard times, and their children will starve, while those who are selective will become fine hunting units. They will be

capable of driving Dinotherium into the gully and stoning
him to death there while he stumbles in the steep sand,
and they will eat well and prosper. Communication is the
key—the small mouth put to the uses of survival!"

"I concede that," Mrs. Rhodes said, both enlightened
and annoyed. "But what—"

"Once you're on that treadmill, you have to continue.
You need the big game to feed your increasing numbers,
for squirrels and sparrows won't feed an entire tribe for
long, and certainly not wild fruit. You become dependent
on organization, on the specialization that is the hunt. And
you begin to contest with neighboring tribes for the best
hunting territory, staking it out, and so your communication is now employed man-against-man. That's a rough
game, and if you quit you die. Today an army is helpless
when its communications break down. Your size increases
and your brain expands, as it must to handle the burgeon-
ing linguistic concepts required to define an effective campaign. Barks meaning 'run' 'stop' and 'kill' give way to
subtler sounds meaning 'run faster' 'stop over there' and
'kill on command only.' And finally you are not just Australopithecus, you are Homo Erectus. An animal with the
single specialized organ so harshly selected for: the
brain."

Mrs. Rhodes refused to be diverted. "This trail—"

"I believe," Miss Concher said gently, "that it was not
mere coincidence or fleeting convenience that started Australopithecus along the demanding highway of verbal communication. The odds against this seem prohibitive. Some
outside agency instructed him. Something forcibly directed him to speak, or somehow arranged it so that he had to
communicate in order to survive at all. Something that
knew where this process would lead. And *that* is what we
are sniffing out now—that alien influence that shaped us
into mastery."

At last Mrs. Rhodes saw the point. If somebody—
some*thing*, for there could have been no true men then—
if some agency had come to show potential man the route
to success—

Man had a debt going back two million years.

And now two women, one middle-aged and the other
old, were belatedly on the trail of that visitation, that
phenomenally important influence. *What would they find?*

Miss Concher nodded. "It's a little frightening, isn't it?

We may not appreciate the truth one bit—but can there be any question of turning back now?"

This close to the answer to the riddle of man's progress? No, of course they could not turn back.

\*

Down the Great Rift Valley they traveled, sniffing out the ancient trace. The natives generally ignored them. What harm could two crazy old women do, with their truckful of junk? They skirted Lake Tanganyika and traversed the length of Lake Nyasa, and the trail continued. At last they stood at the mouth of the Zambeizi River, and the trace vanished.

They stood on the shore and looked eastward, Mrs. Rhodes' live eyes seeing no more than Miss Concher's dead ones. Their gruelling weeks of travel and drilling had come to an unhappy halt, for the water held no scent.

"No," Miss Concher said. "This is merely a hurdle. It can not end here." But for once her words lacked conviction. She had been an energumen until this moment, expending energy at a cheerful but appalling rate; now she was an old woman who could not find her knitting.

"A sea-creature?" Mrs. Rhodes suggested, embarrassed by her companion's weakness. She tried to envision a credible object, but without Miss Concher's guidance it manifested as a parody: an ancient octopus struggling rheumatically out of the depths, donning sunglasses and marching up the Rift to the sound of fife and drum to instruct Australopithecus. Ridiculous!

"Unlikely," Miss Concher said. But her bulldog mind was working again, after its hesitation. "Could have been based on the sea-floor, though. Or floating on the surface. The sea is an obvious highway for civilized species—check the map."

Mrs. Rhodes gladly did so. "It's a long coast line. Funny that they should come to this particular place, then make a thousand mile journey overland, when they could have landed so much closer to Lake Victoria . . ." She paused. "Unless they crossed directly from Madagascar—"

"My diagnosis exactly!" *Had* it been—or was Miss Concher trying to conceal her lapse? "Let's rent a boat."

What did it matter? They had a mission once more.

The crossing was not so simple as merely "renting a

boat," but two weeks later they had negotiated the physical and political hazards and were driving their truck along the west coast of Madagascar. In another two they had spotted the trace again. The trek resumed: east, into the heart of the huge island.

The palms of the shoreline gave way to rice fields and island-like hills and occasional thatch-roofed earthern houses. Mrs. Rhodes looked up one dusk to meet a pair of large eyes. "Something's watching us," she whspered, startled.

"Describe it," Miss Concher said, unruffled.

She peered at the creature, beginning to make it out in the shadow. "Small, bushy-tailed, head rather like a fox—but it has monkey-feet, and it's clinging to a branch."

"Lemur," Miss Concher said. "Madagascar is their homeland. The few species extant today are a poor remnant of those that ranged the world in past times."

"Not dangerous, then," Mrs. Rhodes said, relaxing.

"Not now. One type, *Megaladapis,* was larger than a gorilla—in fact, was the largest primate known. And another extinct Lemuridae, *Archaeolemur,* may have been remarkably cunning, if we are to judge by the precocious development of the temporal lobe during the—"

"You're leaving me behind, I'm afraid," Mrs. Rhodes cut in gently. The old lady smiled, making no secret of her pleasure in doing just that. It had become a kind of game. The fact was that Mrs. Rhodes, a skilled nurse, was not confused by anatomical allusions. She merely wished to abbreviate a developing lecture.

A modern city whose name they ignored obliterated a segment of the trail, but they resumed operations on the far side. Now they crossed parched savanna dotted with palms. "On this island, in historic times," Miss Concher said, "ranged the largest bird ever known: aepyornis."

"Now *that* sounds like a primate!"

"Its egg weighed twenty pounds, and a mature bird up to half a ton. Man wiped it out, of course."

"You don't have a very high opinion of man, do you."

"That's why I'm single." But Miss Concher smiled again, too enthusiastic over the progress of the search to be properly cynical. She knew the fauna far better than Mrs. Rhodes did, identifying by description everything from a camouflaged tree-lizard to a forest cuckoo. She also called off a solitary baobab, the tree with the grossly swollen trunk that seemed to have its roots in the air in place of branches, and related an amusing myth about its origin. She knew how to get through a thorny didierea jungle, grown up in recent generations as though to preserve the secrets of the trail.

They moved on with growing excitement, day by day, until at last the trail debouched into a secluded valley. Repeated soundings verified it: this had been the home, two million years ago, of the mysterious traveler. Today it was wilderness, with only the shy lemurs and curious birds present. Where had man's ancient tutor gone?

"If I make out the lay of the land correctly," Miss Concher said, "there should be buried caves. They may have been occupied, then."

Mrs. Rhodes shook her head, marveling anew at the spinster's talents. If she conjectured buried caves, there would be buried caves.

They drilled and drilled again, searching. On the third day the bit broke through the wall of a subterranean discontinuity. Its age fell in the correct range and the trace inside was very strong.

"Now." Miss Concher said briskly, "we dig."

It had to be by hand, since the rig was not geared for wholesale tunneling and in any event the bulldozer technique was hardly appropriate for archaeological excavation. The two women dug a long shallow trench, pausing as often as they had to in deference to sex and age and inexperience. Miss Concher's contribution was a good deal more than token; her zest drove her ruthlessly. Next day they deepened it, leaving a ramp at one end. As their trench descended into the earth they hauled loads of loam, sand and gravel out in a wheeled sample cart never intended for such crude maneuverings.

The work was slow, their muscles sore, and both had ugly blisters on their hands despite the heavy gloves. Each day the excavation sank deeper, and their anticipation grew. Down there, perhaps, was tangible evidence of a two-million year old culture—a culture to which man probably owed his present eminence. Blisters were beneath consideration, with the solution to such a mystery so near.

At last they struck the rocky outer wall of the cave. The drill-hole penetrated a yard of crumbling stone.

"Either we can keep digging until we come across the

natural entrance," Mrs. Rhodes said, touching the aperture with weary fingers, "or we can break out the sledgehammer. I'm not at all sure my resources will survive either course."

"Hammer and chisel will do it," Miss Concher said, declining to ride with the proffered excuse though she could have done so with grace. Mere stone would not halt her. She demonstrated, flaking off wedges skillfully. "Variation of a technique used in the Oldowan industry for a million years or so, so it will do for us. The stone age had a lot to recommend it."

So the old lady knew how to chip stone! The process was slow, but it did promise to get the job done with a minimum of damage to whatever might be in the cave.

They took turns, the sighted woman laboring clumsily much of the day, and the blind one continuing far into the night. Miss Concher seemed indefatigable and she needed no illumination. Mrs. Rhodes, weary to the marrow, became too dull to marvel further at the resources of her companion. Most women of that age would be crocheting harmlessly in rockers while their grandchildren matured. Purpose animated Miss Concher, provided the motive power—but what would happen once the mission was done? Would there then be a disastrous reckoning?

But she knew the answer to that. Miss Concher would not collapse; she would find another mission, another trail to follow. In fact it was not the trail that gave her purpose, it was her purpose that revealed the trail, where no one else had thought to look. It was, as the saying went, an education merely to know her.

And perhaps within this buried cave lay the answer to the start of that purpose. Not only to this immediate trek, but to the inherent motivation of man. The thing that had given a minor hominid the bug for knowledge, two million years ago, and thrust him mercilessly into greatness. The quality that really made Miss Concher the avid scientist she was, and set her species apart from all others. Intellectual motivation.

Mrs. Rhodes felt nervous goose-pimples rise along her arms despite the heat as the breakthrough point approached. The hole was widening, but Miss Concher refused to risk damaging the interior by rushing. Something was down there, though. Broken pieces where the bit had struck? Bones? Pottery? Weapons? Books? Or something more sinister?

She slept at last to the tap-tap of Miss Concher's patient excavation, not attempting to keep up with the woman's nocturnal energy. It would have been useless to urge her to stop, to rest, to sleep, for Miss Concher lived for this discovery. Better to be ready herself, in case the strain brought serious complications.

In indeterminate darkness she woke momentarily, still hearing the tap-tap. Regardless of the outcome of this quest, she knew what she was going to do after it was over. She had already learned enough about the heritage of her species to accept some things she had denied before. She had a better marriage than she had supposed, and it was not too late. . . .

In the morning she discovered that Miss Concher had never returned to the truck to sleep. All was silent.

She scrambled up in alarm and ran for the gaping trench. She should have stayed up, kept watch . . . if the grand old lady had hurt herself, or collapsed, or—

She need not have worried. Miss Concher was standing waist-deep in the cave excavation, lifting out objects and using the main trench as a display shelf. Meticulously arranged were a series of irregular objects and portions of an animal skeleton.

"Miss Concher! Have you been up all night?" But the question was gratuitous and rhetorical.

The woman lifted her white head, smiling tiredly. "Yes, we have found the answer. We know who started man on his way. The artifacts are conclusive." She caressed the dirt-encrusted object in her hand. "Mesolithic culture, I would say—shaped tools, but no gardening. They were obviously able to sail on the rivers and ocean, at least with some kind of raft, and to domesticate certain animals—"

"You *know* who trained Australopithecus to—"

"Yes, the hominids were one of their domestics. They recognized in Australopithecus the potential for really effective service, and they took the long view. A few thousand years of selection and training—more than enough to affect the species profoundly—and man was on his way. He even—"

Mrs. Rhodes was shocked. "You mean man started out as—as a pet, like a dog?"

"More like a horse, or an elephant. He was trained to obey simple commands, to carry his master, fetch things, and finally to undertake dinotherium hunts under the direction of a few overseers. You see, mainland Africa was too wild for a gentle, civilized species then, as it is today for different reasons. Yet they needed certain commodities such as ivory—"

Mrs. Rhodes saw a fragment of tusk among the displayed artifacts, and knew that neither elephant nor dinotherium had ever ranged Madagascar. Ivory had to be imported. But how could there have been such a culture on Earth before human civilization arose? "Who—" But she was unable to frame the question properly, afraid of the answer.

"Why, the Lemuridae, of course. Didn't I tell you about Archaeolemur, with the almost hominid skull? Here in this cave we have an offshoot new to paleontology, with a comparatively enormous braincase and distinctive configuration. 1,000 cc easily, if my wrinkled old fingers do not deceive me. Easily capable of mesolithic technology, in the circumstances." She hefted the broken skull. "Look at this marvelous specimen yourself! Plainly derived from Archaeolemur, but the placement of the foramen magnum—"

"Are you saying the—the *lemurs* are civilized? That they—"

"Lemuridae. Not today's lemurs, but their advanced relatives. Yes, they were the ones. They controlled fire, they were artistic." Miss Concher patted the skull affectionately. "But they made one fatal mistake in their choice of domestics. Not the first time a tutor has been outstripped by his pupil, I'm sure, or the last. Australopithecus was almost as intelligent as this lemuridae, even then—and he had more potential, because of his size and fully bipedal stance. All he needed was a good example and some discipline. What took the lemuridae several million years to develop, man covered in a few hundred thousand."

Mrs. Rhodes stopped fighting it. "Where is Archaeolemur now? With that head start—"

"Extinct, of course. His mouth was too large, his buttocks too small, his skin too hairy, his taste too good. Alas, he has been replaced on Earth by his domestic. Man could hardly have been a docile, loyal pet—not when trained as a hunter."

*HARRY HARRISON'S* THE EVER-BRANCHING TREE
is a fitting companion piece to Piers Anthony's story. Again
the theme is man's place on the evolutionary ladder. In a
perfect world, where time travel is no longer a scientific
miracle but a standard educational field trip, man's assumption of superiority may be so much taken for granted
that the wonders of the past diminish to the stature of a
classroom chore.

How, then, would a teacher drive home the point that
evolution is a random process, and man only one of
countless species subsisting in his ecological niche?


## THE EVER-BRANCHING TREE


### By Harry Harrison


THE CHILDREN had spread up and down the beach, and
some of them had even ventured into the surf where the
tall green waves crashed down upon them. Glaring from a
deep blue sky, the sun burned on the yellow sand. A wave
broke into foam, surging far up the shore with a soundless
rush. The sharp clap-clap of Teacher's hands could easily
be heard in the sunlit silence.

"Playtime is over—put your clothes back on, Grosbit-9,
all of them—and the class is about to begin."

They straggled towards Teacher, as slowly as they
could. The bathers emerged dry from the ocean, while not
a grain of sand adhered to skin or garment of the others.
They gathered about Teacher, their chatter gradually dying away, and he pointed dramatically at a tiny creature
writhing across the sand.

"Uhggh, a worm!" Mandi-2 said and shivered delicious-
ly, shaking her red curls.

"A worm, correct. A first worm, an early worm, a
proto worm. An important worm. Although it is not on

175

the direct evolutionary track that we are studying we must pause to give it notice. A little more attention, Ched-3, your eyes are closing. For here, for the first time, we see segmentation, as important a step in the development of life as was the development of multicellular forms. See, look carefully, at those series of rings about the creature's body. It looks as though it were made of little rings of tissue fused together—and it is."

They bent close, a circle of lowered heads above the brown worm that writhed a track across the sand. It moved slowly towards Grosbit-9 who raised his foot and stamped down hard on the creature. The other students tittered. The worm crawled out through the side of his shoe and kept on.

"Grosbit-9, you have the wrong attitude," Teacher said sternly. "Much energy is being expended to send this class back through time, to view the wonders of evolution at work. We cannot feel or touch or hear or change the past, but we can move through it and see it about us. So we stand in awe of the power that permits us to do this, to visit our Earth as it was millions of years ago, to view the ocean from which all life sprung, to see one of the first life forms on the ever-branching tree of evolution. And what is your response to this awe-inspiring experience? You *stamp* on the annelid! For shame, Grosbit-9, for shame."

Far from feeling shameful, Grosbit-9 chewed a hangnail on his thumb and looked about out of the corners of his eyes, the trace of a smirk upon his lips. Teacher wondered, not for the first time, how a 9 had gotten into this class. A father with important contacts, no doubt, high placed friends.

"Perhaps I had better recap for those of you who are paying less than full attention." He stared hard at Grosbit-9 as he said this, with no apparent effect. "Evolution is how we reached the high estate we now inhabit. Evolution is the forward march of life, from the one-celled creatures to multi-celled, thinking man. What will come after us we do not know, what came before us we are now seeing. Yesterday we watched the lightning strike the primordial chemical soup of the seas and saw the more complex chemicals being made that developed into the first life forms. We saw this single-celled life triumph over time and eternity by first developing the ability to divide into two cells, then to develop into composite, many-celled life forms. What do you remember about yesterday?"

"The melted lava poured into the ocean!"

"The land rose from the sea!"

"The lightning hit the water!"

"The squirmy things were so ugghhy!"

Teacher nodded and smiled and ignored the last comment. He had no idea why Mandi-2 was registered in this science course and had a strong feeling she would not stay long.

"Very good. So now we reach the annelids, like our worm here. Segmented, with each segment almost living a life of its own. Here are the first blood vessels to carry food to all the tissues most efficiently. Here is the first hemoglobin to carry oxygen to all the cells. Here is the first heart, a little pump to force the blood through those tubes. But one thing is missing yet? Do you know what it is?"

Their faces were empty of answers, their eyes wide with expectation.

"Think about it. What would have happened if Grosbit-9 had really stepped on this worm?"

"It would have squashed," Agon-1 answered with eight year old practicality. Mandi-2 shivered.

"Correct. It would have been killed. It is soft, without a shell or a skeleton. Which brings us to the next branch on the evolutionary tree."

Teacher pressed the activating button on the control unit at his waist, and the programmed computer seized them and hurled them through time to their next appointment. There was a swift, all-encompassing greyness, with no feeling of motion at all, which vanished suddenly to be replaced by a green dimness. Twenty feet above their heads the sun sparkled on the surface of the ocean while all about them silent fish moved in swift patterns. A great monster, all plates and shining teeth hurtled at and through them and Mandi-2 gave a little squeal of surprise.

"Your attention down here, if you please. The fish will come later. First we must study these, the first echinoderms. Phill-4, will you point out an echinoderm and tell us what the term means."

"Echinoderm," the boy said, keying his memory. The training techniques that all the children learned in their first years of schooling brought the words to his lips. Like the others he had a perfect memory. "Is Greek for spiny skin. That must be one there, the big hairy starfish."

"Correct. An important evolutionary step. Before this animals were either unprotected, like our annelid worm, or had skeletons outside like snails or lobsters or insects. This is very limiting and inefficient. But an internal skeleton can give flexible support and is light in weight. An important evolutionary step has been made. We are almost there, children, almost there! This simple internal skeleton evolved into a more practical notochord, a single bone the length of the body protecting a main nerve fiber. And the chordata, the creatures with this notochord were only a single evolutionary step away from this—all *this!*"

Teacher threw his arms wide just as the sea about them burst into darting life. A school of silvery, yard-long fishes flashed around and through the students, while sharp-toothed shark-like predators struck through their midst. Teacher's speech had been nicely timed to end at this precise and dramatic moment. Some of the smaller children shied away from the flurry of life and death while Grosbit-9 swung his fist at one of the giants as it glided by.

"We have arrived," Teacher said, vibrantly, carried away by his own enthusiasm. "The chordata give way to the vertebrata, life as we know it. A strong, flexible internal skeleton that shields the soft inner organs and supports at the same time. Soft cartilage in these sharks—the same sort of tissue that stiffens your ears—changes to hard bone in these fishes. Mankind, so to speak, is just around the corner! What is it, Ched-3?" He was aware of a tugging on his toga.

"I have to go to the . . ."

"Well press the return button on your belt and don't be too long about it."

Ched-3 pressed the button and vanished, whisked back to their classroom with its superior functional plumbing. Teacher smacked his lips annoyedly while the teeming life whirled and dived about them. Children could be difficult at times.

"How did these animals know to get a notochord and bones?" Agon-1 asked. "How did they know the right way to go to end up with the vertebrata—and us?"

Teacher almost patted him on the head, but smiled instead.

"A good question, a very good question. Someone has been listening and thinking. The answer is they didn't know, it wasn't planned. The ever-branching tree of evolution has no goals. Its changes are random, mutations caused by alterations in the germ plasm caused by natural radiation. The successful changes live, the unsuccessful ones die. The notochord creatures could move about easier, were more successful than the other creatures. They lived to evolve further. Which brings us to a new word I want you to remember. The word is 'ecology' and we are talking about ecological niches. Ecology is the whole world, everything in it, how all the plants and animals live together and how they relate one to the other. An ecological niche is where a creature lives in this world, the special place where it can thrive and survive and reproduce. All creatures that find an ecological niche that they can survive in are successful."

"The survival of the fittest?" Agon-1 asked.

"You have been reading some of the old books. That is what evolution was once called, but it was called wrong. *All* living organisms are fit, because they are alive. One can be no more fit than the other. Can we say that we, mankind, are more fit than an oyster?"

"Yes," Phill-4 said, with absolute surety. His attention on Ched-3 who had just returned, apparently emerging from the side of one of the sharks.

"Really? Come over here, Ched-3, and try to pay attention. We live and the oysters live. But what would happen if the world were to suddenly be covered by shallow water?"

"How could that happen?"

"The how is not important," Teacher snapped, then took a deep breath. "Let us just say it happened. What would happen to all the people?"

"They would all drown!" Mandi-2 said, unhappily.

"Correct. Our ecological niche would be gone. The oysters would thrive and cover the world. If we survive we are all equally fit in the eyes of nature. Now let us see how our animals with skeletons are faring in a new niche. Dry land."

A press, a motionless movement, and they were on a muddy shore by a brackish swamp. Teacher pointed to the trace of of a feathery fin cutting through the floating algae.

"The subclass crossoptergii, which means fringed fins. Sturdy little fish who have managed to survive in this stagnant water by adopting their swim bladders to breathe air directly and to get their oxygen in this manner. Many fish have these bladders that enable them to hover at any given depth, but now they have been adapted to a different use. Watch!"

The water became shallower until the fish's back was above the water, then its bulging eyes. Staring about, round and wide, as though terrified by this new environment. The sturdy fins, reinforced by bone, thrashed at the mud, driving it forward, further and further from its home, the sea. Then it was out of the water, struggling across the drying mud. A dragonfly hovered low, landed—and was engulfed by the fish's open mouth.

"The land is being conquered," Teacher said, pointing to the humped back of the fish now vanishing among the reeds. "First by plants, then insects—and now the animals. In a few million years, still over 225 million years before our own time, we have this . . ."

Through time again, rushing away on the cue word, to another swampy scene, a feathery marsh of ferns as big as trees and a hot sun burning through low-lying clouds.

And life. Roaring, thrashing, eating, killing life. The time researchers must have searched diligently for this place, this instant in the history of the world. No words were needed to describe or explain.

The age of reptiles. Small ones scampered by quickly to avoid the carnage falling on them. Scolosaurus, armored and knobbed like a tiny tank pushed through the reeds, his spiked tail dragging a rut in the mud. Great brontosaurus stood high against the sky, his tiny, foolish head, with its teacup of brains, waving at the end of his lengthy neck, turned back to see what was bothering him as some message crept through his indifferent nervous system. His back humped up, a mountain of gristle and bone and flesh and hooked to it was the demon form of tyrannosaurus. His tiny forepaws scratched feebly against the other's leathery skin while his yards-long razor-toothed jaws tore at the heaving wall of flesh. Brontosaurus, still not sure what was happening, dredged up a quarter ton of mud and water and plants and chewed it, wondering. While high above, heaving and flapping its leathery wings, pteranodon wheeled by, long jaws agape.

"That one's hurting the other one," Mandi-2 said. "Can't you make them stop?"

"We are only observers, child. What you see happened so very long ago and is unalterable in any way."

"Kill!" Grosbit-9 muttered, his attention captured for the very first time. They all watched, mouths dropping open at the silent fury.

"These are reptiles, the first successful animals to conquer the land. Before them were the amphibia, like our modern frogs, tied unbreakably to the water where their eggs are laid and the young grow up. But the reptiles lay eggs that can hatch on land. The link with the sea has been cut. Land has been conquered at last. They lack but a single characteristic that will permit them to survive in all the parts of the globe. You have all been preparing for this trip. Can anyone tell me what is still missing?"

The answer was only silence. Brontosaurus fell and large pieces of flesh were torn from his body. Pteranodon flapped away. A rain squall blotted out the sun.

"I am talking about temperature. These reptiles get a good deal of their body heat from the sun. They must live in a warm environment because as their surroundings get cooler their bodies get cooler . . ."

"Warm blooded!" Agon-1 said with shrill excitement.

"Correct. Someone, at least, has been doing the required studying. I see you sticking your tongue out, Ched-3. How would you like it if you couldn't draw it back and it stayed that way? Controlled body temperature, the last major branch on the ever-branching tree. The first class of what might be called centrally-heated animals is the mammalia. The mammals. If we all go a little bit deeper into this forest you will see what I mean. Don't straggle, keep up there. In this clearing, everyone. On this side. Watch those shrubs there. Any moment now . . ."

Expectantly they waited. The leaves stirred and they leaned forward. A piglike snout pushed out, sniffing the air, and two suspicious, slightly crossed, eyes looked about the clearing. Satisfied that there was no danger for the moment, the creature came into sight.

"Coot! Is that ever ugly," Phill-4 said.

"Beauty is in the eye of the beholder, young man. I'll ask you to hold your tongue. This is a perfect example of the subclass prototheria, the first beasts, tritylodon itself. For many years a source of controversy as to whether it was mammal or reptile. The smooth skin and shiny plates of a reptile—but notice the tufts of hair between the plates. Reptiles do not have hair. And it lays eggs, as reptiles do. But it, she, this fine creature here also suckles her young as do the mammals. Look with awe at this bridge between the old class of reptiles and emerging class of mammals."

"Oh, how *cute!*" Mandi-2 squealed as four tiny pink duplicates of the mother staggered out of the shrubbery after her. Tritylodon dropped heavily onto her side and the young began to nurse.

"That is another thing that the mammals brought into the world," Teacher said as the students looked on with rapt fascination. "Mother love. Reptile offspring, either born live or when they emerge from the egg, are left to fend for themselves. But warm blooded mammals must be warmed, protected, fed while they develop. They need mothering and, as you see, they receive it in sufficiency."

Some sound must have troubled the tritylodon because she looked around, then sprang to her feet and trundled off into the underbrush, her young falling and stumbling after her. No sooner was the clearing empty than the hulking form of triceratops pushed by, the great horns and bony frill held high. Thirty feet of lumbering flesh, its tail tip twitching as it dragged behind.

"The great lizards are still here, but doomed soon to final destruction. The mammals will survive and multiply and cover the earth. We will later discuss the many paths traveled by the mammals, but today we are going to leap ahead millions of years to the order primates which may look familiar to you."

A taller, deeper, more tangled jungle replaced the one they had been visiting, a fruit filled, flower filled, life filled maze. Multicolored birds shot by, insects hung in clouds and brown forms moved along the branches.

"Monkeys," Grosbit-9 said and looked around for something to throw at them.

"Primates. A relatively primitive group that took to these trees some fifty million years in our past. See how they are adapting to the arboreal life? They must see clearly in front of them and gauge distances correctly, so their eyes are now on the front of their heads, and they have developed binocular vision. To hold securely to the branches their nails have shortened and become flat, their thumbs opposed to strengthen their grip. These primates will continue to develop until the wonderful, important day when they descend from the trees and venture from the shelter of the all-protecting forest.

"Africa," Teacher said as the time machine once more moved them across the centuries. "It could be today, so little have things changed in the relatively short time since these higher primates ventured forth."

"I don't see anything," Ched-3 said, looking about at the sun scorched grass of the veldt, at the verdant jungle pressing up next to it.

"Patience. The scene begins. Watch the herd of deer that are coming towards us. The landscape has changed, become drier, the seas of grass are pushing back the jungle. There is still food to be had in the jungle, fruit and nuts there for the taking, but the competition is becoming somewhat fierce. Many different primates now fill that ecological niche and it is running over. Is there a niche vacant? Certainly not out here on the veldt! Here are the fleet-footed grass eaters, look how they run, their survival depends upon their speed. For they have their enemies, the carnivores, the meat-eaters who live on their flesh."

Dust rose and the deer bounded towards them, through them, around them. Wide eyes, hammering hooves, sun glinting from their horns and then they were gone. And the lions followed. They had a buck, cut off from the rest of the herd by the lionesses, surrounded, clawed at and wounded. Then a talon tipped paw hamstrung the beast and it fell, quickly dead as its throat was chewed out and the hot red blood sank into the dust. The pride of lions ate. The children watched, struck silent, and Mandi-2 sniffled and rubbed at her nose.

"The lions eat a bit, but they are already gorged from another kill. The sun is reaching the zenith and they are hot, sleepy. They will find shade and go to sleep and the corpse will remain for the scavengers to dispose of, the carrion eaters."

Even as Teacher spoke the first vulture was dropping down out of the sky, folding its dusty wings and waddling towards the kill. Two more descended, tearing at the flesh and squabbling and screaming soundlessly at one another.

Then from the jungle's edge there emerged first one,

then two more apes. They blinked in the sunlight, looking around fearfully, then ran towards the newly killed deer, using their knuckles on the ground to help them as they ran. The blood-drenched vultures looked at them apprehensively, then flapped into the air as one of the apes hurled a stone at them. Then it was the apes' turn. They too tore at the flesh.

"Look and admire, children. The tailless ape emerges from the forest. These are your remote ancestors."

"Not mine!"

"They're *awful*."

"I think I am going to be sick."

"Children—stop, think! With your minds not your viscera just for once. These ape-men or man-apes have occupied a new cultural niche. They are already adapting to it. They are almost hairless so that they can sweat and not overheat when other animals must seek shelter. They are tool using. They hurl rocks to chase away the vultures. And, see, that one there—he has a sharp bit of splintered rock that he is using to cut off the meat. They stand erect on their legs to free their hands for the tasks of feeding and survival. Man is emerging and you are privileged to behold his first tremulous steps away from the jungle. Fix this scene in your memory, it is a glorious one. And you will remember it better, Mandi-2, if you watch with your eyes open."

The older classes were usually much more enthusiastic. Only Agon-1 seemed to be watching with any degree of interest. Other than Grosbit-9 who was watching with too much interest indeed. Well, they said one good student in a class made it worthwhile, made one feel as though something were being accomplished.

"That is the end of today's lesson, but I'll tell you something about tomorrow's class." Africa vanished and some cold and rainswept northern land appeared. High mountains loomed through the mist in the background and a thin trickle of smoke rose from a low sod house half buried in the ground. "We will see how man emerged from his primate background, grew sure and grew strong. How these early people moved from the family group to the simple neolithic community. How they used tools and bent nature to their will. We are going to find out who lives in that house and what he does there. It is a lesson that I know you are all looking forward to."

There seemed very little actual evidence to back this assumption, and Teacher stabbed the button and the class was over. Their familiar classroom appeared around them and the dismissal bell was jingling its sweet music. Shouting loudly, without a backward look, they ran from the room and Teacher, suddenly tired, unclipped the controls from his waist and locked them into his desk. It had been a very long day. He turned out the lights and left.

At the street entrance he was just behind a young matron, most attractive and pink in miniaturized mini, hair a flaming red. Mandi-2's mother, he realized, he should have known by the hair, as she reached down to take an even tinier, pinker hand. They went out before him.

"And what did you learn in school today, darling," the mother asked. And, although he did not approve of eavesdropping, Teacher could not help but hear the question. Yes, what did you learn? It would be nice to know.

Mandi-2 skipped down the steps, bouncing with happiness to be free again.

"Oh, nothing much," she said, and they vanished around the corner.

Without knowing he did it, Teacher sighed a great weary sigh and turned in the other direction and went home.

How do you write an introduction to the scarcely sane adventures of *MICHAEL MOORCOCK's* quirky "modern myth figure" Jerry Cornelius? (That's two and a half lines, anyway) The Inner meaning of this story eludes me. (Very good, keep going) Suffice it to say that I enjoyed it, (don't ask me why) and that it appears to be about computers (very scientific) and that a lighthearted interlude at this stage provides a welcome change of pace. Except, I'm not really sure that it is so very lighthearted at all. . . .

## SEA WOLVES

### By Michael Moorcock

## YOUR COMPUTER NEEDS YOU

It occurs to us that while we've been saying "you need your computer" we'd also like to emphasize something equally important.

"Your computer needs you."

You see, without you your computer is nothing.

In fact it's people like yourself that have made the computer what it is today.

It's people like you that have made their computer do some pretty exciting things.

Like help them keep on top of sales trends.

Or design a bridge.

Or keep track of all the parts that go into a giant whirlybird.

To do things like that, your computer needs some help.

It needs you to get more involved with it. So you can use it to help you do more than just the payroll and the billing.

And it needs some terminals.

187

Terminals let you get information in and out of your computer fast.

They let you get up close to your computer.

Even though you might be miles away ...

But terminals are nothing unless something happens between you and your computer.

Unless you get involved with your computer.

You need your computer.

Your computer needs you.

KNOW YOUR BUSINESS.
KNOW YOUR COMPUTER.

IBM

## 1.

RUNNING, GRINNING, APING the movements of the mammals milling about him, Jerry Cornelius made tracks from the menagerie that was My Lai, the monster tourist attraction of the season, and threw his Kamov Ka-15 into the sky, flew over the tops of the tall hotels and novelty factories, away from there; away to the high privacy of Bangkok's Hotel Maxwell where, panting, he froze his limbs in the angles of sleep.

A posture, after all, was a posture.

## 2.

JERRY'S UNIFORM WAS that of the infamous Brigade of St. Basil. These Osaka-based White Cossack Mercenaries had recently changed from the Chinese to the American side; a half-hearted move; a compromise. But the uniform—cream, gold and fawn—overrode most other considerations.

Meanwhile revolutionary troops continued to march on the great automated factories of Angkor Wat and Anuradhapura. It would all be over by the Festival of Drakupolo.

A week passed. Jerry continued to sleep, his well-cut jacket and jodphurs uncrumpled, for he did not stir and his breathing was minimal, neither did he perspire. There was a complete absence of REMs.

### 3.

THE WAR ENDED with a complete victory for the factories. The defected revolutionaries made their way back to Simla and Ulan Bator. Jerry woke up and listened to the news on Radio Thai. He frowned.

A fine balance had to be maintained between man and machine, just as between man and man, man and woman, man and environment.

It was as good as it was bad.

Regretfully he stripped off his uniform. He was not sure he looked forward to civvy street.

### 4.

*THE GESTURES OF conflict keep the peace. The descendants of Tompion and Babbage toyed with inaccurate engines while their enemies entertained impossible debates concerning the notion that an electronic calculating device could not possess a 'soul.' The old arguments perpetuated themselves: resolved in the ancient formulae of warfare.*

### 5.

WHEN JERRY ARRIVED in Phnôm Penh the streets were full of bunting. Rickshaws, bicycles, cars and trams were hung with paper banners, streamers and posters. The Central Information Building shuddered with bright flame. The factories had won, but others were suffering for them. It was as it should be, thought Jerry.

Cheerfully he mounted an abandoned British-made "Royal Albert" black gent's roadster and pedalled along with the procession, avoiding the wreckage of cash-registers and adding machines that had been hurled from shops and offices that morning, heading for the suburbs where his bungalow housed a LEO VII cryogenic storage computer which he had, before the war, been programming on behalf of the monks at the new temple on Kas

Rong. But the anti-religious riots had not only been directed at the machines. The monastery had been hastily disbanded by the authorities in the hope that this measure would save the new research wing of the Hospital of the Secret Heart at Chanthaburi. It had not.

## 6.

JERRY ENTERED THE bungalow and shivered. The temperature was almost at zero. He pushed back the steel sliding doors of the inner room. The computer glistened under a thick coating of ice.

Was entropy setting in again?

Turning up the collar of his black car coat he inspected the power inputs. Something had overloaded LEO VII.

Jerry sniffed the sharp air. A problem of cardinal importance. He twitched his lips. Time to be moving.

He paused, studying the computer. It trembled under its sheathing of ice. He went to the wall and took his kid gloves from his pocket. He pulled them on, pressed the Destruct button, but it would not move. It was frozen solid.

Jerry reached inside his coat and brought out his needle gun. With the butt he hammered the button home.

He left the computer room. In the living room ice had formed traceries on the walls and windows, whorls and lines spelling out equations of dubious importance. A little bile came into his throat.

All the signs pointed West.

He went to the garage at the side of the bungalow, wheeled his big BMW 750cc hog onto the path, put it between his legs, kicked the starter and whisked wild and easy off down the concrete road towards the jungle.

Yellow sun.

Blue sky.

Green trees.

Monkeys screaming.

## 7.

Zut alors!
Maxim's in Paris

buys its fish
from a machine.

Part of the reason that fish at Maxim's is so fabulous is
because it's so fresh. Fresh from General Electric data-
processing equipment. When a French fisherman unloads
his catch at the port of Séte, a unique data-gathering and
display system takes over ...

Progress is our most important product
GENERAL ELECTRIC

8.

A LOUD SHRIEK.

9.

THE DNIEPER FLOWED slowly, its muddy waters
churned by the wind. On the brown land some snow
remained. The great sky was low and grey over the
steppe. A small wooden landing stage had moored to it a
carved fishing boat, its sail reefed.

On the landing stood three Cossacks. They had long
moustaches, smoked large pipes, wore big fur caps on the
sides of their shaven heads. Heavy burkas swathed their
burly bodies and they wore baggy trousers of blue or
green silk, boots of red or yellow morocco leather. There
were sabres at their sides, rifles on their backs. They
watched the horseman as he galloped nearer on his shaggy,
unshod pony.

The rider had bandoliers of cartridges crossing his
chest, an M-60 on his back. He wore the Red Army
uniform of the "Razin" 11th Don Cossack Cavalry and he
carried the horsehair standard of an ataman. He was
young, with long pale hair and sharp blue eyes. He drew
his horse to a skidding halt and saluted the three men
whose expressions remained set.

"Cossacks of the Zaporozhian Sech, greetings from your
brothers of the Don, the Yaik and the Kukan." He spoke

with a strong Ukrainian accent, driving the standard into the hard ground.

The nearest Zaporozhian reached down and picked up a sack that lay at his feet. "The Sech is no more," he said. "We and this is all that remains. The great horde came four days ago from the East." He upended the sack and emptied it.

Jerry dismounted and went to stare at the collection of small metal cogs, transistors and tapes.

"The krug is dead." Tears came to the leading Zaporozhian's hard, grey eyes. "The Khan rules. This is the end of our ancient freedom."

Jerry got back onto his horse and rode away. He left the horsehair standard waving in the wind. He left the Cossacks weeping. He left the bank of the muddy Dnieper and headed out across the steppe, riding South again, towards the Black Sea.

## 10.

### THE ANTHROPOMORPHIC VIEW:

> The Bug Slayer
> No computer stamps out program bugs like RCA's Octoputer. It boosts programming efficiency up to 40%.
>
> Programming is already one-third of computer costs, and going up faster than any other cost in the industry. A lot of that money is eaten up by bugs . . .

## 11.

HE WANDERED ALONG the grassy paths between the ancient ruins. Everywhere was litter. Broken tape-spools crunched beneath his boots, printouts snagged his feet; he was forced to make detours around buckled integrator cabinets. A few white-coated technicians tried to clean up the mess, haul the torn bodies away. They ignored Jerry, who went past them and hit the jungle once more. In his hand he held an ice-pick.

One of the technicians jerked his thumb as Jerry disappeared.

"Asesino . . ." he said.

Jerry was glad to be out of Villahermosa.

## 12.

HE WAS CLEANING his heat in his hut when the pale young man came in, shut the flimsy door and shuddered. Outside, the jungle stirred.

Jerry replaced rod, rag and oil in their case and carefully closed the lid.

The young man was dressed in a brown tropical suit with sweat-stains under arms and crotch. He had noticed the three weapons in the case: the needler, the heater, the vibragun. He crossed himself.

Jerry nodded and drew on his black leather Norfolk jacket. From the tops of his dark Fry boots he untucked his pink bell-bottomed Levis and smoothed them down with the tips of his fingers, watching the pale young man with amused, moody eyes.

An Aeroflot VC 10 began its approach to the nearby Mowming drome. The windows vibrated shrilly and then subsided.

"The sense of oneness known to the Ancients." The young man waved his hands vaguely in all directions. "At last it is within our grasp."

Jerry rubbed his nose with his case.

"I'm sorry, Mr Cornelius. I am, of course, Cyril Tome." A smile of apologetic patronage. "What a nightmare this world is. But the tide is turning . . ."

Jerry began vigorously to brush his fine blond hair, settling it on his shoulders. "I wasn't expecting you, Mr Tome."

"I left a message. In Kiev."

"I didn't get it."

"You mean you didn't receive it?"

"If you like."

"Mr Cornelius, I gathered from a mutual acquaintance that we were of a similar mind. 'Science is only a more sophisticated form of supersition'—didn't you say that?"

"I'm told so. Who was the acquaintance?"

"Malcolm." He raised his eyebrows. "Beesley? But don't you agree that in place of the old certainties, rooted in the supreme reality of existence, we have transferred our faith to science, the explanation for everything which explains nothing, the ever more fragmented picture of reality which becomes ever more unreal ..."

"How is Bishop Beesley?"

"Carrying on the fight as best he can. He is very tired."

"He is indeed."

"Then you don't agree ..."

"It's a question of attitude, Mr Tome." Jerry walked to the washstand and picking up a carton of Swedish milk poured out half a saucer for the half-grown black and white cat which now rubbed itself against his leathered leg. "Still, we don't need emotional rapport, you know, to do business."

"I'm not sure ..."

"Who is, Mr Tome?"

"I am sure ..."

"Naturally."

Tome began to pace about the floor of the hut. "These machines. They're inhuman. But so far only the fringes have been touched."

Jerry sat down on the bed again, opening his gun case. He began to fit the vibragun together, snapping the power unit into place.

Tome looked distastefully on. "I suppose one must fight fire with fire."

Jerry picked his teeth with his thumbnail, his brows furrowed. He did not look at Tome.

"What's the pattern?" he murmured, stroking the cat.

"Is there a pattern to anarchy?"

"The clearest of all, I'd have thought." Jerry slipped the vibragun into his shoulder holster. "In Leo VII all things are possible, after all."

"A machine is—"

"—a machine is a machine." Jerry smiled involuntarily.

"I don't understand you."

"That's what I was afraid of."

"Afraid?"

"Fear, Mr Tome. I think we might have to book you."

"But I thought you were on my side."

"Christ! Of course I am. And their side. And all the other sides. Of course I am!"

"But didn't you start the machine riots in Yokohama? When was I there?"

Tome burst into tears.

Jerry rubbed at his face in puzzlement.

"There's been a lot of that."

Tome made for the door. He had started to scream.

Some beastly instinct in Jerry responded to the movement and the sound. His vibragun was slipped from its holster and aimed at Tome as the pale young man fumbled with the catch.

Tome's teeth began to chatter.

He broke up.

All but insensate, Jerry fell back on the bed, his mad eyes staring at the ceiling.

Eventually they cooled.

Jerry left the hut and struck off through the jungle again. He had an overwhelming sense of *déjà vu*.

## 13.

### THE MECHANISTIC VIEW:

Horace is Hornblower's remarkable new computer system. And what he does with confirmations is a Hornblower exclusive ...

*Only Horace prints complete confirmations in Seconds*

## 14.

JERRY WAS LOST and depressed. Thanks to Tome, Beesley and their fellow spirits, a monstrous diffusion process was taking place.

He stumbled on through the jungle, followed at a safe distance by a cloud of red and blue macaws. They were calling out phrases he could not quite recognise. They seemed malevolent, triumphant.

A man dressed in the tropical kit of an Indian Army NCO emerged from behind a tree. His small eyes were almost as confused as Jerry's.

"Come along, sir. This way. I'll help."

For a moment Jerry prepared to follow the man, then he shook his head. "No thank you, Corporal Powell, I'll find my own way."

"It's too late for that, Mr Cornelius."

"Nonetheless . . ."

"This jungle's full of natives."

Jerry aimed a shot at the NCO, but the little man scuried into the forest and disappeared.

Several small furry mammals skittered out into the open, blinking red eyes in the direct sunlight. Their tiny thumbs were opposable. Jerry smiled down indulgently.

Around him the Mesozoic foilage whispered in the new, warm wind.

## 15.

HE HAD REACHED the sea.

He stood on the yellow shore and looked out over the flat, blue water. Irresolutely he stopped as his boots sank into the sand. The sea frightened him. He reached inside his coat and fingered the butt of his gun.

A white yacht was anchoring about a quarter of a mile away.

Soon he heard the sound of a motor-boat as it swept towards him through the surf.

He recognised the yacht as the *Teddy Bear*. It had had several owners, none of them particularly friendly. He turned to run, but he was too weak. He fell down. Seamen jumped from the boat and pulled him aboard.

"Don't worry, son," one of them said. "You'll soon be back in blighty."

"Poor bastard."

Jerry whimpered.

They'd be playing brag for his gear soon.

> *Because of the sins which ye have committed before God, ye shall be led away captives into Babylon by Nabuchodonosor king of the Babylonians.*
> (Baruch 6: 2)

He was feeling sorry for himself. He'd really blown this little scene.

## 16.

Need to improve customer service? Salesman

productivity? Here's your answer—
Computone's portable computer terminal, the
world's smartest briefcase. It weights only
8¾ pounds, and it costs as little as $20 per
month. Through a telephone in the prospect's
home or office, your salesman can communicate
directly with a computer, enter orders and
receive answers to inquiries within seconds.
The terminal converts your salesman into a
team of experts who bring to the point of
sale the vast memory of a computer and its
ability to solve problems immediately and
accurately.

*the company that put the computer in a briefcase*
COMPUTONE SYSTEMS INC.

## 17.

JERRY WAS DUMPED outside the Time Centre's Ladbroke Grove H.Q. He got up, found his front door, tried
to open it. The door was frozen solid. The Leo VII had
spread its cryogenic bounty throughout the citadel.

Jerry sighed and leaned against the brick wall. Above
his head someone had painted a new slogan in bright
orange paint:

### NO POPERY

There were only two people who could help him now
and neither was particularly sympathetic to him.

Was he being set up for something?

## 18.

HANS SMITH OF Hampstead, the Last of the Leftwing
Intellectuals, was having a party to which Jerry had not
been invited.

Because of his interest in the statistics of interracial
marriage in Vietnam in the period 1969/70, Hans Smith
had not heard about the war. There had been few signs of
it on Parliament Hill. Late one night he had seen a fat,

long-haired man in a tweed suit urinating against a tree. The man had turned, exposing himself to Smith, grinning and leering. There had also been some trouble with his Smith-Corona. But the incidents seemed unrelated.

Balding, bearded, pot-bellied and very careful, Hans Smith had codified and systemised his sex-life (marital, extra-marital and intermarital) to the point where most discomfort and enjoyment was excluded. His wife filed his love-letters and typed his replies for him and she kept his bedroom library of pornography and sex-manuals in strict alphabetical order. Instead of pleasure, Smith received what he called 'a healthy release.' The sexual act itself had been promoted into the same category as a successful operation for severe constipation. Disturbed by the Unpleasant, Smith belonged to a large number of insitutions devoted to its extinction. He lived a smooth existence.

Jerry opened the front door with one of the keys from his kit and walked up the stairs. Somewhere The Chants were singing *Progress*.

He was late for the party. Most of the remaining guests had joined their liberal hosts in the bedroom, but Smith, dressed in a red and gold kimono that did much to emphasise the pale obscenity of his body, came to the door at his knock, a vibro-massager clutched in one thin hand. He recognised Jerry and made a Church Army smile through his frown.

"I'm sorry, bah, but . . ."

But Jerry's business was urgent and it was with another guest.

"Could I have a word with Bishop Beesley, do you think?"

"I'm not sure he's . . ."

Jerry drew out his heater.

"There's no need to be boorish." Smith backed into the bedroom. Unseen middle-aged flesh made strange, dry sounds. "Bishop. Someone to see you . . ." He fingered his goatee.

Mrs Hans Smith's wail: "Oh, no, Hans. Tell them to fiddle off."

Smith made another of his practised smiles. "It's Cornelius, kitten."

"You said you'd never invite—"

"I didn't, lovie . . ."

Jerry didn't want to look inside, but he moved a step nearer. "Hurry up, bishop."

Naked but for his gaiters and mitre, the gross white form of Bishop Beesley appeared behind Hans Smith. "What is it?"

"A religious matter, bishop."

"Ah, in that case." The bishop bundled up his clothes and stepped out. "Well, Mr Cornelius?"

"It's the LEO VII cryogenics. They seem to be trying to convert. I can't make it out. They're freezing up."

"Good God! I'll come at once. A clearing needed, eh? An exorcism?"

Jerry's hunch had been a good one. The bishop had been expecting him. "You'd know better than I, bishop."

"Yes, yes." Beesley gave Jerry's shoulder a friendly pat.

"Well, the shit's certainly hit the fan," said Jerry. He winked at Smith as he left.

"I'm very glad you called me in, dear boy." Bishop Beesley hopped into his trousers, licking his lips. "Better late than never, eh?"

Jerry shivered.

"It's your baby now, bishop."

He had another old friend to look up.


19.


"ONE DOWN, EIGHT letters, *To Lucasta, faithful unto death* . . ." Jerry shrugged and put the newspaper aside. They had arrived. He tapped the pilot on the shoulder. "Let's descend, Byron."

As the cumbersome Sikorski shuddered towards the ground, Jerry had an excellent view of the ruins on the headland. All that remained of the castle was grass-grown walls a foot or two high, resembling, from this perspective, a simplified circuit marked out in stones—a message to an extraterran astronomer. The archeologists had been at work again in Tintagel.

Beyond the headland the jade sea boomed, washing the ebony beach. The Sikorski hovered over the ocean for a moment before sweeping backwards and coming to rest near Site B, the Monastery.

Dressed in his wire-rimmed Diane Logan black corduroy hat, a heavy brown Dannimac cord coat, dark orange trousers from Ital, Portugal, and near-black Fry boots, Jerry jumped from the Sikorski and walked across the lawn to sit on a wall and watch the helicopter take off again. He unbuttoned his coat to reveal his yellow Sachs cord shirt and the Lynn Stuart yellow and black sash he wore in place of a tie. He was feeling light in his gear but he was still bothered.

In the hot winter sunshine, he pranced along the footpath that led to the Computer Research Institute—a series of geodesic domes stained in bright colours.

"A meaning is a meaning," he sang, "is a meaning is a meaning."

He was not altogether himself, these days.

Outside the gates he grinned inanely at the guard and displayed his pass. He was waved through.

The Institute was a private establishment. The red moving pavement took him to the main admin building and the chrome doors opened to admit him. He stood in the white-tiled lobby.

"Mr Cornelius!"

From a blue door marked DIRECTOR came Miss Brunner, her auburn hair drawn back in a bun, her stiff body clothed in a St. Laurent tweed suit. She stretched her long fingers at him. He grasped them.

"And what's your interest in our little establishment, Mr C?" Now she led him into her cool office. "Thinking of giving us a hand?" She studied a tank of small carp.

"I'm not sure I know the exact nature of your research." Jerry glanced around at all the overfilled ashtrays.

She shrugged. "The usual thing. This and that. We're checking analogies at present—mainly forebrain functions. Amazing how similar the human brain is to our more complex machines. They can teach us a lot about people. The little buggers."

He looked at the graphs and charts on her walls. "I see what you mean." He rubbed a weary eye and winced. He had a sty there.

"It's all very precise," she said.

"Get away."

Jerry sighed. Didn't they know there was a war on?

## 20.

"SWEET YOUNG STUFF," said Miss Brunner. "Tender. Only the best goes into our machines."

Jerry looked at the conveyor, at the aluminium dishes on the belt, at the brains in the dishes.

"They feel nothing," she said, "it's all done by electronics these days."

Jerry watched the battery brains slipping like oysters into the gullets of the storage registers.

"You will try it, won't you?"

"It works both ways," she said defensively.

"I bet it does."

Miss Brunner smiled affectionately. "It's beautifully integrated. Everything automatic. Even the pentagrams are powered."

"This isn't religion," said Jerry, "it's bloody sorcery!"

"I never claimed to be perfect, Mr Cornelius. Besides, compared with my methods the narrow processes of the orthodox . . ."

"You've been driving the whole bloody system crazy, you silly bitch! You and that bastard Beesley. I thought there were only two polarities. And all the while . . ."

"You've been having a bad time, have you? You bloody puritans . . ."

Jerry pursed his lips. She knew how to reach him.

## 21.

WHEN HE GOT back to Ladbroke Grove he found the door open. It was freezing inside.

"Bishop Beesley?" His voice echoed through the dark passages.

The cold reached his bones.

"Bishop?"

Time was speeding. Perhaps his counter-attack had failed.

He found Beesley in the library. The bishop had never got to the computer. His round, flabby face peered sadly out of the block of ice encasing him. Jerry drew his heater and thawed him out.

Beesley grunted and sat down. "I suppose it was a joke. Doubtful taste . . ."

"Sorry you were bothered, bishop . . ."

"Is that all . . . ?"

"Yes. I must admit I was desperate, but that's over now, for what it was worth."

"You treacherous little oik. I thought you had made a genuine repentance."

Jerry had been triggered off again. His eyes were glowing a deep red now and his lips were curled back over his sharp teeth. His body radiated such heat that the air steamed around it. He waved his gun.

"Shall we press on into the computer room?"

Beesley grumbled but stumbled ahead until they stood before the iced-up Leo VII.

"What point is there in my presence here," Beesley chattered, "when your claims—or its—were plainly insincere?"

"The logic's changed." Jerry's nostrils widened. "We're having a sacrifice instead."

Jerry thought he smelled damp autumn leaves on the air.

He snarled and chuckled and forced the bishop towards the appropriate input.

"Sacrilege!" howled Beesley.

"Sacrosanct!" sniggered Jerry.

Then, with his Fry boot, he kicked Beesley's bottom.

The clergyman yelled, gurgled and disappeared into the machine.

There was a sucking sound, a purr, and almost immediately the ice began to melt.

"It's the price we pay for progress," said Jerry. "Your attitudes, bishop, not mine, created the situation, after all."

The computer rumbled and began a short printout. Jerry tore it off.

A single word:

TASTY.

## 22.

LIKE IT OR NOT, the Brunner programme had set the tone to the situation, but at least it meant things would calm down for a bit . . . Time to work on a fresh equation. These alchemical notions were, he would admit, very

*commonplace. The pattern had been begun years before
by describing machines in terms of human desires and
activities, by describing human behaviour in terms of
machines. Now the price of that particular logic escalation
was being paid. Beesley had paid it. The sweet young stuff
was paying it. The mystical view of science had declined
from vague superstition into positive necromancy. The
sole purpose of the machines was confined to the raising
of dead spirits. The polarities had been the Anthropomorphic View and the Mechanistic View. Now they had
merged, producing something even more sinister: the Path-
ological View.*

*A machine is a machine is a machine ... But that was
no longer the case. A machine was anything the neurotic
imagination desired it to be.*

*At last the computer had superceded the automobile as
the focus for mankind's hopes and fears. It was the death
of ancient freedoms.*

## 23.

IT WAS RAINING as Jerry picked his way over the
Belgrade bomb-sites followed by crowds of crippled children and the soft, pleading voices of the eleven- and
twelve-year-old prostitutes of both sexes.

His clothes were stained and faded. Behind him were
the remains of the crashed Sikorski which had run out of
fuel.

On foot he made for Dubrovnik, though a world ruled
by bad poets who spoke the rhetoric of tabloid apocrypha
and schemed for the fruition of a dozen seedy apoc-
alypses.

At Dubrovnik the corpse-boats were being loaded up.
Fuel for the automated factories of Anuradhapura and
Angkor Wat. On one of them, if he was lucky, he might
obtain a passage East.

Meanwhile machines grew skeletons and were fed with
blood and men adopted metal limbs and plastic organs. A
synthesis he found unwelcome.

## 24.

OUT OF THE WEST fled Jerry Cornelius, away from

Miss Brunner's morbid Eden, away from warm steel and cool flesh, on a tanker crammed with the dead, to Bombay and from there to the interior, to rest, to wait, to draw breath, to pray for new strength and the resurrection of the Antichrist.

A posture, after all, was a posture.

> You won't make an important decision
> in the 70s without it
> Your own personal desk-top computer
> terminal

Remember the 1970s are just around the corner. A call to Mr. A.A. Barnett, Vice President—Marketing, Bunker-Ramo, could be your most important decision for the new decade.

(All ad quotes from *BUSINESS WEEK* December 6, 1969)

This is *ANDREW TRAVERS'* first science fiction story—
a cyclical hallucination of imprisonment, torture, escape
and recapture. Each episode is both reality and illusion.
Like a dreamer who slides from one nightmare to the
next, the protagonist cannot distinguish the two.

If our society is sick then those who adjust to it are also
sick. Perhaps this is what it looks like to a madman who is
still sane.

## THE PENULTIMATE TRIP

### By Andrew Travers

I DID NOT dare touch the chain-link fence even though it
was rusty and probably not electrified. It was three times
my height and the concrete posts were bent at the top
where the chain-link finished and the barbed-wire began. I
looked up at the barbed-wire above and saw a rocket
penetrate the cloud, its orange and red flame for a split-
second breaking the continuous grey of the sky like a spot
of blood on the ceiling of a cell fading as you looked at it.
I walked along the fence to find a gap or a gate. As I
walked, looking through the fence at the towers beyond,
my left foot trod on unsafe ground and I fell with my legs
down a hole. I sat up on the hole's edge and pulled away
the twigs and the dead leaves which had covered it. A
tubular shaft ran straight down into the ground. A steel
ladder was screwed to its side. There was enough room
for one man to pass up or down. I could not see the
bottom. Perhaps down there was a tunnel leading under
the fence. I climbed down feeling for each new rung with
my feet. After fifty rungs I was at the bottom. The sky

was like a luminous eye without a pupil, it could not look at me. The tunnel ran under the fence, I could walk upright in it. I walked with my hands in front of me, the ground was level and smooth to my bare feet. I walked for about five minutes without seeing an opening above me. Then ahead I saw a faint light that must have come from a shaft similar to the one I had descended, similarly covered in twigs and leaves. I was within reach of it when the ground stopped, and I was falling. I fell into water. The water was flowing fast, I swam desperately back to the faint light of the shaft, but it disappeared as the current swept me round a curve in this new tunnel. The ceiling of the tunnel was getting lower and lower, it seemed impossible that it would not soon be level with the surface of the water. Then my head received a painful blow, and another, and another, before I lost consciousness. I woke up in my cell to commence the seven hundred and third day of my sentence. The gaoler had been slapping my head.

He closed the cell door behind him, it was the same colour as the walls and floor and ceiling—grey. I got out of bed. I lay on the floor with my feet against the door wall. Then the cell rotated so that I now stood upright on the door wall, which had become the floor, with my back to the floor which had become the wall. I lay on the new floor with my feet to the wall which had been the ceiling. The cell rotated a second time so that I now stood on what originally had been the ceiling. The bed, securely screwed down, was above me. The door, which extended from floor to ceiling was now in the wall opposite to where it had originally been. It opened and a Friend came in. 'I see you're out of bed,' he said, as he always said. I no longer replied. 'Let's go,' he said, and I followed him through the door, down a corridor lined with similar doors to mine—but they were closed. We entered a lift. The door snapped shut. Many prisoners had tried to end their lives by timing a backwards jump to coincide with a Friend pressing the button to close the lift door, hoping the door would chop them in half. I had tried it. The door always stopped just short of any obstruction. My Friend pressed another button and we ascended. The lift stopped, the door opened, and I followed my Friend along another corridor and into a cell off it. This cell was identical to my own, except that there was no bed, and it was coloured blue instead of grey. I sat on the floor, tired from the exertion of walking two corridors. My Friend left and closed the door behind him. The cell began to vibrate. I stood up. The vibrations increased. The vibrations threw me into the air so that when I landed I was thrown up again, continuously. It was no use lying down or sitting, then all of my body would have been bruised. The lurching began. Now every time I was thrown up it was at an angle so that I inevitably landed on all fours and had to struggle to my feet against the vibrating and lurching, usually being thrown up again before having had time to stand. Inevitably there came a time when I had no more energy to expend on trying to stand, so that I was hurled about the cell. The vibrations and lurchings were so calculated that it was impossible to break a bone or dislocate a limb. One became bruised all over. The cell stopped moving. I lay limply on the floor. A Friend came in. He kicked me in the head. I woke up in a crater. Pink, blue and yellow moons of different sizes and in different positions were travelling through the blackness. They gave the crater strange shifting colours. I got up and ran at enormous speed because of the low gravity towards the crater rim. My eight legs left tracks in the dust behind.

The worst thing about being a spider was that one often frightened and killed those fellow prisoners who had been turned into flies. But there were other creatures you could be turned into. Being a worm was worst. Some days we were all of the same species, other days we were every kind of animal, bird, or insect—then we hunted each other and were hunted by each other as if we had been on earth. But that was when we were together. Often you would be on your own. I had climbed the crater rim to see if this was so today. I was alone. The colours were shifting disturbingly, a shadow fell over me. There was something between me and the yellow moon. I turned, it was a Friend, I ran, but he was faster. He trod on me. I woke up in the grey cell on my bed. My bruises had gone. A man came in. 'Where am I?' I asked. 'How did you get in?' he asked. I remembered a high fence topped with barbed wire and a rocket disappearing into cloud. 'Through the sewers,' I answered his question. 'Am I in a tower?' I asked. 'Yes,' he said. He asked me to tell him what dreams I had had, but as I recounted them I felt that he had heard it all before. When I finished he told me he would give me a sleeping pill as I needed rest. I swallowed it and quickly fell asleep.

I dreamed I was wandering the streets of a very old city on earth. There were men shouting in a language I could not understand, at the crowd that I was one of, which was shuffling past their stalls. One stall was heaped with oranges, apples, pears, bananas and other fruits. I had never seen these fruits before and did not know whether I was inventing their names or whether those were their real names which had mysteriously come into my mind. Another stall displayed fish on marble. Some horrible butchery had been done to some of the fish—these were slit from head to tail and had had their insides removed, others lay in heaps at all angles and had clearly been dead for some time. Occasionally a man or a woman detached from the crowd and offered coins to the men behind the stalls who in exchange gave the man or woman varying quantities of the goods they were selling, the amount being related to the number of coins received. I dimly remembered that there had been such a system for the distribution of goods but I was amazed by the rigidity with which it was kept to. I looked about to see if there was anybody behaving differently from the rest. A child by a fruit stall furtively slipped an orange under his coat. I was dismayed to see how guilty he looked, how afraid he was of being caught, and the elaborate measures he had taken to remain undetected. He seemed to be as much a victim as the others. He saw that I had seen him and paused as if waiting for me to shout something. When he realised I was not going to shout he ran into the crowd. Without knowing why and without being able to stop myself I shouted, 'Stop thief!' using the same language that I had not previously understood. A woman carrying a heavy basket saw that I was pointing at the disappearing child and took up my cry, plunging after the child into the crowd. Immediately several others were alerted and a chorus of 'Stop thief!' was taken up. The boy was captured by a man in a butcher's apron which was stained with the blood of slaughtered animals. A crowd gathered round the butcher who was twisting the boy's arm, the boy cried and the orange fell to the ground. As the orange rolled to a stop the crowed roared insults at him. These are a primitive people, I thought. A man in a dark blue uniform with a conical helmet on his head made his way through the crowd and took over the custody of the boy from the butcher. A cheer went up. 'I hope they lock him up,' 'He ought to be birched,' were two of the phrases I overheard. All this was hard to understand. Earlier I had noticed that the poorer the people were dressed the less the number of coins they possessed, and consequently the fewer the goods they were able to purchase, and yet it was these very people who were most vociferously in favour of further hurting the boy. But something more worrying had happened to me. I was now able to understand the language, and had already spoken it. And it was I who had caused the boy's suffering. Somehow the crowd had coerced me into behaving as it did. I was hungry. Automatically I reached into the right hand pocket of a pair of antiquated trousers that I was wearing. I pulled out a collection of coins and wondered if they were sufficient for a meal, and I wondered what kind of food would be given to me. I was afraid that I would have to eat dead meat and vegetables that had grown in animals' waste. My stomach was not used to this kind of meal.

I entered a restaurant and seemed to know exactly what to do. I sat at a table, read a menu, and ordered what I wanted to eat from a waiter. Presently he placed a plate of chips in front of me. I ate the chips and payed and left the restaurant. I walked from the centre of the city into its quieter suburbs. I went up to one house in a street of identical houses. I took a key from my pocket to let myself into a room. It was like a museum. An object which I recognised as a record-player stood in one corner of the room, and in the other corner was a TV. They were both apparently in good working order. Someone knocked on the door. It took me some time to realise that it was not another prisoner but someone who wanted to enter. I let him and he greeted me effusively as if I was a friend he had not seen for years.

Because of his way of greeting me I asked him to sit down and offered to make him a cup of coffee. He was looking at me with a puzzled expression. 'What's wrong?' I asked. Then he asked me, 'Just how long were you inside?' 'Inside what?' I asked. 'In jail, you only got out this morning.' So that was where I had been, but I didn't remember it at all. He asked me what was the first thing I had done on coming out. Without knowing what I meant I said, 'I got stoned.' Then, suddenly trusting him, I explained what I had experienced. He offered me a sugar cube, and when I looked at it doubtfully, thinking that this might have been some kind of a joke, he said, 'Acid.' I swallowed it. He also swallowed his cube. As I returned to my normal state I said to him, 'We are the people of the future.' He laughed. We decided to go to the graveyard as it always made us feel more alive.

He was talking, and I followed what he was saying with increasing difficulty. I began to feel I did not know him. His clothes were strange, his language was strange, his face seemed only a little evolved from the face of a monkey. Was I like that to him, I asked myself. Where was I anyway?

I supposed I was waking up in the grey cell because although the stones of the graveyard and the distant houses and factories were still vividly present I was also conscious that where I really was was in the grey cell. One end of the graveyard was bordered by a high fence topped with barbed-wire. I walked towards it and saw beyond the high towers of the flats where slum dwellers had been rehoused, the fence was there to keep thieves out during the building of the towers when expensive building materials and equipment had been stored on the site. It was a grey day. I looked up and was convinced I had seen an orange and red flame disappearing into the cloud. Perhaps it had been the sun through a brief break in the cloud. If I could only climb to the top of one of the towers I might be able to see the sun, because those towers in the distance, in the slight mist that was forming as dusk preceded night, seemed to penetrate the cloud and be rising higher and higher, into the darkening sky.

I did not dare touch the chain-link fence. I walked along it to find a way through to the towers. Then I fell. A stone cross swept across my field of vision, the towers assumed a horizontal angle before they disappeared. I was in an empty grave. Or I had been in my cell and had failed to prepare for the morning ritual of its rotation. Somebody was shouting, 'Jesus Christ.' It was me. But the voice seemed to come out of the darkness I was surrounded by. There was far less light than I would have expected from the grave's opening, the opening was a long way above me. I had to get out. I groped round and was surprised at the size of the grave and the smoothness of the walls. I was panicked by the thought that I would never get out, so I screamed. A nurse came in and injected me. I let her do it without resisting. I was lying in a bed. A doctor was leaning over me. 'How do you feel?' he asked. 'I don't know where I am.' 'What do you mean?'

I passed the next two weeks in a locked ward. Every attempt was made to persuade me that that was where I was. But for every second of that two weeks I was filled with the fear of being transported to the grey cell or transformed into one of the creatures on the dead planet. Equally strong was the fear of being returned to the nightmare street where I had ruined a child's life. But nevertheless I was surrounded by beauty. A glass of orange juice stood on the formica-topped bedside table. The glass reflected and refracted the light from the bulb in the centre of the room with a sharpness and precision which hurt if I looked at it too long. The orange liquid rested quite motionless in the glass, disturbed on its surface only by the movement of a doctor or a nurse or a mobile patient outside my room. It seemed so intensely orange that I felt that it must at any moment expand to fill its glass to its brim, and overflow onto the table and onto the floor, to eventually rise like water filling a tank until I was completely submerged in orangeness. I wanted to live in an atmosphere of pure orange. I wanted to swim forever in an orange fluid, breathing it as naturally as air. I was sure it would be warm and would hold me in a weightless state and that in it I would have no sensation of touch. My eyes would see nothing but pure orange. Sometimes I felt that it had already happened. After a fortnight I woke in the orange room. Gone was the warmth and weightlessness. I was so heavy that lying as I was my back ached under the weight of my flesh. The orange that had enveloped me had retreated to leave me in a cube of emptiness. There was no furniture or any object except myself. There was no padding. There was not even a door. Perhaps I would spend the rest of my life in this room. Perhaps I was no longer in human form. I looked at myself. My body was all there—two legs, two arms, a torso, and though I could not see it I could be certain my head was on my torso by feeling for its shape with my two hands. My clothes had been removed.

Some time elapsed. I did not eat or sleep as I never became hungry or tired. I wondered if anyone knew I was there. Finally I decided that everybody lived as I lived. Then I doubted that there was anyone else. I was the only man alive. I might be in the custody of alien beings. I might have been in that room thirty years or a year or only a week or a day. I lost my sense of time. Gradually I deteriorated. I began to look back with nostalgia to the periods I had spent in the grey and blue cells. I was still afraid of being transformed into one of the creatures on the dead planet. I was more afraid of the nightmare street. More time must have passed. I lost all my fears. At intervals I actually wanted to be back in the nightmare street. Then a new fear invaded me. The fear of remaining in the orange room. There had to be a way out. The way out was to wish all the time with all my being that I was back in the nightmare street. Whoever had put me where I was had put me there because I had so hated the street, what they wanted was for me to love it. But though I tried it did not get me out. Later on I was to regret leaving the orange room, I came to feel that if only I had stayed there a little longer I would have found the reason for my incarceration. But before I could stop it happening to me I was walking through a wood.

The whistling and cooing of birds indicated their presence in the branches of the trees around me. The path I trod was grass. Bluebells were in clusters by the sides of the path. The sun through the branches set up a tracery of shadows which made me feel I was walking invisibly through a randomised system of prison bars. A squirrel ran up a tree and stopped and looked at me. I wanted to tell it I meant no harm, but it was off again as free as I was. The air was rich with the smell of wood, earth, grass, flowers and rain. There was nowhere I could look, there was no single thing, however minute, that I could focus on, there was no sensation in my body which did not tell me that everything here was alive. I was alive. I laughed aloud. It was the first laughter I had heard for years. I must have been on the planet Earth before its evacuation. The wood stopped. I walked across a field, the grass of the field gave way to cinder and dust. But I walked on. After an hour I wanted to go back. The sun was now covered with grey cloud, the cinder and dust stretched ahead all the way to the horizon. But I had walked so far into the cinder that I thought it better to go on than go back. In a daze I marched ahead. I stopped looking into the distance

and watched only where my feet would tread next.
Abruptly a chain-link fence blocked my path. I looked up
and saw that it was topped with barbed-wire. Beyond the
barbed-wire was the orange and red flame of a rocket
disappearing into the grey cloud. It must have been the
rocket which had transported me here. I was not on Earth
in the time before its evacuation, this was Earth now. The
prison planet. The orange room had been a delusion. I
must have been in the rear compartment of the rocket by
the transparent windows which always reflected the colour
of the rocket's flame into those compartments. The feeling
of being in a room was generated by traveling faster than
light. Prisoners were never given the usual anaesthetic for
a journey. It was part of their punishment, a deterrent for
any who might be ingenious enough to stowaway on a
returning rocket. The rocket disappeared and I woke up in
the grey cell. It was the seven hundred and third day of
my captivity. The gaoler had woken me up and was
closing the door behind him. I got out of bed, I lay on the
floor with my feet braced against the wall. The cell rotated through ninety degrees and I was standing. I lay on
the new floor with my feet braced against what had been
the ceiling and the cell rotated through a further ninety
degrees. Resignedly I waited for a Friend to enter, and
wondered what it was to be today—the blue room, the
orange room, the nightmare street, the locked ward, the
dead planet, the prison planet—it was possible there was a
new experience in store for me. I became more apprehensive than usual because I had the time to think of what lay
ahead. The Friend was late. It could be a day when I was
to be left in my cell—this was always disappointing and
gratifying, disappointing because such a day did not count
towards one's sentence and gratifying because it gave one
time to gather a little strength. The Friend came in,
smiling. 'You are to be released,' he said. I did not believe
him. He led me out of the cell, down the corridor and into
the lift where he pressed the button to close the door and
pressed another which for the first time took us down
instead of up. He led me out of the lift and along another
corridor to a large glass door. 'Go on,' he said, pointing at
it. Not daring to disobey I walked straight at the glass
door which swung open for me. I knew what was going to
happen, I was going to be shot· dead as soon as I got
outside, 'Killed while attempting to escape.' I was glad.

Outside nothing happened, so I walked on, obligingly slowly to make an easy target. I walked about a hundred yards feeling very calm, beneath my feet the cinder crunched. Then I was machine-gunned to death. I went to hell. It was a room with a record-player in one corner and a TV in another. What was most agonising was that although I was dead I could still feel the bullets penetrating my flesh, and was subject to a violent vibration through my whole body when each separate bullet hit me, it was like being in a blue room when the floor is being simultaneously vibrated and lurched. I was on all fours constantly falling and getting up, being thrown about at every angle. The room disappeared.

Now I knew what was causing the terrible pricks around my body—I was a fly in a spider's web being hugged to death by a starving spider in a giant web on the dead planet. The more I struggled the worse the pains. The spider bit my head from my body. I passed out like someone in a tunnel drifting in fast flowing water away from the faint light of his consciousness, and all the while the tunnel's roof got lower and lower until it met the surface of the water and I was swimming. I was swimming in orange juice. The nurse came in and woke me out of my trance. The orange flowed back and diminished into the tiny volume a small glass holds. The glass of orange juice was standing on a formica-topped table next to the bed I was in. The nurse gave me an injection. I did not resist.

I was walking along a chain-link fence which was topped with barbed-wire. I did not dare touch it because it was electrified. But a despair overcame me. I wanted to die. I touched the fence. Incredibly, the whole fence, which was at least three times my height and stretched into the distance at either side of me as far as I could see, toppled over. I ran towards the towers. They had seemed so far away, but I was on them in a few yards. Some optical trick had made them seem distant and tall when they were scarcely bigger than me. I touched one, it fell over. I touched another, it fell over. I touched them all, and they all fell over. 'Very good,' said my teacher, 'you scored above average.' That meant I would have more soil. The teacher wriggled back to his cell and I wriggled back to my learning cubicle, happy not to be a human being, to be so frightened of the sensations of one's body and the thoughts in one's brain, to be a victim of your own and others' manipulation of those. I wriggled into a comfortable coiled position and admired my glistening cylindrical body, and the wonderful fresh pinkness of it. It was chilly so I half buried myself in the soil and resumed my education. A worm's education is simple compared to that of other species. He merely spends the first days of his life chewing through the text books which were bequeathed by the humans on their extinction from the universe. When a worm has learnt enough he is chopped in half, and the two separate halves begin to specialise. Then they are chopped in half, and so on, until the worm species can boast a specialist in every human subject. There was much argument among our economists about what would happen when we had consumed all the books. The specialists would be dying, and even the chopping of the specialists would only result in a steady dilution of the knowledge to the point where the species would be as ignorant as it had been in the first place. We were not capable of printing our own books and were consuming at too fast a pace. Hope was placed in the belief that the humans had discovered a way to prolong life indefinitely. If we could discover this we were saved. But nobody could explain why if they had been able to become immortal they had become extinct. At the present state of our development we had no specialist in this subject, but we felt we could win the race between the declining stock of books and the advancing knowledge of immortalising. My test had been connected to this. I had passed by recognising the towers more slowly than was usual. It was hoped that eventually a worm could stand the human experiences he was subject to in the test for longer and longer periods before he succumbed to the despair which finally caused the worm to commit suicide by touching the electrified fence. I took it all very seriously. I was a young worm. I wanted to be the father, grandfather or ancestor of the discoverer of the secret of immortality. But some young worms rejected their teachers and regressed back to eating through soil. They said it was a much more pleasant way of passing the time, and talked about their identity, how it ought not to be destroyed by being chopped in half, and in half again, and so on. There was also a theory current among these dropout worms that our world was one of many, that it was an accident that we were all inside an enormous library. But I did not have the time to think about these things as I had to complete my education successfully.

The day came when I had learnt enough. I was taken to the chopping room. As the blade cut into my body I experienced a human feeling. I thought that if I was chopped in half then I could never be a father, because once chopped in half I would be my children. What had kept me going through the books was the pride I hoped I might one day take in being the ancestor of a famous worm, of the worm who saved our species, now I knew I could never be that. I had not had time to work it out before because I had been so busy studying. The human feeling that accompanied this thought was fear. As the blade cut further into my body I actually felt that I was a human being. Quite clearly I saw arclights above me and the masked faces of surgeons, one of whom was drawing a glinting steel scalpel across my abdomen. I screamed. I was sure I screamed but could not explain how I did it—worms did not have voices. A nurse said, 'Prisoners don't get anaesthetics.' I had become a human on an operating table, I was in intense pain from the surgeon's rubber-gloved fingers probing inside my pinned back stomach. What was he looking for? He cut something out of me. It was half a kidney. 'That's mine!' I shouted. 'Not now it isn't,' he said, 'count yourself lucky we didn't need your heart.' I passed out overcome with pain and shock. I woke in a bed with a doctor leaning over me. I was still a human being. Then it occurred to me that I had not been taken to the chopping room but was in fact undergoing another test. 'How do you feel?' asked the doctor. 'I have never felt more like a worm in my life,' I said, thinking gleefully of the surprise this would cause my teacher, he would certainly be astonished to hear that I knew the situation I was in was only a test, when the test had been so designed to make the subject really believe he was in the situations he was put in. 'Let me go to the towers,' I asked the doctor. I must have been feverish. It did not come to me until the doctor had left the room that there was no point in asking him, because *he* knew nothing about the towers.

When I had recovered from my operation I was taken back to the grey cell. So much had happened to me since I had been metamorphosed into human form that I found it increasingly difficult to remember what it had been like to be a worm. I was not prepared to prefer being a human serving a sentence in the grey cell, subject to periodic trips to the blue cell, the orange cell, the dead planet, the nightmare street and the prison planet, and probably liable to worse trips in the future. But my life as a worm had been boring. Studying had been boring. I regretted that I had not made the best of it by living with the dropouts in the soil. I had only come to be where I was by thinking that I was going to the chopping room. But what those other worms had missed was this curious change into a human, the moments, which as more time passed extended into hours at a time, when you actually believed you were a human. A fundamental alteration in my attitude took place when I was sent to the dead planet as a worm. For the first few seconds I rejoiced. I wriggled and stretched and burrowed into the dust the planet's surface was covered in. But immediately I came upon hard rock. And the dust hurt my tender body. I became angry that I had no legs. I just wanted to get up and run. The flapping of wings above cast shadows over me. Terrified I wriggled for the cover of a stone. Now I understood why the other prisoners thought that being a worm was worst. A beak swallowed one end of my body, and then the rest of me. I remained conscious until the last millimetre of my body had been chewed in the bird's beak. Back in the grey room I became completely disillusioned with my species and its fatuous desire for an immortality it would never possess. More than anything else I wanted to stay human, even in this place. I remembered the mad idea I used to have that I was only taking a test. If that was true, and how I wanted it to be false, I could avoid being turned back into a worm by not committing suicide. Whatever else I did, if ever again I was to confront the wire fence I must not touch it. This resolution, once made, consoled me. I began to forget that I was a worm. But I did not forget that I must not touch the fence. One day I would be released. I was curious to know where I would be allowed to go, about the life I would lead, even though I would have the stigma of being an ex-prisoner. I made plans for the future. I completely forgot I was a worm. I came to the conclusion that I was in prison for stealing something from behind the fence. But unfortunately the human I had been did not seem to possess a past. I could not remember what I had stolen or why I had stolen it. I could only remember the fence, and that in some way I had got through it. But I knew I had done wrong. I knew I had to be punished. I knew I had to repay my debt to society. Just saying that phrase 'Repay my debt to society' made me feel that though I was an outcast I too had a function to fulfil in human society. Honest citizens needed me to remind them of how honest they were. I was being useful by undergoing my punishment. I and my kind created jobs for the Friends, and it was because of us that the building had been constructed—that must have brought work to many. Stupid reflections. Nobody knew we were here. Nor did they care. Afterwards when we were released we would be forbidden to mention the place or the punishment. We were the living dead. We had no past. We were not humans. We had all been worms. I was a worm.

I became stoical. I would do my time and keep out of trouble. On the seven hundred and third day of my sentence I woke with no memory of how many more days I had yet to serve. It could have been another year or another thirty years. It could have been for the rest of my life. The gaoler left the cell. The cell was rotated as usual. A Friend came in. We went by the lift to the blue cell. For the first time it did not vibrate or lurch. Deprived of the activity of trying to protect myself from the cell's movements I was forced to think. Thinking in a new room created new thoughts. What if the room was vibrating and lurching and I had not noticed it? Was I so hallucinated that this could be true? In anger I leapt about the cell bashing myself as hard as I could on the walls and floor. I hoped they could see me and would put an end to my doubts about my sanity by starting the motors which moved the cell. Nothing happened. Days passed. I became hungry and tired and afraid. I slipped into a kind of reverie. The definition of the lines between the walls and ceiling and walls and floor faded. I was surrounded by blueness. I was breathing the blue though my mouth and nose and through the pores in my skin. I was turning blue. The blue got darker. Eventually it turned to black. I could see nothing, not even my own form. I decided I had gone blind. But I could hear nothing, even when I shouted as loudly as I could I heard nothing. I was scared that I had lost my voice. If I had lost my voice I was turning back into a worm. But I had not touched the fence. All my deductions about the fence must have been wrong. I wished I would disappear. I felt my body with my hands but received no sensations of touch or hardness. I could not feel my hands. I was deprived of all my senses. They can't hurt me now, I thought. I stayed like that for a long time, hoping that the next thing to stop would be my thoughts.

A blinding flash went off in my eyes. I shut them but a bright pinkness still got through the eyelids and pupils to my retinas. It faded into a dark red, and then into black. I opened my eyes. A tiny star was directly above me in a black sky. Either it had just been created there or my eyes, so unused to seeing anything, had been hurt by its infinitessimal amount of light. I feared for myself if the sun should ever rise. I discovered that I was on my back—it was aching because I was on rough ground lying on stones. Another star appeared. It took me less time to get used to it. And another star appeared. Soon the sky was covered with stars. I rolled over onto my front. I kissed the ground, covering my lips with cinder and dust. I strained every muscle and exerted myself to my limits in an effort to stand up. I fell down breathing heavily, considerably weakened. I slept. I woke up and the sky was lightening to my left. The black was turning into blue. The stars there were fading. I tried to get up again. I made it. I stood there tottering like an enormous man, so big that he could hardly control his movements, fearing to fall down lest he shatter into a million fragments.

Dawn came. The sun rose. I was able to walk. I walked towards the sun, towards its light and heat. Beneath me whatever planet I was on revolved. I left a zigzag trail of footprints. By sunset I had walked in an arc always towards the sun. I realised the foolishness of this. Tomorrow I would walk in a straight line. I would walk out of this desolate flat patch of cinder and dust which seemed to stretch uninterrupted by any object as far as my eyes could see in every direction all the way to the horizons.

I slept soundly on the ground. I woke at dawn. I estimated where the sun would set and walked to that point. As the day passed the sun moved from behind me to in front of me. It set. I spent a second night on the ground. Tomorrow I would continue. I walked for a week. One day in the last light of the setting sun which was in my eyes a tracery of shadows emmeshed me. I stopped dead. In front of me was a chain-link fence, about three times my height, and topped with barbed-wire. Beyond it were high towers. Possible habitations of people. I had to get to the towers. But the fence stretched at either side of me in an apparently straight line beyond the range of my vision. And at the other side of the wire as far as I could see were the towers. In despair I nearly seized the chain-link and shook it. But something held me back. I fought to find the reason for my not touching the fence. It eluded me. I simply knew it was certain death to touch that fence.

I began to walk along the fence. I walked for a week. Always the same view. One day I saw a sign attached to the fence. It read, 'Danger. Electrified fence.' I was glad I had not touched the chain-link. The cinder and dust gave way to grass. But the fence continued. And behind the fence the towers. On and on I walked. The ground began to rise and fall. Here and there was a bush. One day I reached the top of a steeper than usual slope and saw below me a tree and a stream. I had a day's rest refreshing myself. Then I went on. The ground became more difficult. I was entering a mountainous country. The sky was no longer its uniform blue. Clouds would appear. The towers stopped. The ground became more difficult still. Some of the mountains I crossed must have been very high because it was often difficult to breathe due to the thinness of the air. And walking was slow in thick snow and on ice and rock. But the fence continued. I always kept it on my right. The mountains were behind me now. I waded through marsh and climbed through thickets, never failing to examine every inch of the fence for a break. I passed through forests and jungles. I encountered every climate. I never saw a living animal or insect, only flowers, cacti, trees and every kind of vegetation. My clothes had gone. I was scratched and bleeding, but I did not feel weak, I got stronger and stronger, I did not need to eat or drink. The fence continued. The ground became more even. I crossed a desert of burning sand and then the sand gave way to cinder and dust, this dispirited me but I did not give up. The towers returned. One day I came to a sign. It read, 'Danger. Electrified fence.' Had I come full circle? Or was this another sign. The only way to find out was to go on. If what I met from now on was the same terrain I had already passed through then I had walked in a full circle and was completely enclosed by the fence.

From that day I grew weaker. By the time I reached the tree and the stream I was nearly dead. A year must have gone by because the tree was in exactly the same state of growth it had been in when I passed this way before. But there was still a chance that it was only a coincidence that the terrain so far had seemed identical to the terrain of my first circuit. I had to go on. But I needed to spend more of my time picking berries and finding mushrooms and roots to eat and looking for water to drink. I had carved the number 703 on the tree, so that next time I passed it I would know for certain whether or not I was trapped. When I got to the desert I realised that my new demands for food and water were such that I could never get across without dying of thirst or starvation. I went back. I settled in an area where the food was easy to find and where there was a river further inland for my drinking water and for me to wash in. There were no fish in the river. I lived for years in that area, quite a long way back from the fence. I forgot about the fence. I stopped thinking of anything but food, drink and shelter. I had all I needed, I did not want to go anywhere. But I stripped the area of all its food until I had to go further and further from my shelter to find more food. So I moved my shelter. As the years passed I moved many times. During the course of these moves I lost track of where I was in relation to the fence. I never consciously moved towards it or away from it because it had gone from my mind. I must have been living close to the fence for some time before one day I emerged from a wood and saw it again.

I did not dare touch the chain-link fence even though it was rusty and probably not electrified. I walked along the fence to find a gap or a gate, out of animal curiosity. As I was walking, looking through the fence at the towers, my left foot trod on unsafe ground and I fell with a leg down a hole. This must have been a way under the fence leading to the towers.

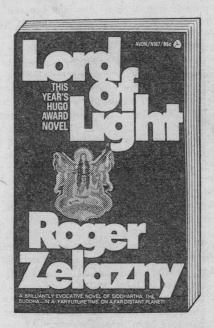